Tidewater Blood

Other Fiction by William Hoffman

Novels

The Trumpet Unblown

Days in the Yellow Leaf

A Place for My Head

The Dark Mountains

Yancey's War

A Walk to the River

A Death of Dreams

The Land That Drank the Rain

Godfires

Furors Die

Collected Stories

Virginia Reels

By Land, by Sea

Follow Me Home

Tidewater

Blood

a novel by **William Hoffman**

Algonquin Books of Chapel Hill   1998

Published by

Algonquin Books of Chapel Hill

Post Office Box 2225

Chapel Hill, North Carolina 27515-2225

a division of

Workman Publishing

708 Broadway

New York, New York 10003

Library of Congress Cataloging-in-Publication Data
Hoffman, William, 1925–

Tidewater blood : a novel / by William Hoffman.

p. cm.

ISBN 1-56512-187-2

I. Title.

PS3558.O34638T53   1998

813.'54—dc21   97-32434

                                                        CIP

10 9 8 7 6 5 4 3 2
First Edition

For Susan and Bill, who taught me French

Man is born into trouble, as the sparks fly upward.

—Job 5:7

Prologue

I RECONSTRUCT AND set the scene in my mind of how it must've happened.

First my oldest brother, John Maupin LeBlanc III, strides out and stands on the portico of the three-story dormered brick mansion. He looks down across the five-acre lawn sloping to Virginia's Axapomimi River, a winding tidal stream that on that mid-August Thursday afternoon would not seem to flow as much as to lie soaking up sun before sliding on, reptile-fashion, into the day's hazily moist heat.

A kingfisher might cry and a great blue heron squawk as it glides to a graceful landing in greenish shade of the far bank. The infrequent breeze likely fails to rouse the weather vane on the crown of the slate mansard roof.

John, head of the family, is tall, fit, in his mid-thirties. He has the blunt LeBlanc chin of all the murky portraits inside the house. His wife, Eleanor, appears wearing a voluminous white skirt. I remember from my few glimpses of her a small pinched mouth in a doll-like face. I expect John wishes she'd slow to a more dignified gait, though it's his complete domination of her that makes her scurry around like a cornered mouse. Above all, John believes in composure.

Maybe he watches his blond son Paul, age five, whacking striped croquet balls on the lawn or rolling with the English setter's puppies. John hopes the boy will be a horseman. It's in the blood, he assumes. What isn't in the blood?

The occasion is the annual celebration honoring Jean Maupin LeBlanc, who in 1740 sailed from La Rochelle to escape increasing Huguenot harassment by Louis XV. On this day the family dresses in eighteenth-century costume—the ladies in rustling floor-length silk gowns, snug bodices elaborately hand stitched, puffed sleeves with lace ruffles; the men in cravats, waistcoats, breeches, polished boots—all without a shred of irony.

The idea was our father's, but the whole thing took on the feeling of a much older tradition even before he died. "In America ours is the bluest of blood," he'd told us.

John, who hates lateness, waits for our other brother Edward, Edward's wife Patricia, and their three-year-old daughter, Marise, to arrive from Richmond.

"You'd think a person of Edward's nature would be prompt for this gathering," I hear John say, checking his gold pocket watch, a LeBlanc heirloom.

"He's usually on time," Eleanor would answer, since Edward's a fussy, time-driven man. Eleanor would've taken my mother's place, and I imagine her fluttery hands smoothing an Irish linen cloth on the oak trestle table carried out and set at the portico's east end. Would she also rearrange the centerpiece of red roses as I saw my mother do years before?

"*Usually* is a word that ought to be dropped from the dictionary," John would quote our father. "It's a cover to evade the exact."

Exactitude was my father's hard lesson to John, Edward, and me, among other things, though I don't believe my brothers ever felt his fist as I did.

Now I see old Gaius walk on stage to set the table with the family Limoges. He and Juno also wear period clothing—Gaius a sagging vest and badly fitting frock coat, Juno a long gray calico dress and a white kerchief knotted around her hair.

Maybe Gaius nearly topples crystal from his silver tray. John might reach to rescue the goblet brought over the sea from France. His composure perhaps conceals a wish to retire Gaius.

I close my eyes and conjure up a raincrow's plaint and a mockingbird's intricate parody of a cardinal. I remember Bellerive's sultry Augusts and insects chirring drowsily in the mown grass and along limbs of scaly water oaks.

John will be growing more irritable about Edward's lateness and would again lift his watch. I see him cross to the hunt board at the portico's west end to fix himself a bourbon over cracked ice and crushed mint.

For two hundred and fifty years, he might well be thinking, the LeBlancs have owned the land. And here, I have him invoke his sense of gratitude to Jean Maupin LeBlanc as well as to our own father and the long line of ancestral blood.

The river's course bounds the long front of his property. My land now, John must muse, and feel the full goodness of it. I picture him standing on the portico, his stance like a liege lord waiting for fealty. "My land, my son's, and my son's sons," he'd whisper, for certain.

The family is scheduled to gather at one o'clock. After drinks and conversation, they'll step to the table for a meal that never varies: chilled honeydew melons, sugar-cured ham, black-eyed peas, rice topped by raisin-thickened gravy, blackberry wine, and a chess pie served warm from Juno's oven.

When all are seated, John will stand at the head of the table and say grace. He'll lift his wineglass and repeat the words spoken annually by my father:

"We are gathered here at Bellerive to remember Jean Maupin LeBlanc, our illustrious forebear who possessed the courage to cross the great ocean. He planted the seeds of this family in rich Virginia soil to provide for his descendants the means to secure the blessings of a bountiful life—"

But before he can finish rehearsing the words, John experiences a sensation of weightlessness an instant before he feels the searing force of being hurled upward, and his world wrenches into a whirling disruption of glass, bricks, and flagstones.

1

I ROWED THE leaking skiff through a muddy, brackish gut that snaked among reeds of the green, steamy marsh, the boat's bow pointed toward a low spit of land where my cabin stood among ragged cedars. Some cabin—a plank shack I'd hammered together using unmatched pieces of lumber found along the eroding shore.

My inlet off the Chesapeake was too small and shallow for work- or pleasure boats and had no identification on the charts. I'd named it Lizard. A red sun glinted across the murky water and off the flattened beer cans I'd tacked to my tar-paper roof to plug leaks.

Lizard Inlet bordered a swamp grown up with cypress, myrtle, and elder. Cottonmouths and the last canebrake rattlers in Virginia made it home. The swamp water lay still and darker than the tidal rise that flowed over the mudflats twice every twenty-four hours. Nights I'd hear the cry of a lynx and squeals from its prey.

Months ago I'd found the skiff half stoved and sunk on a sand shoal and dragged her ashore. I'd repaired, caulked, and tarred the bottom. Using a drawknife, I'd fashioned oars from split lengths of a cedar felled by a nor'easter. In purring coals I'd heated leaf springs swiped from a wrecked Chrysler at the junkyard and hammered myself a pair of oarlocks.

Gill nets, crab pots, floats, poles, buckets, and scrap lumber had collected around my shack. I'd dug a pit, lined it with oyster shells, and covered it with angle iron and wire mesh. I used it to do my cooking except during rains or the coldest weather.

A stovepipe stuck from the shack's roof. My outhouse I'd framed and covered using two-by-fours and galvanized sheets salvaged from the dump. When the crapper's stench became so strong I gagged at my own foulness, I shoveled out another hole and moved the frame. Not often. I could tolerate lots of stink.

I hauled the skiff among reeds and made the painter fast using a clove hitch around a pine stump. Laughing gulls had followed me in, and they squabbled overhead. A rockfish lay at my feet. The striper had to weigh eight pounds. As I hooked a finger under its gill to lift it, a man stepped from cedar shade.

He wore shin-high black shoes, light brown uniform trousers that had dark brown outer seams, a white V-collared sport shirt, and a white Panama hat. The butt of a Colt .38 Police Special gleamed from an oxblood leather holster. He ambled toward the skiff, his full cheeks jostling with each step. Sweat shone on either side of a lumpy, porous nose.

Fear rose in me like a rotted log stirred up from the swamp's bottom.

"Nice catch," he said, his face half turned, a mocking look that positioned his eyes at the edge of their sockets. He smiled, yet only the left side of his mouth raised.

He wasn't the local game warden, whom I knew by sight. Maybe the new Drake County sanitarian. Were they armed now?

The Health Department and fire-breathing environmentalists wanted my privy gone, though any pollution I caused to seep into the bay was nothing compared to what the yachtsmen flushed overboard—classy air-conditioned turds. The real filth was fucking man himself, occupying the earth and seas.

I didn't speak. I crossed to my cleaning bench, a heavy plank nailed and braced between cedars. I drew my fish knife from its sheath attached to my belt, which I'd made by stitching together strips of leather carved out of a discarded army boot. I cut into the striper just below a gill slit. Blood welled over the blade I kept honed on a whetstone. At Lizard Inlet I lived by my knife.

"Ain't the taking of stripers illegal this time of year?" the man asked. He knuckled back the Panama. His red hair was short and kinky. He hooked thumbs over his hip pockets. Not a sanitarian, I decided, but more police shit.

"Found him floating dead," I said and made the next cut across the tail of the fish, whose last life quivered against my fingers. Stripers were strong and gave themselves reluctantly to death. I'd meant to slice off two fillets and use the carcass and innards to bait a crab pot. Maybe not today.

"Sure, and him still wiggling under the knife," the man said. "Make a better story to tell he just jumped into your skiff."

He acted as if we shared a joke. He was too redneck to be a Fed. He watched me pare between the initial cuts to remove a slab of mostly clean white flesh. I'd planned to grill and eat it with greens picked from my garden.

"You good with that blade," the man said. "Appears you don't care much for the law."

"The law's not cared much for me," I answered and felt the chunk of fear rise and shift around inside my belly. I'd learned terror from gliding, deadly shapes in black places.

"Oh I don't know," the man said, and a finger flicked a drop of sweat from the tip of his nose. He was younger than I'd first judged, no more than in his forties. "You been a guest at a first-class government hotel according to your record."

My hands didn't shake as I peeled the striper's outer skin from the fillet. Why would this shitkicker be looking into my record? Maybe the rich bastards at Sailors Cove put the law up to it. They'd been wanting to wipe my ass off this earth.

"Who you?" I asked.

"The question is, who you? Jesus, this place smells. You ever clean it up?"

I lifted a yellow plastic bucket from a nail pounded into the side of my cleaning bench. I'd found the bucket floating in the bay. I crossed to the water's edge and dipped it. I dunked the fillet to wash away blood smears, which looked too red against the white flesh.

"I been taking an interest in you," the man said and allowed the rest of the smile to work across his mouth.

"You must got time to waste."

"Nah, Charley, you make good reading," he said.

Charley, Charles, names shed, on no piece of identification in my frayed wallet, a memory seen only in flashes and quickly quelled.

I flipped the striper over to slice the second fillet. A shudder disturbed the blade's cut.

"Don't be dumb," he said. "Just check out your dance card and let us know who you was two-stepping it with August sixteenth last."

"Why?"

"This why," he said and slipped his wallet from a hip pocket. The cloth of his pants had worn glossy over his big, rounded butt. He opened and extended the wallet with its badge and glassine enclosed identification. "Sheriff Lewis Rutledge from King County."

I dunked the second fillet in the bucket before speaking. Words were traps.

"You come all that way down here from King County to ticket me for a fish?" I asked, but fear slogged. I gripped the knife.

He stepped back and whistled between his teeth—the way you'd call a dog. A second man emerged from cedar shade. He wore a brown-and-tan uniform and campaign hat.

"Might add the illegal fish to the list," the sheriff said and repocketed his wallet. "Now you fixing to talk to me or not? August sixteenth, 'bout one in the P.M."

"I don't keep calendars. And I got no watch."

"'Fraid that won't buy it," the sheriff said and hunkered good-ole-boy fashion, his smile leveled to a slit. The tip of his holster prodded salt grass.

"I not been anywhere except to Sailors Cove," I said.

"You produce verification of that statement?"

"You probably noticed I don't live in a place that keeps verifications handy."

"You a bona fide hermit, huh? You scare children with that ratty beard. They smell you coming."

"I don't study times or dates. I not left here except for the Cove."

"But you coulda. Nobody round here'd miss you. You might be gone a week and who'd notice? Just slip away and back unseen."

"Why'd I do that?"

"Because your name ain't Jim Moultrie at all but Charley LeBlanc. That good enough reason?"

"A name's no reason for anything," I said and dipped the knife blade to rinse it.

"Well what you think about this? I'm carrying a piece of paper here signed by a circuit-court judge that invests me with the authority to take you into custody and ride you back up to King County for questioning."

The sheriff stood and drew the folded paper from the other hip pocket. He tapped a stubby index finger against the writ.

"Not a hell of a lot," I said.

"You can pack a bag, but I got to watch everything you stick in."

"Don't own a bag."

"Charley, what say we then just put our feet on the path?"

"My fillets?" I asked and held them across my palms.

"Let's wrap and take 'em. They be too tasty to waste on them frigging gulls."

2

THE SHERIFF TOOK my Old Timer and sheath knifes. He and his deputy patted me down, emptied my pockets, and snapped on the cuffs before sitting me in the rear of a black Ford Galaxie that unlocked from outside only. Rat wire separated the seats. The interior door and window handles had been removed.

The Ford lacked air-conditioning. The sheriff and deputy had rolled down their windows. The deputy's brown shirt bore Confederate gray epaulets. His plastic nameplate read COLE.

"Should've hosed him off first," Cole said to Rutledge and held his nose. He was chunkily muscled and had hamlike thighs. Likely he pumped iron.

Cole drove the sandy road between pines dusty and drooping under the yellow day's gathering heat. I felt thirsty but didn't tongue my lips or raise linked wrists to rub my throat. I'd eaten nothing since yesterday evening—a dinner of uncooked Crowder peas from my garden and half a dozen shoreline oysters shucked and tipped salty off shells into my mouth.

I tried to figure what they'd landed on me for. I'd told the truth about not leaving Lizard Inlet except to hoof it to Sailors Cove. Not that I gave a damn about the truth, which had become for me anything that slid you around the bad stuff. I rarely set foot in the Cove, and only to purchase or lift what couldn't be done without—flour, baking soda, hooks, nylon line to repair nets. The thing about the law, though, was once it sunk its teeth in your flesh and bone, you never tore free.

The distance from Lizard Inlet to King County was 112 miles, and another 11 to Jessup's Wharf, the county seat, bordered by the Axapomimi River. Once steamers and trading barges had navigated upstream to docks along forested banks and taken on cotton, tobacco, lumber, and grain, often bartering these for finished goods from the industrial North.

By the time I was born, most docks and landings had already fallen in from disuse or been dragged away by high water, leaving jagged piling sticking up from black bottom muck. The river couldn't compete with railroads, and the shrill feminine whistles of the Baltimore steamers no longer roused the ospreys that perched cooling among white-limbed weltering sycamores.

Bellerive lay three miles upriver from Jessup's Wharf, and I'd either ridden into the village on my pony, Mosby, or walked the distance alone Saturdays if a tent show arrived or a movie was shown in the Farley Brothers warehouse, which after standing vacant for years had been converted into a shabby theater. Patrons would sit on backless wooden benches while bats dipped through shafts of light from the grinding camera, their lurching images darting across the sheet tacked to a crumbling wall.

Jessup's Wharf centered around the brick courthouse, the drug, general, and feed stores, the doctor and lawyer offices, the Dew Drop Inn, the moldering warehouses, two churches for whites, one bank, and the sawmill.

The belfried courthouse and its dependencies had been built during the late eighteenth century. The frame Dew Drop Inn, prior to what many locals termed the War of Northern Aggression, had schooled genteel ladies. The Virginia Short Line RR had run straight down River Street, laying the scent first of coal smoke and later diesel along the length of humpbacked brick pavement—odors not even the heavy wash of summer rains could sluice away into gutters.

Nothing appeared much changed since I left, except the rail tracks had been dug up, the street repaved. The Virginia Short Line had gone bust. In the town square water from an iron faucet still collected in a stone trough, though on law days horses would no longer be tied to hitching posts in front of the elm-shaded courthouse. Those trees that had once seemed so towering and grand to me as a boy now appeared sickly and just hanging on to life: Dutch elm disease, or maybe just weariness.

Cole drove around the courthouse to a graveled parking lot beside a new one-story jail built of cinderblocks painted light brown. He opened the Galaxie's door and reached for me. His fingers around my biceps were more than staunch. They meant to punish.

As I stepped out, my ragged tennis shoes retrieved from the Cove's landfill crunched gravel. For a second I believed I could smell smoke from long-vanished locomotives.

"I hate touching you," Cole said.

"Likewise," I answered, and he jerked me hard alongside him.

The cinderblock looked raw and wrong next to the old courthouse, its bricks seasoned by the years to a pale red, the mortar chipped, the white paint of windowsills bleeding. Behind the jail's horizontally louvered panes moved the phantom shapes of prisoners. I tasted puke. A voice called, "Come on in, we having a party."

The sheriff opened the spring-loaded door, and Cole guided me roughly along a corridor past a squad room to the steel entrance of the holding cells. The bars, walls, and floor were painted battleship gray. The prison odors of sweat, Lysol, piss, vomit, and fear fused into reek. There were six cells on either side of the barred walkway. Three held prisoners.

Cole removed the cuffs, pushed me forward, and locked me in. The cell held a seatless commode, a sink with one faucet, and two fold-down bunks made of canvas stitched around half-inch pipe.

"Fucking child killer," Cole said and checked the door by rattling it. He stabbed a hand upward and yanked it down as if closing a switch. "Zz-z-z," he hissed. The sound of high-voltage electrical current.

Bolts jammed into place and clanged as he left—universal sounds of entombment.

Two black prisoners watched. They slouched, their fingers curled around bars. Young, maybe twenty, they laid on me the death stare. The third prisoner was an old man who sat on a bunk, his expression hopeless and sad.

"He it?" one of the young ones asked.

"He look like shit," the second said.

"What he look like is dirty shit," the first said. Both had dreadlock hair. They wore jail-issue orange coveralls.

"Man, you ever wash?" the second asked. "You putrefying our environment here."

I turned away and crossed to the window. Beyond the bars and louvered glass slats, I glimpsed a wedge of River Street—the awninged Jessup's Mercantile, its sidewalk displaying bins of fruit and vegetables, and the King County Bank, a miniature classical Greek building with an American flag hanging listlessly over the doorway.

I unlatched the lower bunk from the wall, swung it down till the link chains at each end stretched taut, and sat. I looked at my begrimed tennis shoes. I wore no socks, and a smudged toe showed through a hole. My Big Boy overalls had been boiled so often they'd become bleached and flimsy. My green cotton shirt snitched from a Goodwill collection box had a ripped left sleeve. Sweat had collected in my beard's tangle.

Through the window a humid, drifting breeze carried the tidal mud scent of the Axapomimi, an odor I'd wakened to morning as a boy at Bellerive. I heard the ancient cry of herons.

The two prisoners no longer watched me. They played cards through bars of adjoining cells. I closed my eyes and felt the waterlogged stump slopping around inside. "Fucking child killer," Cole had called me. What did that mean? I rubbed my throat and tried to gather myself against the panic of again being jail-bound. I'd sworn after Leavenworth I'd never again let a steel door shut on me.

Heat thickened as air stilled. I stood to turn on the sink's faucet. A pitiful stream of rusty water twisted into the bowl, its enamel stained dark brown by a constant drip. When the flow cleared, I palmed myself a drink. At Lizard Inlet I used a fifty-gallon barrel as a cistern to collect rain off my roof. This water from the Jessup's Wharf's silver-painted tank tasted of sulphur and iron, common to wells of Tidewater. It'd been the same at Bellerive.

Banging along the corridor. Cole swaggered back carrying keys. He unlocked my cell and fastened on the cuffs, this time with my wrists behind me.

"Party time," the first prisoner called from his cell.

Cole used the keys to jab me forward.

"Bye," the second added. "You all come see us now, heah?"

3

FLUORESCENT TUBES BOLTED to the ceiling pitilessly lighted a windowless gray room off the corridor. Three brown metal folding chairs had been set at one side of a rectangular table, a fourth placed opposite and alone. Two microphones were centered on the table. Sheriff Rutledge and a man wearing a seersucker suit and a narrow, limp black tie stood waiting.

"Off the cuffs," he said.

After Cole removed them, the man stepped forward and held out his hand. "I'm Benson Falkoner, Commonwealth's Attorney."

"Can I have a glass of water?" I asked. Rear-guard action to provide time to size up the terrain before they jumped me. Falkoner's nostrils twitched. He'd had to force himself to touch me.

"You surely may. Cole here will oblige."

Cole was fitting the cuffs into the black leather pouch attached to his belt. He didn't appear obliging but left.

"Sit down, Charley, and rest your bones." Falkoner, a soft, ruddy man who talked slow and easy, indicated the lone chair before the table. His eyelids hung heavy, as if he needed sleep or had just risen from the bed. As he sat, his flesh settled.

A ceiling ventilator blew in uncooled air. I flexed my fingers. Falkoner, too, had called me Charley. Cat-and-mouse time. He lifted a briefcase from the floor, released the straps, and drew out a manila folder.

Cole returned carrying a Dixie cup of water. I drank, emptying it, and Cole took and crushed the cup in his fist before tossing it into a brown metal wastebasket. Curly hairs covered his knuckles.

"Let's all get comfortable here," Falkoner said. He opened the folder. His hands were fat. A wedding band pinched into the skin of a finger.

The sheriff lowered himself next to Falkoner and held his holster to keep it from bumping the chair. He hadn't taken off his Panama hat. Cole stood at the door. I felt the closeness of walls. A howl formed in my throat. I choked it down.

"Now, Charley, we haven't brought you here to beat you up in any fashion," Falkoner said. "We're small-town folks who try to get along and go along. You surely remember that, being a local boy. Why if you and I went back far enough we'd likely find ourselves to be cousins. My wife, Helen, could research it. She can trace blood-lines to Adam and Eve."

My eyes drifted upward to the wall behind Falkoner. The gray paint didn't entirely mask the word *Jesus* scratched into a cinderblock.

"Before we go down the road any further, I'm going to read you the Miranda," Falkoner said. "I don't want you or anybody claiming later we tried to trick you. I'm asking Sheriff Rutledge to turn on a recorder so as we can keep things straight and aboveboard. Now, you understand you have the right to remain silent. . . ."

Rutledge had leaned to the recorder on the floor and clicked a toggle switch. Wires led to the microphones the sheriff arranged in front of me and Falkoner. I knew the Miranda by heart. The tape spools spun. My life being wound onto them. Tape bound tighter than chain. . . .

"Do you?" Falkoner asked.

"Don't know why I'm here," I said and struggled not to show fear at continued thoughts of closing doors.

"But do you understand the Miranda?"

"Like to be given the reason why you hauled me in," I said, words worth nothing. I had learned long ago you never really beat the law. If it didn't fuck you one way, the legal sonsabitches came around corners and found another.

"We'll get to that," Falkoner said, talking so slow he might nap before finishing a sentence. "But I'd like you to state for the record you've heard and fully understand your rights."

"What if I don't?"

The sheriff shifted on his chair and thumbed back his Panama. His kinky red hair had become sweat-snarled.

"We have it on the recorder," Falkoner said, the pace of his voice unchanged, but the loose flesh of his face firmed. "You try to deny you heard it, we produce the tape."

The faint shriek of a steam whistle penetrated the room. I remembered Axapomimi Lumber, where timberhicks skinned trucked-in logs, sawed them, then ricked the lumber high to season under the sun. Southern breezes used to carry that whistle's sound all the way to Bellerive. My father had become the company's major stockholder.

"I heard it," I said and felt as if bones of my body were softening and giving way.

"Good," Falkoner said. "Got that out of the road. I want to emphasize at this time we're not yet officially charging you with anything. We just trying to find out facts about what happened at Bellerive. Want to keep things low-key and amiable."

"What things?" I asked. His graying hair was so thin the scalp's pink showed through.

Not only Falkoner, but also Rutledge smiled, the sheriff again using just the left half of his mouth. They cut their eyes at me as if we were kidding each other.

"Course you don't know 'bout that," Falkoner said and clasped his hands on the table. He interlaced the pulpy fingers.

"No."

"Charley, it's not going to help anybody to play footsie with this business," Falkoner said.

"What's the business?"

The smiles thinned and withdrew. The sheriff again shifted his weight. He reached to his holster and adjusted its heft. Cole stirred behind me. I glanced back. His mouth had tightened as if ready to spit.

"You not going to keep pretending you don't know when it's been in all the papers and on TV?" Falkoner asked.

"Gave up reading papers. Got no juice for a TV."

Falkoner sighed and turned to face the sheriff. Rutledge nodded. The creases on either side of his lumpy nose lengthened.

"You can't go anywhere in the state without knowing," he said.

"I don't go anywhere in the state if I can help it."

Despite the ventilator, air of the closed room felt too sticky to draw into my lungs.

"You claiming here and now you don't know or never heard anything about the blast at Bellerive?" Rutledge asked.

"I'm not claiming anything," I said, sitting straighter.

"Your brother John, his wife Eleanor, their son Paul, and a black servant named Gaius blown to kingdom come?" Rutledge asked.

"No," I said. What shit was this?

"Ah, Charley," Falkoner said, all the folksiness sloughed from his face, "I got to tell you everybody's apt to find that impossible to believe."

"For damn sure," Rutledge said.

"You'd have to live under a rock not to've heard," Cole said.

"Maybe I been living under a rock."

Before running off from Bellerive I'd only briefly met Eleanor, whom John was dating, and later at my mother's funeral had glimpsed her holding their baby son.

Falkoner and Rutledge fastened their eyes on me as the tapes whirred. Falkoner sighed a second time and fingered the open folder. He studied it. He set his elbows on the table and rested his chin on bridged fingers.

"The portico at Bellerive, Charley, destroyed. Looks like a battleground and was outright slaughter. Even the dog killed."

"Duchess, a bitch setter with a soft mouth for birds," Cole said.

My hands clenched my thighs to keep both from shaking. My high-and-mighty older brother John I'd not seen since my mother's funeral. He'd once held my head underwater in the Axapomimi till I believed I'd died.

"He knows," Cole said.

"Stay out of it," Rutledge said.

"I can see he knows," Cole said.

"Button it," Rutledge said.

I thought of Bellerive and the last words I'd had with John before I left home. After dinner, for which I'd been late, we'd walked down from the house to the landing, on an October evening when wind rustled not only leaves but bark of the birches. The river's dark flow soughed against piling.

"Why can't you do right?" John'd asked. He was tallest in the family, middleweight champ at the university before attending law school, a fox hunter and expert slayer of the geese that swept in honking each winter to feed on Bellerive's wheat-sown fields.

"You've caused enough pain," he said. He had an easy, casual way about him and a controlled voice even when aroused. "You ever try to stay out of trouble?"

"You don't know everything," I'd answered, and my arms lifted because I believed he meant to hit me.

"You ought to think of others before you do the crazy stuff. Giving Daddy and the whole family grief."

John had laid guilt on me there in the gathering darkness, he who never had to recall the picture I couldn't escape or endure for the thousandth part of a second.

"Charley, it'd be better all the way around if you'd come clean," Falkoner continued. "We could work through this and make it bearable as possible for everybody concerned."

"You wanting me to do exactly what?" I asked, but knew. I'd heard the words before.

"Just take your time and tell us in your own way what happened out there," Rutledge said.

I looked at my hands. They were as rough as unplaned lumber and badly needed washing. Grime mooned under broken fingernails.

"Maybe you been thinking they mistreated you all these years," Rutledge said.

"You've had plenty of reason not to be beholden to your brothers," Falkoner said.

"They got it all and you nothing," Rutledge said.

"Enough to make a man bitter," Falkoner said.

"Maybe you had a few drinks and slipped up here one night and laid the charge," Rutledge said.

"A terrible thing, but understandable," Falkoner said. "Hurt and hate rancoring all these years."

"They living rich and you poor," Rutledge said.

As I stared at my gripped fingers, they were accusing me of murdering blood kin, a woman and her child, Gaius. The ventilator's raw air stirred against my face and reeked not of their deaths but my own.

"I want a lawyer," I said.

4

COLE RETURNED ME to the cell and shoved me in so hard I bumped the wall. He'd cuffed my wrists. Again he held his nose.

"Got to hose you down 'fore you contaminate the whole jail with your fleas, crabs, and lice," he said. He locked the cell and left, his step flat and plodding.

"You got a buddy there," one of the prisoners said.

"Tell he crazy 'bout you," the second added.

Cole came back carrying a towel, a bar of brown soap, and clean folded orange coveralls. He unlocked the cell.

"Get your smelly ass out here," he said.

He walked me cuffed to the shower room—one dripping nozzle and slatted floorboards over damp unpainted concrete. A single bulb burned inside a ceiling cage.

I knew the routine. When Cole removed the cuffs, I untied my tennis shoes, stripped down, and laid my shirt and overalls on a wooden bench before stepping under the nozzle. No water sprayed out as I turned the hot-water handle.

"We don't run no fancy hotel," Cole said, pleased. He'd lifted a booted foot to the bench.

I twisted the other handle. Needlelike streams struck my chest.

I disappointed him by not flinching. I was used to cold water, and this felt good coursing my body. The jail shower was near luxury after the way I'd been living at Lizard Inlet.

"Want to see mad-dog lather head to toe," Cole called and quickly underhanded the bar of soap. I caught it.

At the side of my shack I'd hung a punctured five-gallon lard can from a cedar limb. When I wanted a shower, I climbed a patched-up stepladder and poured in water from my cistern before hurrying to stand beneath the short-lived sprinkling. Summers the water stayed sun-warmed. I stole soap from the Sailors Cove Amoco station rest room or the shelf of the Dollar General. During the dry season when I needed a wash, I walked to my dock, the piles of which I'd mauled into mud. Using a painter tied to the bucket handle, I scooped up brackish water to dump over myself. I checked first for nettles. The inlet water left me feeling gummy.

I now soaped my head, face, beard, chest, stomach, crotch, arms, legs, feet. I also raised my mouth to the shower and drank. Water ran into and filled my eye sockets.

"Reckon that's enough for a piece of shit," Cole called. He'd lit a cigarette.

I cut off the shower and crossed the slippery floorboards to the bench. Cole pitched me the brown towel. It was stiff, the nap worn off—like using sandpaper.

"You've lightened up a shade or two," Cole said. "Why, you almost a white man."

"You a Rudd, ain't you?" I asked as I dried myself, aware of my skinny build. But it was tough skinny, no excess load.

"Yeah," Cole answered, surprised. He dropped his foot from the bench to floor. His boot sole squeezed out water. "How'd you know?"

"I remember Rudds from when I lived in King County," I said. They'd been considered common, knockers on Bellerive's back door, the father a jackleg blacksmith, the numberless younger ones farmhands or millworkers. All had brawn and ham thighs, even the women.

"Sure, my daddy worked at Bellerive some," Cole said and pinched out the cigarette. "Took care of machinery. Lost a hand to a hay binder he was fixing. Your daddy treated him right, though. Got him a pension and found him light chores till he give up the ghost."

I pulled on the orange coveralls and battered tennis shoes. No underwear provided, but I'd given up its use anyway except for long johns during winter. The coveralls, like the towel, felt unyielding.

"Yeah, your daddy and your brother John was all right for rich men, but you got to **be** one dirty sonofabitch," Cole said and squinched his nose at my overalls and shirt on the bench. "I ain't touching those."

He snapped on the cuffs tight, prodded me to the cell, removed the cuffs, locked me in. The two prisoners stood watching, their hands gripping the bars.

"You bad," the first said. "Bad, bad, bad."

"They gonna have a big party for you," the second said.

"Cake and presents too," the first said.

"'Lectric entertainment," the second said.

I sat on the bunk. I knew they shouldn't be holding me without a hearing and charge, yet rules didn't count much in hick Southern towns. Family and relationships were everything. The whole county knew your genes from back before time was written.

I rubbed my face. My pores had again filled with sweat. Brother John, his wife and son, killed. Their deaths fully sinking in. I felt no sorrow, only more fear. Falkoner and Rutledge meant to feed me into the legal machinery's maw. I could be ground up, spit out, fried. What a goddamn fool I'd been to hope I could ever break free of men and laws.

Scratched into the cinderblock wall opposite the bunk: *Jesus Gave Himself For Mankind.* Bad trade, I thought.

Bolts clanged. A stout, aging woman wearing a tan uniform shirt and skirt rolled food in on a wooden cart that had rubber wheels. She ladled red beans and two hotdogs onto each tin plate. She served me before the others by sliding my plate through a horizontal slit at the bottom of the cell door.

"Get no cat-soup?" the first prisoner asked.

She acted as if she hadn't heard. When she pushed the old man's plate toward him, he slowly, achingly, reached for it, set it on his lap, but seemed too spent to lift the white plastic spoon.

"No chili and onions?" the second asked.

"You want ketchup, chili, and onions, go to the Dew Drop," the woman said. She handed paper napkins between bars. The old man dropped his and watched it flutter to the floor.

"Right on," the first said. "Let us out, and we come back right after we eat."

"Bring you a hot fudge delight," the second said.

"In your dreams," the deputy said and turned to me. "You ain't changed. You still trouble."

Something familiar about her pug nose—then I saw the nameplate pinned to her shirt—MARY BETH BAINS. *Bains* another county name, she likely to have been among a gang of women who each spring arrived to pick Bellerive's strawberries, which were graded by hand and placed in crates to be trucked to Richmond and the best hotels.

"They still have strawberry fields at Bellerive?" I asked.

"They kept a patch for the house and family," she said. Gray hair fit tight against her skull. Her earrings were also tan, shaped like barn swallows with white beaks. "Coons'll take 'em now. Eat everything except the bean poles."

She walked away, leaving the cart. The plastic spoon bent under pressure of my fingers. Food and fear tangled into a hard lump. Yet I felt hungry. If the others hadn't been watching, I would've licked the plate.

"No soda pop to wash this caviar down?" the first prisoner asked Deputy Bains when she came back. She wore low-heeled brown oxfords and brown cotton hose.

"God's own water in the spigot," she said.

"Rather have a cup of jiving java," the second said.

"*Rather*s don't count," she said.

She collected the plates, stacked them, and moved off pushing her cart. The old man hadn't eaten. The tin plates rattled, and the cart's wheels created sibilance over concrete.

I lay on the bunk, the pasty taste of store food foul in my mouth. I'd rarely bought rations. Mostly I'd lived off the land and water— crabs, oysters, fish, clams. For meat I'd loaded up my single-shot twelve-gauge Savage and sat hidden in reeds till a teal, mallard, or tundra swan flew past. I took only sure shots because for shells I had to lay money down. Stores in Sailors Cove locked up ammo.

When nothing flew, I trapped possum, groundhog, coon. I never disdained a snake. I'd cut puff adders into chunks and fried them with potatoes from my root cellar.

I bought no hunting license, and game wardens leveled binoculars to watch and stalk me. One sonofabitch named Carl Wiggins passed within six feet of where I lay sprawled in muddy marsh grass. I read the L.L. Bean trademark on his boot heel. Wardens considered me a trophy.

I snared rabbits and baited birds. They didn't have to be partridges: I ate crows whose flesh was rubbery and flavored of fish and mussels. I cooked a mess of robins I shot on the ground during the January thaw. To me taste was nothing, and all food simply fire for the boiler.

"Did I not see yonder high-in-the-sky LeBlanc eat beans and dogs just like poor folk?" the first prisoner asked. He'd lifted his hands to grip bars above his head and seemed to hang more than stand.

"He don't talk," the second said and shuffled cards. "LeBlancs don't mouth with trash."

"He look trashy himself lying there," the first said. "In fact he look like shee-it."

When I used the john, they commented and hooted.

"Didn't know LeBlancs had to piss water," the second said. "You reckon they human like people?"

"Nah, they got they own private air to breathe," the first said. "Washed and perfumed."

The old man began coughing loudly. He wheezed. His knees drew up. Cole entered the cell to look. He took the man's pulse and left fast. Within minutes, two members of the King County Rescue Squad wearing white coveralls followed Cole into the cell and carried the old man away on a stretcher.

The two youths whispered. They'd stolen a car. Despite the way they talked, they were scared. They bowed their heads together and appeared smaller.

I'd gone past everything except fear. Once you learned that, the real terror deep, it never left but lodged permanently in the flesh, bone, and heart—if you had any heart left.

5

BOTH IN 'NAM and at Leavenworth I'd learned to rest keeping part of myself alert—an outer fringe of consciousness that sensed movement and alien sounds in darkness.

The cell block's lights had been cut off except for one caged bulb. The whispering of the two youths ended. River Street traffic ceased except for the passage of an occasional truck rumbling through. The barking of dogs became half-hearted, and a breeze barely roused the courthouse elms.

I thought of Lizard Inlet and wondered what Sheriff Rutledge had done with my striper fillets. Likely fed them to a wife and children.

I tried to center my mind on the thing that'd happened at Bellerive on August sixteenth, date of the LeBlancs' annual celebration of themselves. I'd once been a part of it and watched my father raise his wineglass to give the toast. He hadn't liked my looking at him.

Brother John had taught me to box college-style and became furious when instead of following his gentlemanly rules I ducked under his fists and tackled him. He sat on my chest and battered my face. "You ever going to learn?" he hollered down at me.

I waited for the release darkness gave to daylight, the noises of morning: barnyard cocks, crows squabbling in pines, doves twittering, pigeons cooing as they searched for grain spilled from loading docks at Southern States Co-op, outboard engines sputtering to life, the whistle at Axapomimi Lumber, the awning being lowered over the sidewalk at Jessup's Mercantile, tires again rasping River Street's dew-dampened pavement.

Deputy Bains rolled in her cart with a breakfast of two sugared doughnuts and a tin cup of black coffee for each prisoner. I'd brewed my own eye-openers at the inlet, using washed roots and the shaved bark of wild sassafras, which I dried on my roof. I'd nibbled myrtle buds and whittled points on holly sprigs to clean my teeth.

I used the crapper. This time the others made no comments. They were to stand before the judge this morning, and fear bound them.

I wanted a cigarette. I'd learned to control most desires but never shook the need for smokes. I collected butts on Sailors Cove's sidewalks or lying mashed in gutters. I'd shred the tobacco and spread the fibers to dry on a board nailed under a shack window with a southern exposure. I rolled my own.

I washed my hands and sat looking up at the window. A radio played in somebody's car. Johnny Cash. Not that I had a preference. All man-made music had become yapping or whining to me. Silence was man's best and rarest offering. My music rose from the staccato cry of rails among reeds, the scoggin's screech, the tide lapping the shore.

Cole came for my fellow inmates at mid-morning. He cuffed and motioned them ahead of him along the corridor.

Toward noon Benson Falkoner padded into the block. Cole opened the cell door and stood outside. Falkoner sat heavily beside me on the bunk. His hands hung between his spread knees. He worked his mouth as if needing to unlimber it before use.

"Treating you right 'round here?" he asked.

"I still want a lawyer."

"You mean to make it tough huh?"

He smelled of aftershave. His weight and the day's early heat had already wrinkled his seersucker.

"I know you got to charge me to hold me."

"Oh it's always easy to find something to charge a man with," Falkoner said and listlessly flapped his hinged hands. "Taking stripers out of season, shooting swans, illegally raiding a county landfill. A whole passel of reasons lying in a law book right there on Lewis Rutledge's desk. The book grows every year. You understand how the game's played."

"Never thought of it as a game."

"Metaphor. Been hoping you had time to run our situation through your mind. Don't it make sense you'd make life better for all concerned if you gave us a statement? I can tell you my office and every law official down the line would feel a lot more kindly about your continued welfare."

"You allowing me to see a lawyer?"

"Oh you can have yourself a lawyer, but once you got him your predicament is guaranteed to become lots more complicated and nasty. Myself, I hate mess and complication. I go a long way to aid a fellow who assists me avoiding them. He'd have the Commonwealth's continued goodwill. The way the system works."

"Think I ought to care about the fucking system?"

"My guess is the system's not going to care much for you," Falkoner said and stood by pushing down on his knees. His flesh repositioned itself around his frame. "I been intending to do some fishing. I could become downright put out with a man who kept me out my boat during the August heat."

"Get me my lawyer."

"You always been bad news around here," Falkoner said and lifted a hand to signal Cole to unlock the cell.

6

THE AFTERNOON COOKED up, the bars and louvers blasted with sunlight. Saws shrilled at Axapomimi Lumber. Gulls flapped slothfully toward the river, where they'd drop to swoop up bait and shuckings tossed overboard by fishermen. The birds sounded like quarreling hags.

Had I been at Lizard Inlet I'd be checking crab pots or maybe bringing in a blue or another striper from a gill net. I kept a broken La-Z-Boy chair positioned in cedar shade near the water. I'd hauled the chair piece by piece from the dump. Often during flaming July and August days I stretched out and listened to mullet jump in tidal ponds. They were trapped. So was I.

For lunch Deputy Bains brought me a cheese sandwich on unbuttered white bread and a cool Dr Pepper. After I ate, Cole banged into the block, opened the cell door, and snapped on the cuffs. He was chewing gum and popped a bubble.

"Always liked your mama," he said. "At Christmas she passed out silver half-dollars to the chaps who sang carols in front of Bellerive. How'd you go so wrong?"

"Talent."

"Git!" Cole said and jammed knuckles into the small of my back.

He returned me to the interrogation room. The fluorescent tubes created an antiseptic light. On the other side of the table stood a young man well over six feet tall. He appeared as awkward and angular as a heron parading shallows of the marsh. He wore a khaki suit, a blue button-down oxford shirt, and a red-and-blue regimental tie. Some lawyer. My guess, a halfass college boy.

"Need anything, holler," Cole told him and locked us in. The old choking feeling closed on me, and I raised my face to the ceiling ventilator in a need for air.

The lawyer ran hazel eyes over me and palmed back lank light brown hair. He reset his glasses before holding out a hand. On a long bony finger he wore a gold ring that had an onyx stone inset with the Greek letters *KA*. He offered to shake across the table. I didn't want to touch his hand and raised the cuffs for an excuse. He was happy to draw back.

"Word is you needing counsel," he said. "My name's Frampton. Walter Frampton. If you require proof I'm a genuine attorney, a diploma hangs on a wall of my office."

"Why don't we stroll over for a look?"

"Benson phoned," he said and pulled out a chair from his side of the table. He didn't sit so much as unsnarl elbows, arms, legs. From the floor he lifted a leather attaché case. It was unscarred, the initials WBF embossed. "If you're indicted, Judge Pechiney will appoint me anyhow."

"New lawyers get the crap," I said.

"Well put. You can refuse to talk to me. Raise a fuss. Petition the court that you have no confidence in counsel."

"Where'd you go to school?"

"Washington and Lee," he answered, and fingers of the hand wearing the fraternity ring flexed slightly.

"You ever try a capital offense?"

"A man has to start someplace."

"Any sort of case?"

"Just yesterday I pled for a man who'd shot a neighbor's dog. A beagle."

"You win?"

"I got him off with a small fine and felt my voice resonate through the courtroom like Patrick Henry's in the House of Burgesses."

"Didn't your daddy serve in the General Assembly?"

"He did and was often invited to Bellerive. Hunted birds and drank liquor with your father whom he claimed was the best shot who ever lifted a gun."

He reset the glasses on his long, steep nose. I still stood near the door, and he took in the sorry state of my tennis shoes. He was thinking dollars.

"I didn't know about any explosion," I said.

"Well you see, Mr. LeBlanc—"

"Moultrie. Jim Moultrie."

"You change your name legally?"

"I changed it here," I said and raised my cuffed hands to tap a finger against my right temple.

"A citizen can call himself most anything he cares to, but in the eyes of the law you are still Charles MacKay LeBlanc. Furthermore, it's virtually impossible to believe you hadn't heard about Bellerive. In this day how does anyone escape the media's bray and blare?"

He couldn't get his long legs arranged. They kept tangling up around a table leg. He liked hearing himself though. He tasted and juiced words as he spoke them.

"You see where I been living, you'd believe," I said.

"I just might do that thing if it comes to my representing you. Mind if I smoke?"

Without waiting for an answer, he drew a pack of Winstons

from his shirt pocket, rapped it against the table's edge to loosen cigarettes, and as I was hoping, extended them to me. Because of the cuffs, I used both hands to draw one. Frampton held the flame of a blue Bic lighter for me. I drew down smoke, felt it take hold in my lungs.

"Why they landing on me?" I asked.

"You're the only fish in the pool," he said. His glasses wouldn't stay fixed on his nose. He pushed at them.

"Meat to hungry dogs huh?" I asked. I hoped to talk Frampton into giving me the pack of Winstons.

"It's a bit more substantial than your just being handy," Frampton said. He had a dainty way of holding his cigarette reversed between his thumb and a spindly index finger. Like a faggot. "With you they have motive and opportunity."

"What motive's a drifter living on fish and swamp muskrats supposed to have?"

"Experience has taught me for men there are only two—women and money. I suppose we can eliminate the former."

"What money?" I asked and snorted smoke. "Don't tell me my loving brother John remembered me in his will."

"I'm speaking secondhand here. John and his wife's estates reportedly go into trust for payment to a few aged ladies, several black retainers, various charities, the income of the remainder to be paid out to your brother Edward."

"So?"

"Edward also receives Bellerive outright. The trust corpus will dissolve on his child or children, again with various minor bequests. Benson, however, has hinted at a substantial insurance policy with you named the beneficiary."

"John naming me in a policy is about as likely as Yankee dead rising to sing Dixie."

"Don't know details, if details there are," Frampton said. He un-scrambled his legs beneath the table.

"Got to be a mistake. Brother John wrote me off the books long ago."

"Let me repeat this has come to me unofficially. I've examined no evidence. The estate's in the hands of Richmond's Bank of the South. I've not seen a copy of the will or a listing of contents in your brother's safety deposit box."

"No chance him leaving me anything."

"All sorts of talk going 'round," Frampton said and tapped out his cigarette on a shallow metal ashtray that advertised Purina Chow. "It's public knowledge you've been the family black sheep. In your present circumstances, it can be argued that money had be-come irresistibly attractive."

"I'm supposed to have killed four people because of an insur-ance policy I don't know anything about and that might not exist?" I asked and dunked my cigarette, which had burned to my knuckles.

"Even without a policy, you'd still be suspect. The fact you call yourself by another name could be interpreted as proof you have no affection for the LeBlancs and are motivated by envy, hate, re-venge."

"My father and brothers didn't want me, so I didn't want their name."

"Where'd you get it, the Moultrie I mean?"

"On a tombstone in a Tampa graveyard."

"You found a man about your age who'd died and whose name and date you used to apply for a birth certificate and Social Security card."

I shrugged and wanted another cigarette.

"Moultrie has a certain aptness, but let's not get into that," he said. "Can anybody vouch for you on August sixteenth last?"

"Not unless crabs and ospreys learn to talk. But nobody could've spotted me around Jessup's Wharf either because I wasn't here."

"I'll see what I can learn," Frampton said and got himself disengaged to stand. "Don't suppose you'll be able to make even a token payment for my services this day?"

"Get me out of this goddamn hole and I'll keep you in fish, oysters, and crabs the rest of your life."

"Never been wild about seafood. Allergic. Break out in hives."

"How 'bout leaving the cigarettes?"

7

AFTER DARK A squall blew in from the southwest, curls of rain rolling over the jail and splashing the sidewalks and parking lot. Cole cranked the louvers closed. The young prisoners hadn't returned. Late in the night Cole half carried a drunk white man to an end cell and locked it. The man wept and fell off his bunk to the floor, where he lay puking.

"Not me!" he wailed. "Ain't me doing this!"

At dawn a pigeon-toed deputy whose nameplate read RODGER ambled past, looked at the man, and said, "God Almighty, Albert!" He poked the drunk with the toe of a Dingo boot and ordered him to stand.

"I thought I'd done quit," Albert said. He rubbed his bloodless face. Maybe thirty, he appeared borderline respectable in a striped lightweight suit that had a torn lapel. "What'd I do this time?"

"Damn near knocked the hind end out the Dew Drop," Rodger said. "We'll clean you up, and then you take care of the mess you made here."

Deputy Bains arrived with my two sugared doughnuts and coffee. She had no word for me. When Rodger brought Albert back, he'd washed and was carrying a pail and mop. Rodger stood by while Albert swabbed the cell floor.

Rodger locked Albert in and took away the pail and mop. Albert let down on his bunk. He closed his eyes, then opened them to focus on me.

"Admit I need help," he said. "All I stopped for was a Orange Crush. Edith'll kill me."

He smoothed his torn lapel as if he could reattach the fabric.

"Don't know how it happened." He again looked in my direction. "You and me had a fight once."

I couldn't remember. I'd had many fights before being sent to Santee Military Academy and not a few afterward, including the big one with my father.

"Down at the river," Albert said. "My name's Yaw. You hit me up side of the head with butt end of an oar."

"What we fight about?"

The Yaws were a clan located mostly in the western pine woods of King County. Some trooped to Jessup's Wharf to do odd jobs or work at the mill. Others owned small farms and cut billets. There was always another Yaw.

"Found you using my fishing hole."

"You owned the river?"

"Believed I did back then. Like to have kilt me. I fell in and couldn't swim and still can't."

I lay smoking Frampton's Winstons. Raindrops patted and slid down the louvered panes. Gutters overflowed. At mid-morning the courthouse bell rang—an off-key gong. Rodger came to take Albert away. He'd stand him before the General District Court judge.

I thought of Benson Falkoner and Sheriff Rutledge cooking up a legal potion for me. Walls pushed in like at Leavenworth. I had to stop thinking walls. I pictured space and endless green plains. Montana, a place I'd never been.

Deputy Bains fed no lunch. Rain drummed the jail roof. Thunder boomed. I felt tremors other than my own.

Rodger unlocked the cell during the early afternoon. He cuffed and held my arm as we moved side by side to the interrogation room. Falkoner and Rutledge were already seated. Walter Frampton adjusted his glasses and positioned a chair for himself.

Rutledge switched on the tape recorder. He'd set his Panama hat on the table. His kinky red hair looked wiry as steel wool.

"Charley, please state your name for the record," Benson said. Sweat glistened on his half-lowered eyelids.

"Jim Moultrie."

"Your given and surname," Falkoner said.

"Charles M. LeBlanc," I said. No use holing up in that terrain.

"For the record, Charles M. LeBlanc is in the presence of Benson Falkoner, King County Commonwealth's Attorney, Lewis Rutledge, King County sheriff, and Walter Lee Frampton, King County practicing attorney," Falkoner said.

He eyed me.

"Now, Charley, you've had plenty leisure to run events through your head. I'll ask you one more time, do you care to make any statement here of your own free will concerning events out at Bellerive Plantation on August sixteenth last?"

"He doesn't have to," Walter Lee Frampton said. He appeared too much a fraternity boy to be sitting in the room with grown men and pros.

"Your astute attorney is correct," Falkoner said. He didn't look at Frampton. "You see the recording machine. I'll ask Charles M. LeBlanc to state he sees the machine."

"I see it," I said. I also saw again the painted-over *Jesus* on the cinderblock wall. "And I had nothing to do with what happened out at Bellerive."

"Ah, Charles," Falkoner said.

"Whoever set off that charge had to be familiar with the layout of the house," Rutledge said. No smile even on the left half his mouth. "Knowledge of people's routines and how to get under the portico, plant the charge, and when to fire it."

"Don't mean me," I said. They hadn't asked me to sit, and I still wore cuffs.

"You'd know those things and where to hide yourself," Falkoner said. "Maybe lie in wait along that strip of pines down to the river. Have binoculars and watch for the right minute. Or hear the celebration going on. Fire the charge and steal back to that swamp shack of yours down in Drake County."

"Or if you wont hiding and watching, you coulda fired the charge with a timer," Rutledge said. "The LeBlancs held that celebration every year on the same day. Edward and his family would've bought it too except for a belt tearing loose on their car making them late from Richmond."

They watched me. I looked at the wall. I heard the faint breath of the ventilator and the buzz of fluorescent tubes. I turned to Walter Frampton. He'd laid a legal pad on the table and held a pencil poised above it. His glasses slid slowly down his nose. He wasn't about to open his mouth.

"We waiting to hear from you, Charley," Falkoner said.

I shrugged.

"You was in the army, wont you?" Rutledge asked.

I didn't speak or move.

"Got busted out on a bad discharge," Falkoner said.

"Court-martialed and sent to Leavenworth," Rutledge said.

"Always been a burden to your family," Falkoner said.

"Brawling, drinking, carousing," Rutledge said.

"Ever'body 'round Jessup's Wharf knows about you," Falkoner said.

"The fights you had with your daddy," Rutledge said.

"All that bad history on your record," Falkoner said. "How you think a jury'll take to you when you walk in the courtroom?"

"We want to do right for everybody here," Rutledge said.

"You just have to stand before Judge Pechiney whose ear will be whispered in about how you cooperated with law enforcement and the Commonwealth," Falkoner said.

Still I didn't speak. Falkoner and Rutledge stared. Frampton diddled with his pencil above his legal pad.

They were right about a jury. I'd be cooked before the members filed into the box. I felt myself slipping a little and firmed up. Give them nothing, I told myself.

Rutledge shifted. His holstered Colt clunked his chair. Falkoner drew doughy hands from the table.

"But you go hardhead on us, we put our minds full throttle to this thing," he said. "I can guarantee you the Sheriff's Department and Commonwealth will give you our entire attention. Even the tiniest scrap of lying or unlawful behavior will be uncovered as sure as the sun shines on a pig's ass."

"There won't be no goodwill left around this courthouse for Charley MacKay LeBlanc," Rutledge said.

"You know what they doing now down in Richmond Town, don't you?" Falkoner asked.

"They frying again," Rutledge said. "They dusted off that old chair and using it. I wouldn't want to ride that seat into hellfire."

"The Commonwealth will go for the death penalty," Falkoner said. "I guarantee they'll be no plea bargaining."

I looked at the wall. They waited.

"He ain't gonna tell us nothing," Rutledge said. His shin-high black shoes scuffed the floor under the table.

"A crying shame when we done our best to be nice," Falkoner said, his heavy eyelids drooping farther. He worked his mouth and shook his head.

"Git him out of here," Rutledge told Rodger.

8

I LAY ON the bunk. Rain had stopped and the louvers were cranked open. Water still dripped from the roof. A distant thunder. I didn't allow myself to picture that old chair and the hot ride to eternity.

Walter Frampton came to my cell just as the whistle blew to end the day's shift at Axapomimi Lumber. Rodger let him in. Walt set his attaché case on the floor and slouched.

"Want to express my appreciation for the way you stuck up for me this morning," I said, continuing to lie on the bunk.

"Sarcasm from a man in your position."

"You opened your mouth once."

"A time and place for mouthing, which was in Benson's office. More than fifty minutes of yammering. Just might be able to ease you out of here and onto the street."

I sat up.

"Sounds better? Near tied my tongue in knots pleading your situation. Fortunately when they searched your sha—your dwelling at the inlet, they found nothing incriminating. Kept reminding Benson and Lewis they had not a single witness, all evidence was circumstantial, and that the matter of your past would be largely, if not entirely, inadmissible before a circuit judge."

41

I swung my feet to the floor.

"I also let it be known a good defense lawyer could win a change of venue and move the trial out of King County, which would further increase chances of acquittal."

"What you telling me?"

"Rutledge wanted to go for a preliminary hearing and have you bound over for the grand jury. I argued that the Commonwealth Attorney's office might be perceived at a later date to have been hastily presumptuous of guilt and injudiciously eager for conviction and closing of the case."

"And?"

"Funny how I've suddenly captured your complete attention. They told me to wait in the hall and drink a Coke while they talked. I did and partially searched a title in the clerk's office before they called me back."

"Don't be a sonofabitch," I said, by this time standing.

"Say please."

"Please goddammit!"

"That's a bit more than I asked for. But if you'll give your word not to leave King County and to report in to Lewis's office every morning by eight o'clock, they just might cut you some slack."

I didn't believe they'd take my word. If they released me, it was either to allow me freedom to trap myself by fleeing or because of a hope I'd lead them to evidence that'd put me away for good.

"Fail to report in by eight and they'll haul you back where the only sunlight you'll ever see again will have iron bars across it."

"They believe I'll convict myself."

"You will undoubtedly be the center of their absolute attention."

"Okay, they got my word."

"I'll report it to them."

"Where'm I supposed to stay around here if they agree?"

"No more specific than you don't cross the county's confines," he said and lifted the attaché case as unscarred as himself.

"I got no money."

"Don't even think of asking me for any."

"They have a legal right to make me report even if I'm not charged?"

"Probably not, but I wouldn't push that." He called for Rodger.

"Thanks I guess."

"You guess?"

"I don't want to step in a tiger pit dug for me out there."

"You believe I'd be part of that?"

"I gave up believing."

"You and the world," he said and left.

AS I WAITED, I lay listening to locusts reach screeching crescendos in the courthouse elms. I smoked the last of Walt's cigarettes. What the hell was taking so long? I stood and paced the way I'd done at Leavenworth. Animal cage twelve by nine.

Traffic increased on River Street. Citizens on their way home. At Lizard Inlet I'd be stoking up my fire for steaming crabs or frying fillets.

Bolts and doors. Rodger. He carried my overalls and shirt hanging from the end of a wooden billy. They'd not been washed. When he unlocked the cell, he dropped them on the floor.

"Change," he said.

I zipped down and stepped from the orange coveralls. I recognized my odor in my shirt. He returned my Old Timer, thirty-seven cents, and my empty wallet. He held a mimeograph form and pencil to me—a receipt for the possessions I'd received back.

"Where's my fish knife and sheath?" I asked.

"We keeping that awhile. Don't forget to come see us."

His face was larger at the bottom than the top. Small brain. He walked me to the end of the cell block and swung open the steel door. I moved along the corridor past the interrogation and squad rooms, both empty.

When I left the jail, my first thought was to slink off like a kicked dog. I steadied myself and turned toward River Street. The humid air felt heavy—like wearing a wet shroud. The sun, still high, shone hot and red. The chirring elms, the rusting World War howitzer, the Confederate soldier forever striding, all appeared bent by the hazy light.

Jessup's Wharf's business district was now two blocks long, a major advance from my boyhood, yet the character of age and traditions still prevailed—small shops and offices, most one-story brick or white frame except for the classical King County Bank. Nothing modern like a Hardee's, Food Lion, or Revco. Much real estate had belonged to the LeBlancs, Jessup's Wharf existing practically in vassalage to Bellerive before the Great Depression.

Cotton was no longer grown, but a LeBlanc warehouse still stood beside the river, the town's name, once painted on the tin roof as an aid to aircraft, now faded except for the letter *W.* The warehouse had become a scabbed hulk favored by sleek river rats we'd shot with our Daisy air rifles.

I hadn't walked this street in years, yet the pavement felt familiar. My feet remembered. The Planters Drug Store collection of colored apothecary bottles still lined a window ledge. I glanced into the shadowed interior. Ladies of the village still sat on wire-back chairs to drink their lemonade and chocolate sodas at small, round marble-top tables.

People gaped at me along the way, both from the sidewalk and in passing cars. My beard and ratty clothes marked me. I looked into no one's face. Jessup's Wharf's lack of a paper or TV station had failed to slow the spread of news. The local grapevine handled it at a velocity equal to electronic transmission.

I passed under the strip of shade laid on the sidewalk by Jessup's Mercantile's striped awning. I smelled tomatoes, peppers, and cucumbers in the wooden bins. Somebody had hurried inside to buy milk or bread and left the engine of a red Chevy Impala running. I thought of stealing the car and driving hell-bent from the county. My fingers tightened as if they gripped the wheel. I kept walking. Cole and the rest of the courthouse bastards would've been after me in ten seconds.

I hoped Walter Frampton had put up a shingle somewhere along River Street so I wouldn't have to ask about his office. A town policeman stood at the corner by the control box that operated Jessup's Wharf's single stoplight. He watched. I crossed to the other side.

People flowed around me as if I were a rock in a stream, especially the alarmed ladies. Men scowled, and I kept my eyes lowered, not meaning to challenge anybody. I looked at the sidewalk's loaf-shaped bricks channeled with the passing of countless scuffing shoes. A pale moss grew in cracks, and rainwater had pooled in gutters.

I reached the Bridge Street intersection where the old grist mill still stood and beyond was Axapomimi Lumber. The scent of sap from newly sawed loblollies mixed with tidal odors. Yellowish smoke rose from a black metal stack. A powerboat sped under the low, narrow span.

I'd have to ask about Walter. I slowed before a shoe shop, where a black man pounded nails into a lady's slipper fixed on a metal last.

"Lawyer Frampton's office 'round here?" I called through the open door. The cobbler wore a blue apron and never stopped hammering.

"Up Hill Street and a flight of steps."

I thanked him. Jessup's Wharf had no hill. Land rose nearly imperceptibly from the river. A street had to be named something, and this one had seen better days. There'd been stables, a mortuary, the post office, and a three-story frame hotel named the King's Inn that offered a veranda and rocking chairs. When I was a boy, the hotel burned, and we saw the sky lit a flickering reddish orange all the way to Bellerive.

A brick building had belonged to a Dr. Poythress. He used the upstairs to concoct his own medicines and to experiment making braces. He'd been a scary man, gaunt and brooding, and when parents wanted to punish a child for misbehaving, they'd threaten to take him to Dr. Poythress. I'd pictured him binding me in braces and sticking me with long hypodermic needles.

Now an antique store occupied the first level. It was closed. In the dusty window lay a pair of cavalry spurs, a cracked china platter, and empty picture frames. A line of red ants crawled over a wheelless baby carriage topped by a torn and faded pink canopy.

The black metal shingle that read WALTER B. FRAMPTON, II, ATTORNEY hung over wooden steps that led to the second floor, the letters painted in white English script. The entrance had a polished brass knob and letter slot. A printed sign said ENTER.

I opened the door half expecting to see old braces and instruments of torture I'd pictured in Dr. Poythress's chamber of horrors. Instead I faced a high-ceilinged, whelk-colored room with a large desk that had two cane chairs set before it. Walls held framed diplomas and behind the desk hung an outsized photograph of General Robert E. Lee in uniform—boots, saber, but bareheaded. He looked too kindly to be such a magnificent killer. My father would've smacked me for even thinking that.

Walter wasn't working but sat leaned back in his swivel chair, his spindly fingers laced behind his head, his eyes fixed on the ceiling. He'd cocked one loafer on his wastebasket. Open across his chest lay a *Vanity Fair.*

"Believed and hoped I was shut of you," he said, cutting his eyes at but not turning his head toward me.

"I thought you'd be around when I got out."

"You appear to be under the misapprehension I'm still your lawyer. You're no longer being held or charged and thus don't qualify for pro bono services."

"Like telling me I don't need a doctor till I'm dead. They setting me up."

"Good chance," he said and leaned so far back in the squeaky chair he was nearly horizontal.

"Don't seem so good to me. How long can they keep me around and make me report in without a charge?"

"Long as the world turns," he said and raised his arms to stretch them.

"Isn't that harassment?"

"I hear strains of a jailhouse lawyer."

"I read some law. Had time to do it."

"The University of Leavenworth."

"An accelerated course. Also finished my GED and got twelve college credits."

"Commendable," he said. He dropped the foot from the wastebasket to the floor, and the chair sprang him upright. He tossed the *Vanity Fair* to his desk.

"I'm supposed to hang around waiting for them to find a way to burn my ass?"

"It's what you agreed to, and at the moment you have no other recourse," Walt said. He sniffed. "You realize you smell like the skunk works. Might help your public relations to get a shave and haircut."

"How, with thirty-seven cents in my pocket?"

"Let's get one matter straight here and now," he said and spun to face me directly. "I don't intend to continue representing you or give you free legal advice. I don't want you on my hands."

"You could look into the insurance policy thing," I said. "If there's money, I'll pay."

"The policy's only talk. Moreover I believe you're quite possibly guilty and a despicable human being. I don't want to be associated with you in any fashion whatsoever. Has the message gotten through to you?"

"Well fuck you then."

"Actually I screw only for love," Walt said.

9

I LEFT HIS office and followed Bridge Street to the river, where I skirted the public landing. The Axapomimi gently rocked moored pleasure boats. During my youth there'd been few frivolous, gaily painted crafts like these, only the skiffs and johnboats of watermen who ran trot lines and sold their catches at dockside.

I again thought of running. I'd learned that skill, changing my name the first time after a bar fight in Key West, again for the army, lastly following my release from Leavenworth. A police nightstick in Miami had left me addled twenty-four hours. My fingers could still trace a dip in the back of my head. I'd become so hungry I'd sold my dick in exchange for a spaghetti dinner and later mugged fags in a palm-shrouded public park within hearing of the geriatric set's clacking shuffleboard sticks.

I'd begun to feel I'd discovered a long-term refuge at Lizard Inlet, flood-plain land so godforsaken not even the real estate hawkers tried to peddle it. Now I'd never go back, not even for the cracked-stock twelve-gauge Savage I'd left in my shack. Somebody'd probably stolen it anyhow.

I felt the West tug at me—Montana, with its dwindling population, snow-crowned mountains, and broad undulating grasses that stretched forever under a sky like an inverted sea.

I turned to look behind. Was I being followed? Maybe not. They could be giving me a chance to run, then pull in the state troopers with all their computers and tracking gadgetry to drop the net.

Out in Montana I'd hunt and cook over a cottonwood fire. I'd find me a stream that ran fast and pure. Set up my camp on a rise of ground where, like a Sioux, I could view all approaches. Only if I stayed too long in one place, they'd find me. That meant never-ending rear-guard actions to keep them from zeroing in on me. The law would become a python with ever-constricting coils.

A marina had replaced the old landing—slips, Exxon pumps, a store selling nets, rods, and bloodworms. Along the far side, white summer cottages built by people from Richmond or Washington reflected in tranquil pale green water. All had screen porches and private piers with ladders for swimmers.

When I was a boy, ancient sycamore trees had lined the bank. I'd swung out on a rope tied to an upper limb, turned loose at the top of the arc, and dropped into the river from a height so high I plunged to the dark bottom and had to jerk my legs free from billowing, grasping mud.

A path still followed the town side of the bank. My bare feet had patted the slick alluvial soil. There were more houses, not the summer kind across the river, but substantial residences owned by Jessup's Wharf's merchants, professionals, and surely a banker or two.

I reached a chain-link fence across the path. No gate. I hesitated, peered up the lawn to a Dutch colonial, and climbed the fence. A young woman wearing a white shirt and shorts opened the front-porch screen door.

"This private property!" she hollered. "I'll call the police!"

I ran to the second fence and scampered over. When I glanced back, she was shading her eyes to look after me. Ahead, more fences and a collie, who started barking. At a lane between houses, I jogged up from the river to the paved road.

Then out to highway, two broad lanes of asphalt soft and polished under the sun. Breathing hard, I walked the weedy shoulder. Ditches had grown up with honeysuckle and cow vine. My possessions, only thirty-seven cents and the Old Timer pocketknife. Not even a fucking cigarette.

I realized I'd instinctively headed toward Bellerive. There'd once been three thousand acres in the holding. During the 1930s the tract had been whittled down by desperate needs of my Grandfather LeBlanc to survive financially. Not till the money rolled in from High Moor did my father start repurchasing parcels of land as well as begin his long and loving restoration of the big house.

I again blocked his face from my memory.

Though late afternoon, the sun still burned high. I searched for the deer trail I'd followed as a boy. John, Edward, and I'd made it our private shortcut to Jessup's Wharf.

I found it overgrown with broomstraw and briars, which snagged legs of my overalls. I pinched out a thorn stuck in my toe and swatted flies attracted to sweat.

At the pine woods a fence, this one barbwire marking Bellerive's southern boundary. I wanted a look at what the explosion had done to the house. The pines had become huge since I left, uniformly spaced loblollies. They spread a thick shade that had killed or stunted all undergrowth. A dense cover of tags softened the ground. Timber companies would pay high dollars for this stand. The money to go to whom? Brother Edward, the inheritor of Bellerive.

I'd used the word *whom*. Bellerive reaching for and reminding me to watch my language and manners. I found myself conjugating *amo, amas, amat*.

A beating of wings caused me to whirl and throw up an arm. The gobbler flushed from high in a loblolly, its dusky flight among dark, interlaced branches. I'd been a youth who'd never wanted to come in from the woods to learn Latin.

Moving out of shadows into slanting sunlight, I reached a white plank fence and pasture, land that graded downward toward the river, which I couldn't yet see. No cattle grazed, but a salt lick remained, and a green glimmer rose from an ocean of orchard grass.

I ducked through the fence and hoped no bull patrolled the pasture's expanse to protect his harem. I shielded my eyes to spot the grove of water oaks growing from the highest ground of what had been a self-sufficient plantation. Those oaks surrounded the big house, now a hundred and sixty-three years old. I'd climbed them and pretended to spread sail and sword-fight pirates among spars of a three-masted galleon.

I jumped a shallow, winding branch that flowed to a cattle pond and climbed the grade to reach the sandy drive that led to the house. My father had left it unpaved to protect the horses' hooves.

The entrance from the highway was marked by white gateposts topped with stone pineapples. A small brass BELLERIVE had been mortared into bricks. My father had ordered the Kentucky gate be kept closed to prevent strangers from driving in to gawk, and locals knew to stay out unless invited.

The drive wound between rows of black walnut trees whose trunks were pitted from woodpeckers' feeding on insects. Gaius had collected bushel baskets of the nuts each fall for cracking and use in Juno's kitchen. The rest had been raked into a pile and given to any hands that wanted them. I remembered the *tap-tap-tap* of Gaius's hammer.

In fields on either side were barns, silos, equipment sheds, outbuildings. All were white with a midnight green trim. My father had bought the most modern machinery and often operated the big tractors himself. He'd worn dark glasses and a straw hat as he dug his plow blades deep and boiled up clumps of plundered red soil. He'd loved his dicking of the earth.

Nearer the main house, a row of six identical white-brick cabins lined a pasture's crest. They'd been decaying slave quarters my father rebuilt and modernized for Bellerive's tenants, who were required to keep them painted and in repair.

I reached the serpentine wall at the rear of the house. The grilled iron gate had been left ajar. I listened and scanned terrain before I stepped from the line of walnut trees to edge through to the courtyard and the fountain. Sun had dried the gray cobblestones, and no flow splashed from the gaping dolphin's copper-green mouth. Water collected in the fountain's bowl had the yellowish cast of piss.

As yet no visible damage. Red and purple crape myrtles bloomed along the side of the English basement. Courses of bricks laid in Flemish bond rose three stories to arrowhead-tipped lightning rods and decorative ironwork around the slate roof's mansard crown. Surrounded by the ironwork, and added since I was last here, was a weather vane painted in the likeness of my father's piebald stallion, Caesar. A breeze off the river caused it to shift.

Police had strung yellow plastic tape around the house. I spotted no guard. Blinds of the English basement were closed. I walked toward the front and looked down across the lawn. English box bushes lined the path to the river and dock where my father had kept an inboard launch.

Several water oaks had been doctored, their wounds patched with concrete. Ancient limbs were chained to keep them from breaking loose of their weight. This shade was richest of all trees, appearing thick enough to slip fingers under and lift like a carpet.

I rounded the house. When I ran away from Bellerive, there'd been no portico, and the LeBlancs' annual celebration was held on an extensive wooden veranda. I eyed the destruction—a collapsed roof, broken two-story stone columns, crushed iron furniture, glass shattered from broad high windows, bricks and shards of slate flung across the lawn, stricken box bushes covered by debris.

I looked over rubble to the breached double doorway and the yawning wrecked dimness within.

"Hey!" a voice shouted. A wizened man in a blue uniform too large for him hurried around the house. "What you doing?"

"Couldn't resist a look-see," I said, backing off from the tape.

"No looks allowed unless you got written authorization from the sheriff, the bank, or the insurance company," he said, his hand near his army-issue .45 automatic, which was way too big for him, making him appear lopsided. Probably stole the gun from the service. His nameplate read ROY.

"Didn't know I needed permission."

"Oh hell no, and you wouldn't want to steal nothing," Roy said. A shoulder patch shaped like a shield identified him as an employee of the Bulldog Security System. "There's still furnishings inside. Nobody but the law, the bank, and insurance people allowed around here."

"I'm on my way," I said and started back around the house.

"Don't come no more. And give me your name."

"Monroe. James Monroe."

"Where you live?" he asked, following. He pulled a pencil and palm-size notebook from his shirt pocket.

"Just thought I'd do a little fishing in the river."

"Yeah, where's your gear? You don't look like no fisherman to me."

"Got to fetch it," I said. "Been looking for a good spot to wet a line."

I walked along the side of the house to the courtyard and slipped through the gate. It closed behind me.

"You got no right on this land!" Roy hollered.

10

AWAY FROM THE house the drive curved, and I looked behind me before turning down between a gap of walnut trees to intercept a farm road that led to the complex of barns, silos, and equipment sheds.

My father had installed pipe cattle guards between fields instead of gates. Honkers rose gabbling from a pond. Where were the cows?

I passed a multibayed galvanized building that held tractors, harrows, bailers, rakes, a combine. Each had been precisely parked —my father's demand for exactness had been continued by brother John.

I moved on to a barn smelling of alfalfa. A hay wagon had been left in the central passageway near a chute. During winter, hands slid bales down the chute to the wagon, and a tractor hauled it out to fields where bales were dropped off to feed the cattle.

I drank by cupping my hands beneath the all-weather Iowa faucet before climbing the wooden ladder to the loft. Dusk settled over the land. I looked across fields to the row of restored slave cabins. All doors were shut. No lights, pets, children, or tenants moved about. There'd used to be a common garden my father insisted the tenants cultivate to provide vegetables both for themselves and the big house, a kind of tithe required of their produce.

I relaxed on alfalfa bales till darkness seeped into the loft and I could no longer see the roof trusses. I listened for human sounds. What would Roy be doing, and did he or other guards check the cabins?

Whippoorwills tuned up, and far away a dog barked. I climbed from the loft, ran across the pasture, and traversed the drive before circling wide behind the cabins. A half-moon provided a bloodless light. It shone on the common garden, the untended rows sprouting weeds.

Crouched, I moved up to the cabin farthest from the big house and listened before straightening to peek in a window. A deeper darkness inside. Ready to run, I tapped on the back door. No answer. I twisted the knob, and it wouldn't turn. I snuck along trying doors. At the fourth cabin one gave to my fingers.

"Anybody home?" I called and entered.

When my eyes adjusted, I made out and touched a small round table, a straight chair, a cook stove. I looked through the window over a sink. Fireflies glowed above moon-glazed grass.

I tiptoed from the kitchen to a front room. All shades had been drawn. I quietly raised one to reveal a collapsed sofa, a floor lamp, a scatter rug. I checked out two small bedrooms, the first empty, the second offering a bare mattress in place over box springs.

My father had furnished the cabins. Tenants provided their own sheets, blankets, adornments. Undoubtedly brother John had kept up the practice.

Back in the kitchen, I didn't try the lights. If the electricity hadn't been disconnected, even the quick on-and-off flick of a switch might cause a flash that could be seen by Roy or other guards at the big house. I reached to the stove and turned a control. A hiss, then blue fire popped in a rear burner.

When I left Bellerive, neither the cabins nor the main house had been rigged for gas. My father or John might've changed that. Gas could've caused an explosion. Had Redneck Rutledge checked it out?

I tried a sink faucet. Water ran onto my palm. It didn't become hot and was warmed only by a residue of the day's heat. Still I could have myself a wash as well as a night's sleep on the mattress.

I was so goddamn hungry. I cracked the back door. Darkness everywhere except for moon glow and a whitish aura among the water oaks at the main house. The guards would have lights.

Around the garden a closely woven wire fence had been strung on posts to keep out rabbit, possum, deer. Nothing could keep out coons. I opened the gate and dug my hands into soil among withered vines. My fingers clutched potatoes. I picked tomatoes, okra, and used my Old Timer to cut a mess of turnip greens. I pulled up onions and shook dirt from them. Hobo stew on the menu.

At the cabin I again lit the stove's rear burner, and the flame furnished enough eerie light for me to rinse the vegetables in the sink. Searching, I slid out a metal drawer at the bottom of the stove and found a dented tin pot. It didn't leak water. I half filled it and diced in the tomatoes, okra, onions, greens, and thickly sliced unpeeled potatoes.

I hadn't explored the refrigerator. When I opened the door, a light switched on, and I shielded it with my body. Inside, nothing except a single can of Nehi grape soda—a poor man's wine to accompany a dinner of hot hobo stew. As always, the land provided.

I washed a broken wooden spoon lifted from the floor and used it to stir my pot. If I played my cards right, I could live here nights. Hiding someplace else during the day'd be easy enough. After reporting in to the sheriff each morning, I'd laze along the river, catch fish, build a little fire to fry them, sleep in willow shade to escape the heat.

I popped the grape soda. It slid cool down my throat, a fine vintage. At Lizard Inlet I'd made wine out of wild scuppernongs and got so drunk I fell on my face into the slough. I'd wallowed like a grunting hog.

My stew bubbled, and its smell caused my stomach to pinch and ache. I drew the pot off the burner and spooned up a taste. Lord God how good, and I'd have enough for tonight and another meal tomorrow. With the grape soda I toasted myself for surviving the day intact.

The door banged open. A huge shape loomed toward me. I backed to the wall. Very slowly I reached to my pocket for the Old Timer.

"Who in this house?" the shape demanded. "I asking who in this damn house!"

"Didn't know anybody still lived here," I answered as I slid the knife out and pressed it against my leg.

The shape kicked shut the door, became a shimmer in the glow from the blue flame, feinted sideways, lunged, and hurled me into the front room, where I fell over the sofa. I scrambled up. I'd thumbed open the blade.

A match flared. Behind it a black man, his massive face sweaty and gleaming. He spread vast arms low as if to tackle me.

"You ain't told me who yet."

"Needed a place to lay over for the night," I said and backed around the sofa.

"You busted in here," he said and followed me.

"I didn't bust in. The door was unlocked. Believed everybody gone."

"What you think of doing with that pissy little knife?" he asked. The match burned out, and he lit another. "You ain't scaring Rajab Ishmael. Got a blade in my pocket so sharp that it'd slit you head to toe 'fore a drop a blood know it free."

"I don't want trouble," I said. Jesus, a fucking Moslem brother in King County. "Just let me make tracks."

"Nobody want trouble," he said and blew out the match before it singed his fingers. "Thing is trouble sometime want you. What's your name?"

"Carson," I said. He was blackness within blackness. "William Carson."

"Pile of shit," he said. "Rajab Ishmael can smell shit in the dark. I ready to throw you ass out this house."

"Try the stew first," I said, still backing. "Got more than enough for the two of us."

The deeper darkness ceased stalking me. He struck another match, the flame protected by a hand big as a dinner plate.

He crossed to the mantel above a gas space heater. The flame moved to the wick of a candle stuck in an empty Mountain Dew bottle. He didn't try to switch on a light, and his not doing so meant he had no more right to be in the cabin than I did.

"Maybe Rajab taste your stew before he toss you out," he said. In the yellowish candle flicker he now appeared Oriental. He wore black slacks, a black shirt that'd had the sleeves cut off at the shoulder, and a black cap, the bill turned rearward.

He sheltered the flame as he carried the candle to the kitchen and set it on the table. He lifted the pot of stew and sniffed it. Watching me, he lifted and sucked up a spoonful.

"It ain't poison," he said and smacked his thick lips. "Ain't high hog either. Needs salt. You hungry, ain't you? Look like you could eat me."

"I'm hungry," I said and still held the knife, but my fingers eased on it.

Rajab spied the Nehi. He stared at it before yanking open the refrigerator. "You been drinking my goddamn grape soda?" he asked and slammed the door shut.

"I thought it'd been left."

"Been left by me for me," he said and grasped the can, drank deep, and wiped a forearm across his mouth. "This stew all right."

I closed the knife, let it drop into my pocket, and stood by while he ate from the pot and watched me over it.

"Need vinegar. You from 'round here?"

"Just passing through."

"Oh nah, you ain't heard about the 'splosion or thinking maybe they something left lying about you could light-finger."

"I heard."

"Killed Gaius," he said. "Him my uncle."

When I was a boy, many black hands bore names like Gaius, Cyrus, Juno, Priam, Minerva, Achilles, Cornelia, and Darius to please Grandfather LeBlanc, who'd loved classical history and made cash gifts to parents who laid those names on their children.

I remembered Gaius, a slender, graying man who worked in the big house answering doors, polishing silver, waiting tables. He had many children, mostly girls he married off. Born on the place, he'd learned to speak white man's English.

At Bellerive many blacks signed on during harvest season. Most lived down dusty lanes among scraggly scrub pines. Half-buried whitewashed car tires marked entrances. As a child I played and hunted with their children. We took fish from the Axapomimi. The first girl I ever kissed and felt up was black, and she fled giggling.

"You think I got bird brains?" Rajab asked when he lowered the pot. "I 'member you. We work hay together. You Charles, ain't you? Word's around. Everybody know the man after your ass."

He kept eating and without taking his eyes off me finished off the last of the stew.

"I knowed you, but you never needed to know me. You turned

over a skiff that had a big king snake curled under it. Ran around shoving that snake at people. Hung it right in my face till I jump in the river."

"King snakes never hurt anybody," I said. The sonofabitch. I was suffering hunger.

"Yeah, then why they call him snake? You always in trouble. Now sneaking around here after you blow up Gaius. I thinking you ought to have a long swim in that old river. A swim that don't never stop. Make catfish bait."

"I didn't blow up anybody."

"Not what I hear in Jessup's. Everybody calling you turd."

"Calling don't make it true."

"Don't make a damn to me," he said and dropped the pot in the sink. "Uncle Gaius a house nigger—I call him nigger, you can't. Lots of times he more white than whiteys. Thought he better. Wore your daddy's old clothes. Your daddy pay mine to call me Hector. I renounce it."

"I'd do the same."

"You let that snake loose in the big house. Your daddy whip you good for that. Heard you hollering all the way to the shop."

How much fire smoldered in the bellies of Bellerive's blacks? Enough for one to lay a charge under the portico?

"Me, I moving on," he said, the candle's light sliding his lumbering shadow across the wall. He sat at the table. "Ever'body been let go 'round this place. No work at the mill neither. I helped plant the garden. I got rights to pull myself a salad."

I stood waiting.

"Fucking LeBlancs ruined this country," Rajab said. "Took it all and didn't leave nothing for nobody else. Worked the black man to death. Same way up in the mountains."

"The mountains?"

"Word got back. Worked ever'body to death." Rajab belched. "Wearing shiny boots and riding around on fancy horses. Care more for horses than men."

Maybe he meant Caesar, the stallion my father owned that won timber races at the Gold Cup three years running. When the piebald died, the family held a service, Father Lovelace driving out from Christ Church and reading Scriptures on a November morning when oak leaves spiraled down. Caesar had a tombstone in Bellerive's animal cemetery.

"I know about you," Rajab said. "How they send you to military school and you run away after the fight with your daddy. Ever'body 'cept your mama call you bad. She nice lady and didn't have no LeBlanc in her for damn sure."

Again he belched.

"You was a good shot, I remember that. Brought in more birds than the big house could feed. Your daddy send the extra down to the hands. We cook up stews out your squirrels."

I raised my head and gobbled, at the same time flapping an arm to give the call vibrato. I'd built lean-to blinds from pine boughs in the bottom, dressed before dawn, and sat giving hen yelps as mist rose from the river. I'd coaxed turkeys to within twenty feet and seen their surprise and alarm as I pulled down on them with my L. C. Smith twenty-gauge. Dead meat.

"I didn't blow up the place," I said.

"Why I believe your mouf? You a LeBlanc, ain't you?"

"Only half."

"Half plenty."

"My brother John ever mistreat you?"

"He didn't need to mistreat nobody. He had other people do his mistreating."

"He was also involved in lots of land and business transactions. Could've been a cause of bad blood."

"How I know? Kitchen door closest I got to the big house except when they give parties on the lawn and I'd hide and watch. Hung lanterns in the oaks. Shine colors on the grass and river."

"My brother have any special friends?"

"Gaffreys," Rajab said. "They ride horses right through a man's seeded fields. Wearing red coats. Thirty or forty hounds chasing a poor fucking fox. Gaffreys keep the hounds."

"Where they live?

"Up King's Tavern. Run hounds and horses right over a man's field and never leave a dollar for the crop they tramp on."

"Gas used for heating in the big house?" I asked.

"No gas. Burn Number Two fuel oil."

"Cooking?"

"Juno have the two stoves—one wood, the other 'lectric. She never like 'lectric. Said nothing come out a wire good for food."

I knew about the big Kalamazoo wood burner. I'd come in wet from hunting, and she'd stand me beside it to warm and dry. With black, ladylike fingers, she handed me buttered biscuits still hot from her oven. She'd be at least eighty now.

"Juno not her real name," Rajab said. "Name your granddaddy lay on her. She 'Lizabeth."

"How bad was she hurt?"

"Cut some. She pack up and gone."

"Where to?"

"Down Richmond way with her cousin Mary. Now I gonna sleep. Don't try nothing. I be hearing you. I be knowing where you is every second." He stood. "I leaving tomorrow. Everybody gone. This place cleaned out. The bank take the cattle. I rolling down to Norfolk town. Get me a job building ships. The mattress mine."

He lifted the candle, and his lumbering shadow followed him to the front bedroom. He used the toilet.

"I for the fucking fox!" he called as he closed and locked the bedroom door.

I waited till he snored before I slipped out to the garden for a second picking of tomatoes, okra, onions, potatoes, and greens to pacify the claws raking my belly.

11

I TRIED THE sofa, but it tilted and rocked each time I turned, so I stretched out on the back bedroom's floor. I'd known harder sleep. Through plasterboard walls Rajab continued his growling, bearlike snore.

I'd raised the shade and window. So many years since I'd lain hearing night sounds of Bellerive. No cattle lowed, but I listened to whippoorwills, pond bullfrogs *ba-whomp*ing, the continuous, throbbing insect drone. Wind off the river stirred black walnut leaves and carried smells of honeysuckle, orchard grass, and wisteria.

Without a word Rajab clomped through the cabin and left before dawn on his way to Norfolk, ships, the sea. I stripped down and gave myself a whore's bath using the bathroom sink and a sliver of soap. I walked around naked to dry.

At first pearly light I looked toward the big house. Nothing. I shut the window, pulled the shade, and opened the back door. Mist collected and stirred in the low ground. I dressed and ran to the garden. No corn ears on the stalks, and cucumbers had rotted. I picked a zucchini, which I washed and peeled at the cabin sink before eating raw.

I crossed moist pasture to the plank fence, climbed it, and followed the deer trail through pines to the paved road. No traffic along the blacktop. Somewhere a hound gave tongue, and a chain saw snarled. In rural Virginia you could always hear a hound or chain saw. I looked behind me. My tennis shoes had left prints on damp asphalt.

The distant shrill of the mill whistle. Cars and pickups passing, the employees on their way to work at Axapomimi Lumber and Southern States. Above the tree line rose the town's silver water tank, the courthouse belfry, and the white steeple of the Ebenezer Baptist Church.

Life rousing on River Street. The twirling peppermint pole of the barber shop augered upward. A black cook wearing a rolled-up paper sack for a hat hauled trash from the Dew Drop Inn. Two barefoot boys carrying fishing rods ran toward the bridge. Cars stopped in front of the post office, where the flag hadn't been raised.

At the jail Rodger sat in the sheriff's office reading the sports page of the *Daily Press*. Chest hairs spilled over the open neck of his shirt. A wisp of steam lifted from a half-empty mug of coffee.

"You damn near late," he said and pushed a legal pad and pencil toward me. "Sign."

"Why? You see me, don't you?"

"Do it."

I did as the radio scanner behind him crackled. The wall had been used as a dartboard, the target a tacked-up magazine photo of Ayatollah Khomeini. On a two-burner hot plate a pot of coffee heated, and the bastard could've offered.

"Where you staying?"

"Only five-star hotels," I said and wondered whether they'd tried to follow me yesterday but had been thrown off when I used the deer trail.

"We got to know how to reach you."

"Slept down by the river," I said, only half a lie. "The river don't have an address."

"You be back tomorrow."

"Sip of coffee?"

"Nope," he said and looked at the humming electric clock on the wall before writing down the time beside my name. The clock advertised the Axapomimi Funeral Home. Police humor.

I left his office and town. Farmers passed trucking livestock to market, cows bawling and hogs squealing. A covey of birds flushed from Queen Anne's lace growing along the shoulder. Instinctively I tracked them as if I held my L. C. Smith. Could've brought down a double.

I crossed through pine woods, thinking of chiggers and ticks. At the fence I scouted Bellerive before following the wagon road to the barn. I climbed to the loft to watch the big house.

A car entered the lane. I couldn't make out the driver. A few moments later a pickup drove away. A changing of the guard.

The sun brightened water oaks. Pigeons circled the white ventilation spire of the stable. A box stall had once held my pony Mosby and later a chestnut gelding called Red Warrior. I'd raced brother John down the lane, across fields, over fallen trees. We swam horses in the river.

A two-and-a-half-ton Ford truck turned off the county road, its bed loaded with plywood sheet. Then three pickups. Workmen sent in by the bank or insurance company.

Hammering and the screeching of saws. I dozed in the expanding loft heat. How long did Falkoner and Rutledge expect me to stick around Jessup's Wharf? They'd maneuvered me into a chess game—my move, the law's, mine again.

I sat up quick at the sound of an engine. At the equipment shed two black men fastened a tractor to a mower. One drove it off, the second held to the seat and stood behind him on the hitch.

My stomach gurgled, yet I couldn't take a chance during daylight of raiding the garden. I still had the thirty-seven cents. I left the backside of the barn and kept it between myself and the big house till I reached the woods. At the country road I turned north.

My father had owned a store that sold groceries and dry goods to locals. I pictured a can of succulent Vienna sausage. The label carried a red rose.

I found the frame building caved in under heavy growth of creeper and honeysuckle vines the size of my arm. The vines had pried off the tin roof, which had rusted through. Weeds covered a broken concrete stump that'd supported a single Pure gas pump. I used to ride Mosby here to buy a penny's worth of horehound candy I'd share with the pony.

I continued along the road. Grasshoppers warmed by the sun sprang from weeds. Pickups passed, farmers who sized me up, a few who raised their hands after the fashion of country people. The land on both sides still belonged to Bellerive for at least another quarter mile. My father's doings.

A GMC slowed and stopped to wait for me.

"Save your shoe leather," the driver called through the window, a bespectacled man wearing a red Southern States cap. His smile vanished. "Hold it. Ain't you—?"

He shifted gears and drove on fast. I looked after him, spat, and worked down through the pine woods to the riverbank. Sun glittered on mid-channel water. The shorelines lay shaded by overhanging willows. I sat and unlaced my ragged tennis shoes before lying back and watching an osprey circle. From Bellerive came faint sounds of pounding.

I again thought about the insurance policy. Whether it existed or not, didn't I have a right to know? Dumb question. Rights belonged to respectable people, not swamp-dwelling felons who raided dumps and scared children.

"Ain't you learned anything?" I asked myself.

A fish jumped in the river, not a shad who would've finished migration but likely a smallmouth bass gulping down an unlucky grasshopper or June bug. I wished I had a line.

I stood and walked the bank till I found a growth of cattails. I pulled them, peeled young shoots, and ate them and the pith from the rootstalks where they joined. They tasted like muddy celery.

I laced on my shoes and hiked the bank toward Bellerive. Close, I stopped every fifty paces to listen. Across the river crows squabbled after a hawk. An outboard skiff ran upstream, two fishermen inside trolling.

I let down on all fours and crawled to the white plank fence bordering the big house's lawn. Grass needed mowing. More rapid hammering. I squinted toward the knoll, able to make out workers nailing sheets of plywood over broken windows.

Hunger again gnawed me. I slipped back to the river where I found mussels growing along the shore. I wrenched them free and used my Old Timer blade to lever open shells. The meat resembled yellow mucus, but I sucked it up. They, too, tasted of mud. I swallowed a dozen.

When shadows lengthened across the water, I sneaked back to Bellerive's broad lawn. I saw and heard no activity. I scouted the bordering fringe of pines. Where was Roy? I watched and waited.

A breeze lifted from the south, and the piebald weather vane adjusted. Sheets of new plywood nailed over the front windows and doorway gave the house the stark expression of an outraged grand dame.

Roy walked around the corner of the house, stopped to remove his cap and wipe his face, continued on to the rear. He set a white iron lawn chair at the gate, lowered himself into it, stretched his legs. Yawning, he used the cap to fan his face.

I moved down toward the river till the house hid me from him, then ran straight up across the lawn to the destroyed portico. I edged around the house and crouched behind a box bush to spy out Roy still sitting by the gate. He again yawned, began leafing through a magazine, slapped a skeeter.

I backed along the English basement to the portico, where I stepped carefully around chunks of broken columns. A single door had been cut through the plywood covering the smashed front entrance. The door was held closed by a hasp that had a ten-penny nail bent through it.

Quietly I climbed rubble and drew out the nail. The strap hinges were new and shouldn't squeak. Inch by inch I pulled till I had just enough space to squeeze through. I closed the door behind me.

I stood in the wrecked hallway. Pendants of the teardrop chandelier were shattered, and the brass support chain had partly pulled loose from the ceiling. Shards of white plaster covered the heart-of-pine floor. Walls were pocked. Portraits had been removed, the furniture shoved and crowded to the rear of the house. A pale yellowish dust lay thick over all.

To the left, the parlor, its oak double doors shut. Grit crunched under my shoes. I opened a door just enough to see across the high-ceiling room with its Oriental carpets, grand piano, and Georgian highboy.

Over the fireplace hung the oil painting of Jean Maupin Le-Blanc, first squire of Bellerive—a tall, bewigged man with a narrow face who posed holding the barrel of a grounded musket, an Irish setter at his side.

As a boy I'd wondered why any man would hunt wearing a wig and what looked like green satin breeches. A convention of the times, my mother explained.

I crossed the hallway to the dining room. The floor-to-ceiling windows were covered at the front by plywood, but light splayed through shuttered panes at the side. The great cherry table still held a candelabra, stacks of china, a punch bowl. On a walnut hunt board, silver platters used for the breakfast buffets were set out and filled with dust.

My mother's oil portrait was centered above the marble mantel. She wore a pink summer dress and sat in a red wingback chair, a white angora kitten on her lap. The kitten, named Flora, had grown into a large arrogant cat that stalked birds. My mother had fastened a collar and bell around its neck.

Acquiescent in most things, my mother tried to stand between my father and me. She helped me up the back stairway to hide me from him when I arrived home drunk. She snuck into my bedroom nights to lay her small hand on my brow, worried I suffered fever.

"Everything will work out" was her soothing, whispered refrain.

I walked the obscure hallway to the library, where I found no destruction except a single crack in the south wall. Leather-bound books still gave off a gloss, most having belonged to Grandfather LeBlanc, who'd recited Cicero while sipping his tods.

Grandfather LeBlanc had loved the Roman Empire. Insisting John, Edward, and I study Latin, he hired a tutor named Augustus Longworth. John had obediently complied, and Edward had relished the language. I'd bucked.

A walnut desk in the center of the room held a brass banker's lamp and a silver inkwell from which angled a feathered quill. A *Wall Street Journal* dated August fifteenth lay spread across the green leather-edged blotter.

On wainscoted walls hung portraits of kinsmen I once could've identified, generations of LeBlancs stretching back across the sea to Provence, their ancient turtle eyes now seeming to pronounce judgment. From earliest times, there were always eyes.

Across the hall to what we called the den—less formal than the parlor—easy chairs, a leather sofa, TV, fox-hunting prints, and the outsize framed LeBlanc coat of arms, its motto *Fortudo et Vires*—oversimply translated "courage and strength."

Here, the portrait of my father: tall, brown hair silver at the fringes, the blunt LeBlanc chin. He wore his scarlet hunting coat and held a whip that had a crooked staghorn handle joined by a silver band. I turned my eyes.

Next the breakfast room, the pantry, and the kitchen, where copper pans hung from hooks screwed into a pine beam above Juno's massive Kalamazoo. The white modern electric stove appeared frail and unused. I touched the chopping block where Gaius had cleavered beef, poultry, game. The double sink still held plates and glasses dirtied from what must've been the day of the blast. Flies spiraled.

I searched for food. The refrigerator had been emptied, all condiments were gone from the shelves. There wasn't even a moldy loaf in the bread cupboard. I found an unopened bottle of Rhine wine under the pantry counter. I slipped it and a corkscrew into my overall's hip pocket.

Instead of using the grand staircase in the front hall, I climbed the back steps to the landing. I looked out the leaded window. Roy sat reading the magazine.

I continued to the second floor and what had been my room. As I touched the knob, I felt a rush of sorrow so strong my eyes burned. I didn't cry. I'd not done that since early winter days at Santee Military Academy. So much had gone wrong. I gathered myself to open the door.

Inside nothing of me remained. The bed I'd slept in had been replaced. The turkey fans, mounted red-tailed hawk and the gray fox gone, as was my L. C. Smith. Antlers of the eight-point buck I'd killed had been taken from the wall, the screw holes filled and repainted. A dresser and wardrobe were as impersonal as motel furniture.

I backed out. Across the hall, Edward's scholarly bedroom, holding his books, a clarinet, student's desk, a microscope. Everything in its place. Before money snared him he had considered becoming a scientist. His dried, glass-covered butterfly collections still decorated walls.

Next, John's old room, transformed for his son, my nephew Paul, whom I'd never met, the boy a builder of model fighter planes and bombers, which dangled from the ceiling by nylon line so fine as to be nearly invisible. He'd flown, all right—the longest flight of all.

I hesitated at the master bedroom, my mother and father's domain, undoubtedly passed down to John and Eleanor. I didn't open the door but remembered the walnut tester bed, the Empire chiffonnier, the egg-and-dart molding.

More than that, I remembered the night my parents returned from a Christmas party at Judge Pechincy's house. I lay in bed hearing snow pat my window. I was thinking about duck hunting early along the river and wanted my father to go along.

I slid from beneath my goose-down comforter and walked the hall to their bedroom. Light edged the doorway. For a moment I couldn't understand. He wore his tuxedo, and my mother was trying to pull free. He snatched her back by her hair and thrust a hand up under her yellow taffeta gown and her panty hose and pumped fingers into her. The hair drew her face taut, slitted her eyes, and she appeared painfully and hopelessly saddened and submissive.

At that instant my father glimpsed me, released her, and kicked the door shut. He knew I'd seen. After that night whenever he looked at me, he knew.

I never told and fought off remembering. I tried to convince myself it'd not really happened, yet at odd moments obscene images sickened me, and the fury against my father took root.

The last door I entered had been my mother's place of refuge, what she'd called her sewing room—two dormered windows to the east, a table holding a pink porcelain lamp, her ladder-back chair, a wooden chest to keep mementos, her drop-leaf desk where she wrote letters, a plain, unpainted cradle in which she'd rocked me, and her wicker sewing basket itself set on a cushioned window seat.

I touched her darning needle. She'd been happiest in this room, and I'd watched her fingers so deliberate and tender as she threaded needles. She'd also read *Robinson Crusoe* to me, the book I loved best in the world, both of us sitting in the window seat, she speaking the words in her gentle, whispery voice as if fearing to bruise them.

On walls, snapshots and photographs, each framed, though a few hung crooked, perhaps disturbed by the blast—dogs, horses, family gatherings, John and Edward, cousins, friends, picnics by the river. My face appeared in none because I'd been erased.

I opened the desk, touched her stationery, leather stamp box, and slim golden pen. Papers stuck from blue, felt-lined pigeonholes. I slid out drawers, and in the bottom one, under old letters neatly bound with red twine, I found a manila envelope that held silhouettes she'd drawn on black masking paper and scissored.

Profiles of John, Edward, Juno, Gaius, Grandfather LeBlanc. As I shuffled through them, my fingers recoiled as if burned. The last profile was a young boy, perhaps twelve, most likely kept hidden by her from my father, who at the end wanted no reminders of my existence. I placed it back in the drawer.

At the landing I again stopped by the window. Roy had rolled up the magazine and was tapping it against a crossed knee. Along the hallway I flinched at my reflection in a gilt mirror. I needed clothes, a haircut, shave. I resembled a haggard, half-starved sharecropper from Grandfather LeBlanc's snapshots of Depression days.

In the guest bathroom I pocketed a bar of soap and a tarnished Gillette razor. I took the scissors from my mother's sewing basket. Next I raided a first-floor closet off the back hall and gathered belted khaki pants, a blue denim shirt, and a pair of high-top work-shoes. I tied the laces and hung the shoes around my neck.

From the kitchen window I checked Roy. He was smoking and swatting flies with his magazine. My feet grinding dust, I sidled through the plywood front door, closed it, and inserted the bent ten-penny nail into the hasp. I ran down across the lawn to the pines.

Deep in the shadowed woods I stopped, held to the trunk of a tulip poplar, and bent forward to breathe, all the while sweating and trembling—not from fear, a constant, but because I'd looked over the chasm to a distant world where during another life I'd abided.

12

AT FULL DARK I carried my tote to the unlocked tenant cabin. Rajab's candle still stuck from the Mountain Dew bottle on the kitchen table. I lit and carried it to the bathroom. Standing before the empty medicine cabinet's mirror, I used the scissors to trim my beard and cut my hair, which fell around my shoulders and into the sink.

I heated water on the stove, soaped up, and dragged the razor an inch at a time down my face. I nicked my LeBlanc chin. By candlelight, I appeared unearthly, as spectral as if risen from the grave.

I crossed to the garden and again pulled up stew makings. While the pot boiled, I used the corkscrew to open my Rhine wine. I blew out the candle to conserve it and sat in the blue glow of the gas flame. Drinking from the bottle, I allowed no childhood memories to take full shape. When they attempted to emerge, I dismembered them.

I lay on the mattress but couldn't sleep. I thought of Juno and brother Edward. Also of what Rajab had said about word coming back from the mountains. What had happened up in West Virginia?

I roamed the dark cabin, glad at last to hear a cock's crow, but when I switched on the stove to heat what was left of my stew, no flame popped to life. Either the propane tank had emptied or somebody had closed a valve. I looked toward the big house. Dawn absorbed the floodlights.

I still had water pressure. I spooned up the last of the cold, congealed stew. I pulled on my rank, torn shirt, overalls, and tennis shoes. The razor and scissors I rolled inside the clothes I'd stolen. I bound them with the belt.

The gas being cut off could mean a guard or maintenance man might come to check the cabins. They'd find evidence of use. I ran across the pasture to the pines and slowed to cross down to the river. It murmured under mist. A pair of wood ducks flushed, their flapping takeoff leaving ripples spreading over dark water.

I set the clothes from the house in a dry cavity of a dying sycamore. My flight garments. I hiked back to the paved road and walked toward town, still thinking of where I should turn next. I reached into my pocket to finger the thirty-seven cents.

Pigeons circled the Confederate statue, which had a striped cast in the first sunlight to work past elm branches. Cole had the duty at the sheriff's office.

"Some haircut," he said. "They'll shave your head for you down in Richmond town and cap it too. A small charge."

I signed the legal pad and left.

Juno and Edward. I wanted to talk to her, and shouldn't he especially have been questioned by the police? He and John had never gotten on well. Edward stood to inherit Bellerive, as well as the income received from John's estate through the trust.

They'd been different—John the sportsman, a winner of trophies, Edward more refined, a bringer home of the best grades, honor student at Yale and president of a debate society. Unlike my frequent clashes with John, Edward and I'd had only one fight and I whipped him.

I returned to the river. At the sycamore I uncovered my cache of clothes and changed. John's brogans were too large. I had no socks. I tightened the laces to keep the shoes from slipping. I'd try to reach Richmond and return to King County before morning. The promise I'd made Falkoner and Rutledge meant nothing. Fucking up and getting caught did.

I worked upstream among peeling birches till I was a good mile and a half north of Bellerive. I then stood back among scrub oaks at the side of the road, and each time I saw a vehicle approach that carried no rack of lights I stepped out and thumbed.

An old man whose palsied head shook on a skinny neck stopped his brown 1972 Dodge for me. He was clean-shaven and wearing his Sunday-go-to-meeting dark wool suit. Speaking caused his lips to quiver.

"Name's Ned Yancey," he said. "Sears having a sale."

Ned never drove faster than forty-five and kept both hands high on the wheel. Everything passed the Dodge.

A blue-and-gray police cruiser sped toward us. I pretended to have a coughing fit and bent forward to cover my face. The cruiser swept by.

Richmond was seventy miles from Jessup's Wharf. Office buildings finally took shape on the skyline. They appeared washed, shiny, pinkish. Twice a year my mother had brought us to the city to buy clothes.

My father took us to Battle Abbey, where we stood awed by the knives, guns, and shredded regimental flags under glass as well as the great painting of Lee and his generals. Edward could recite all their names. We'd felt we stood in church.

I didn't know where Edward lived. When Ned drove off Interstate 64 into the city, I asked him to let me out at the corner of Fifth and Broad. I watched him enter traffic and almost cause a pileup. He wound on, his head still wobbling.

I looked up the name Edward DeVere LeBlanc at a pay phone in the Marriott's lobby. There it was: 1517 S. Wellington Road. I asked the black doorman, who wore a red tunic and shako with a white plume, about Wellington. He hesitated before deciding to show me on a city map.

"Uptown's uptown," he said. "West End Bus comes by ever fifteen minutes. Step aboard and transfer to Wyndam Forest. They treat dogs and lawns out there better'n people."

I waited at the corner bus stop until a bus arrived. When I climbed on, a ticket cost sixty-five cents. I dropped my thirty-seven cents into the toll box, held up my palms in a plea, and said "Wyndam Forest." The driver looked me over and turned his eyes up and away. I sat.

He was also good enough to give me a transfer slip and to signal the stop where I should wait to board for Wyndam Forest. The other riders on that bus were all black women, domestic help on their way to work for inhabitants of uptown's uptown.

Maple branches arched over South Wellington. No litter marred the genteel shade. Georgian and Tudor houses became grander and were protected by walls. Sprinklers whirled over weedless emerald lawns glimpsed through gateways. The box bushes shone with the midnight greenness of being given bone meal and perpetual care.

I stepped off the bus at the 1500 block of South Wellington and checked addresses on gateposts. Mercedeses glinted from shadowed bays of garages. Silky dogs aroused by my passing had cultured barks. No flea-bitten baying hounds allowed.

I'd last seen Edward and his wife, Patricia, at my mother's funeral. A cold, blowing shower flapped and beat the scalloped canopy over the flower-bedecked casket. I'd stood opposite them across the grave, my wrists bound, an armed guard at my side. Afterward, Edward had only one sentence for me: "I'm glad she no longer has to witness the thing you've become."

He was a couple of years older, and during my last year at

Bellerive we had our fight behind the smokehouse. I'd pushed his face into dirt and made him eat it. He'd been too humiliated to tell, but I found the red-tailed hawk I'd mounted in my room stomped and broken.

I walked the circular drive edged with blooming verbena. The shakoed lackey at the Marriott had been right: such fine grass, the blades delicate and pampered. No dead limbs in the dogwoods and sugar maples. My mother wrote me a few weeks before she died that Edward had become a vice-president at Boone & Massey, an investment advisory firm. Undoubtedly order ruled there as here.

A brass fox-head knocker on the front door. I hesitated before using it. I'd become a user of back entrances. A cap was customarily doffed and held in my hand.

Juno surprised me by answering the door. I'd believed I'd have to find her at her cousin Mary's. Despite her age Juno was still tall and erect, her skin the color of horse chestnuts and drawn taut over distinctive facial bones. She was part American Indian, Pamunkey, and her braided black hair had become gray. She wore a white-collared green uniform and a white apron.

"Miss your hot biscuits," I said.

She glanced into the house, then stepped out and pulled the door to behind her.

"Mr. Charles, you best get down the road."

"Didn't know you worked here."

"I live in a room over the garage. Mr. Edward don't want you 'round."

"I'll give him the chance to tell me that."

"He at work downtown. You looking thin, Mr. Charles." Again she glanced behind her. "Can't feed you at this place. You need money, I try to sneak you some."

She stood with hands folded, and her dark, purplish eyes appeared all pupils. She'd slipped me a loaf of her bread after my mother's funeral. The guard and I'd eaten it on the flight back to Leavenworth.

"I'm all right for the moment, Juno. You don't believe I blew up Bellerive, do you?"

"I thought Judgment Day come. All the pots and pans fall in the kitchen. Me too. I afraid for you."

"I'm afraid for me too. They ganging up."

She was about to reply, but Patricia opened the door.

"Juno, what in the world—?" she asked and looked frightened when she recognized me. Patricia was heavier now, more settled, a matron, her face rounded, her off-blond hair restrained by a recent permanent. She wore clean, neatly pressed blue overalls and a straw hat, her stylish gardening clothes. She drew Juno inside and would've shut the door.

"Patricia, listen a second," I said.

"You'd come here?" She fastened the night chain. "I'm calling the police."

"Just tell me how to reach Edward, and I'll leave."

"You think I'd tell you so you can go downtown and hurt him?"

"All I want is to talk."

"You've never brought anything except heartache to this family."

"Would you phone and tell him I'm here?"

"I don't want him to see you," she said. Juno, features dimmed by the hallway, stood behind her.

"Put it up to him," I said. "It's a decision he'd want to make."

She closed and locked the door. I left fast for the street and jay-walked at the corner. I turned into a service alley bordered by flower-draped walls on one side, privet hedge on the other. I pressed back deep into the hedge, yet could still watch traffic. If I saw a po-lice car or heard a siren, I'd run for it through the alley.

I heard tennis balls being struck. There would be swimming pools, patios, and croquet courts behind houses of this neighborhood. The insulated world of the rich who'd never known shitting terror or the leering, stinking face of death.

How long would it take for Edward to get home from downtown Richmond if Patricia phoned? I figured twenty minutes. At the end of the alley a green metal barrel had yellow smiling daisies painted on it. Even trash in this community had to be prettied up.

Each time a car passed, I peered from the hedge. A black Audi sped along the street. The front end dipped as it braked for the corner. I stepped away from the hedge, crossed the street, and walked toward Edward's gateposts.

The Audi had turned in. Edward stood on the drive, the Audi's door left open. He was talking to Patricia, who'd come out onto the stoop. As I approached, she saw me, pointed, and hurried inside.

Edward shielded himself behind the Audi's door.

"The bad penny," he called. "Don't come nearer."

He hadn't cut off the engine, and he hunched ready to duck inside the car.

"Knew you'd be glad to see me," I said and stopped.

"I want you away from this house. I've got a phone here." He held it up. "I'm prepared to notify the police."

"You could offer your brother a cup of coffee first."

Patricia peeped through the front door, and at a second-story stone-encased window a child stared down at me before disembodied hands drew her away.

"My brother," Edward said. "When were you ever that? Now get out of here, and I'm not fooling. I have the phone in my hand."

He held the phone above his head. He wore a pale gray summer suit and subdued blue tie. His shoulders were stooped, his skin pale. He had a talent not only for languages but also math, yet never helped me with the algebra I flunked twice at Santee Military Academy. He'd always seemed older than his actual years.

"Afraid I'll blow you up? That I got a bomb in my pocket?"

"Leave me and my family alone," he said and pointed the phone at me as if he held a pistol.

"You can search me. Satisfy yourself I'm not armed."

Patricia opened the front door. She hadn't taken off the garden hat.

"You all right? Should I ring the police?"

"Just stay in the house," Edward answered.

She again shut and locked the door. Her face appeared at a downstairs window.

"I mean it when I told you not to come closer," Edward said. An index finger was poised over the phone. "A nightmare's what you've become to this family."

"Surprised you went into investments," I said. He'd won the Woodberry Forest Latin Prize. "Thought you'd become a college professor."

"I try never to think of you. No closer."

"I'm standing still."

"I'm afraid to let my daughter out of the house. We're living here besieged."

"I just came to get your version of what happened at Bellerive."

"My version? Christ, what a word to use. Version. If Patricia, my daughter, and I hadn't been late because of a timing belt, we'd be dead too. We were walking into the house by the side entrance. A few more steps. Version. A slaughter."

"First time under fire huh? And you blaming me?"

"I believe it's only a question of how you did it," he said and glanced at Patricia who stood at the window and also held a phone ready.

"I hadn't been to Bellerive since Mom's funeral."

"Your saying that doesn't make it so."

"What reason would I have for blowing up the place?"

"Money's an obvious answer."

"That coat could fit you. If I didn't do it, who'd have the best mo-tive and opportunity?"

"You're accusing me?"

"Tell me about the will."

"I don't have to tell you anything," he said and lifted a foot back into the Audi. "You think I'd expose my family to the danger of that explosion? I'm shaky yet remembering what almost happened to us."

"Besides you, who'd profit? You're the number one LeBlanc and about to inherit big. You were always envious of John, just not man enough to whip his ass, or mine."

"Get away from here," he shouted and waved an arm as if to wipe me off the earth.

"You moving out to Bellerive now? Becoming lord of the manor?"

"I'm calling the police," he said and bent into the car. He shut and locked the door. He held the phone to his ear. Inside, Patricia did the same.

I ran.

13

I SPRINTED DOWN the drive, out the gateway, and to the corner, where I crossed the street to the bisecting alleyway. I broke free at the end of a tree-shaded avenue and small park furnished with sliding boards and swings. I made a zigzagging run among them.

Ahead an expanse of green—a golf course, water hazards, a distant white clubhouse. A three-man crew had chain-sawed a dead oak felled along the fairway's edge. I glanced behind, slowed to a walk, and joined them. They wore yellow hardhats.

"Use some help?" I asked a beefy man who appeared in charge. He stood with hands on his hips.

"You got to be insured," he said. "You know you on private property?"

"Thought maybe I could earn a dollar," I said. "They hiring caddies?"

"Ask at the pro shop," he said and pointed.

I thanked him and walked toward the clubhouse. As soon as I curved out of his sight I picked up a rake leaning against a bench at the eighth hole. I angled across the fairway toward hardwood trees beyond the rough. I hoped I looked like an employee.

It was ladies day. They rode their carts over the tended grass.

Sunshine glistened along their bare, shaved legs. They didn't really see me.

I reached the trees and another stone wall, which bordered a narrow, sun-dappled street. I sat in shade, my back against the wall, and let my breathing quiet. I thought of Juno. She'd been about to tell me something. I could phone. With luck, she'd answer.

I also thought of the insurance policy. Walter Frampton had told me Richmond's Bank of the South was executor of John's estate.

I hadn't money for bus fare back into the city. I looked over the wall before climbing it, then, carrying the rake, hurried along the shaded sidewalk. John's shoes hurt. The tight, stiff leather rubbed blisters. Ahead, an elderly white man wearing white tennis togs held a hose to water scarlet sage growing on either side of an entrance.

"Sir, here's a first-class rake that'd cost you eight or ten dollars at a hardware store," I said. "I'll let you have it for five."

He eyed me and the rake. Without a word he twisted the nozzle to shut off the water, dropped the hose, and took the rake. He tested its heft before lifting his shirt. He carried a wallet hinged over his pants waist. He handed me three one-dollar bills. The sonofabitch was probably a lawyer or banker who suspected I'd stolen the rake but knew a good deal when he saw one.

No time to bargain. I accepted the money and left. At the end of the block, I waved down a bus, which hissed to a stop. As I settled into a seat, a city police cruiser sped by in the opposite direction, siren wailing.

I got off on Franklin Street, a block beyond the Jefferson Hotel. The day had become a boiler, the buildings absorbing and reflecting heat. A vendor sold newspaper-wrapped bunches of yellow flowers on a corner. I cut to East Main, which provided parking lots and doorways to step into if I needed cover. Approaching the financial district I met suited men and chic women.

Richmond had changed from the last time I walked its streets. Glassy buildings bright as gigantic zircons overwhelmed the gray, fortresslike structures of an older, more stately time. Despite the heat, the air had quickened and bore within it the excitement and velocity of money.

I passed bistros, stores selling leather goods, bicycles, running shoes, fashionable clothes. Haughty, intent ladies clicked past on high heels. Men flushed from trading hurried to keep up with the tape. They stared at my ragged hair, khaki slacks, and brogans. They swept wide of me.

Richmond's Bank of the South wasn't housed in one of the tall, dazzling buildings that had tinted windows, fountains, and decorative banners hung over spacious entrances. It remained the guardian of old money, granite not concrete, refusing to tempt gravity or bad taste beyond seven stories, advertising itself only by a nameplate shaped like a shield embedded in a gray Doric column.

A uniformed guard stopped me just inside this cool marble temple of money's baronial lobby, which was amberly illuminated by iron Teutonic chandeliers. Currency clinked behind grilled tellers' cages.

"You have business here?" he asked, an overweight, lumbering man whose arms hung ahead of him.

"Trust department," I said, using my snotty cultured voice. I made myself hold his rheumy eyes. Maybe he'd think I was an eccentric millionaire.

"Seventh floor," he said, showing a moment's doubt before nodding me toward the rear of the lobby.

I choked the impulse to thank him. Doing so would voice the subservience I felt in the presence of even menial authority—a lesson learned at Santee Military, in the army, and from the best teacher of all, Leavenworth's grinding death of the spirit.

I walked the marble floor and heard echoes of my own footsteps. The elevators had bronze doors. I watched the clocklike indicator above them, each arrival announcing itself with a muted musical chime.

I stepped among men wearing correct money suits. The speed of the rising elevator was soberly persistent. Its brass had been polished, its walnut panels waxed. Those around me carried attaché cases and smelled of cleanliness and aftershave. They were careful not to stand near me. Perhaps they believed I'd come to carry out trash, repair a faucet, or wash windows.

At the seventh floor the doors slid quietly open onto subdued banking grandeur—pale gold carpeting, a creamy corridor hung with Audubon prints, vases of freshly cut flowers set about, no blooms too extravagant. This was a place where money's hair was washed, trimmed, and parted.

A slim, crisp brunette guarded admittance to a corridor of closed gray doors. Her beautifully kept hands rested above the ivory keyboard of an electric typewriter her painted red nails made decorative. She looked up and turned on a smile that was another furnishing of the department.

"I want to see the officer handling the John Maupin LeBlanc estate," I said.

"LeBlanc?" she asked. "And you are—?"

"Charles M. LeBlanc," I answered, the words still reluctant and alien on my tongue. Little choice—either use the name or be turned away. I'd risk the assumption the bank had at the most heard I'd been held for questioning in King County.

"Just a sec," she said, and her eyes measured both the way I was dressed and my probable net worth. She lifted a rose-colored phone and spoke so softly I couldn't make out her words. She pressed the phone against her breasts.

"Mr. Bartlett will see you," she said. "If you'll be seated."

I chose a genuine leather club chair among several arranged around a circular coffee table that held ashtrays, matches, and a Grecian bowl containing cigarettes. The Bank of the South undoubtedly held hogsheads of old tobacco money in storage. When she wasn't looking, I pinched up half a dozen Marlboros and stuck them in my shirt pocket. I reached for another and lit it. She watched while pretending not to.

I listened to the listless ticking of the clock. Wealthy legatees entered and left after checking on their inheritances. Trusts were primarily a way of beating taxes and frustrating the real world's way of separating fools from their money. I felt a sneer coming on.

Mr. Bartlett was a fit, sandy-haired man who moved with the assurance of a person for whom life had turned out as expected. Two to one, a scratch golfer. He had sleekness and grace with just the hint of the liquored softness his flesh would patiently transform itself into one day.

He spoke to the receptionist before turning to me. I again felt the impulse to run. He held out his hand. It was possible he knew I shouldn't be here and had notified Edward or the police.

"An unexpected pleasure," he said, his voice Southern, yet cultivated. "Sorry to keep you waiting but I was on the line. Adjourn to my office?"

He waited for me to snub out my second cigarette and walked me past the receptionist to a door with his name on it in very small white letters. He palmed me inside. His broad window offered a view of the muddy James and chalky rocks breaking its flow. Gulls circled above a bridge across which beetle-like traffic scampered.

"Hope you had a good trip down to see us," Bartlett said. He glanced at the Marlboros I'd slipped into my shirt pocket. He knew where I'd gotten them.

"Us?"

"We consider the bank us," he said and laughed. He indicated I was to sit before his desk, on which lay a black lacquered cigarette box.

"You looked me up," I said and sat.

"Correct," he said, jerking at the pants of his subdued blue suit as he lowered into his chair. "I thought for a moment Gail might be mistaken about your name or that you were Edward. What can we do for you?"

"We can provide information about my brother John's estate such as a copy of the will and appraisal of his holdings."

"Afraid we can't comply at the moment even if you're authorized to receive them. The estate is considerable, the holdings not fully gathered. Appraisal might take months. I can inform you unofficially that you're mentioned neither in the last will and testament of your brother John nor his wife Eleanor."

"That's all you'll tell me?"

He repeated the information Walter Frampton had given me— Edward to receive Bellerive, John and Eleanor's other assets to go into trust, the income to be paid to Edward during his life, and at his demise the corpus distributed to heirs *per stirpes.*

Per stirpes. Legal Latin. Through or by what? I pushed back to a time of being tutored by cranky old Augustus Longworth. *Per stirpes?* Through stem or order of bloodline? Jargon that wouldn't affect me.

"What about an insurance policy with my name on it?" I asked.

"Absolutely nothing in your brother's estate," he said, his hands resting on the desk. He wore a gold wedding band, and his nails were immaculate as a surgeon's. His right index finger twitched slightly—an involuntary movement indicating a message from a private place.

"There's more," I said.

"More of what?"

"You're holding back on me."

"Every word I've spoken is the truth."

"Then you got more words. Just answer yes or no. Is there an insurance policy of any kind in my name?"

"Not in your brother's or sister-in-law's estate."

"In anybody's estate?"

He brought his hands slowly together and touched his fingertips above the blue blotter. He turned from me to gaze out the window, a stalling tactic. A helicopter flew past, its rotors silent in the insulated office but not in my blood.

"Possibly," he said.

"Possibly isn't much of an answer."

"Everything will come out when the entire estate's quantified."

"The way you talk doubly makes me believe there's something else."

"I repeat not in your brother John's or his wife's estate."

"Whose then?"

"I don't know that I'm at liberty to speak."

"If you don't, I go to a lawyer. I have a right to know if my name's on a policy."

"Excuse me," he said and stood. He needed to talk to somebody higher up, the way of bankers. "Help yourself to the cigarettes."

He slid the box forward on the desk and left. When I opened it, I smelled cedar. More Marlboros. The bank must hold bundles of the stock. I helped myself to a fistful, arranged them in my pocket, and lit up.

Gulls circled the rapids. At Lizard Inlet they knew me. I'd hold up my hand offering a piece of crab bait, and they'd swoop to snatch it, their beaks kind to my palm.

Bartlett came back. Again he hitched at his pants legs before sitting. Grandfather LeBlanc had told me when I was a boy that a gentleman never did that. Only salesmen and people in trade.

"A policy with your name on it was discovered in your brother John's safety deposit box but not purchased by him," Bartlett said.

"Well then who?"

"Your mother."

For a moment I couldn't get it straight.

"My mother bought a policy on her life to be paid to me?"

"Apparently. The contents of the box are under review."

"My mother's been dead a number of years."

"So we understand."

"But the policy was discovered in brother John's box?"

"Yes."

"Never presented for payment?"

"No."

"Wouldn't that seem to indicate John kept it from being paid to me when she died?"

"It's not in the province of the bank's responsibilities to draw a conclusion in the matter."

"How much?"

"Initially in the sum of one hundred thousand. Over the years the increase in value has been significant."

"How significant?"

"I can't speak for the insurance company but possibly in the range of one hundred and twenty-eight or so."

"Or so."

"Yes."

"When do I get paid?"

"At her death that policy should've been part of your mother's estate. Bank of the South had no knowledge of it, and as I stated the discovery is under review."

"How long?"

"In matters this complicated time's required to determine a proper course of distribution. You weren't mentioned in your mother's will, which is being restudied by our legal department."

"When will you know?"

"Some weeks. Trust Departments don't set speed records."

"You sweet-talking bastards rule the world."

"I know it must appear so to you," Bartlett said.

14

I **HAD TO** haul ass back to King County but before leaving Richmond I dropped a quarter of my remaining $1.48 into a pay phone in front of the Pig House where I'd laid down eighty-seven cents for a pork barbecue and glass of water. Patricia answered, not Juno, and I hung up.

I climbed on a city bus and paid another sixty-five cents to ride east to the end of the line in Henrico County. I walked to a traffic signal a block away from a ramp that led to the Interstate 64 and twice stepped back among parked cars when I sighted bears.

A White Freightliner stopped for a red light. Painted on its side was AXAPOMIMI LUMBER. I reached up to tap the door.

"Give a lift to Jessup's Wharf?" I called to the black driver. He eyeballed me good before nodding. I hurried around the hot diesel's rumble to climb aboard. His name was Norman, and he wore a GI shirt that had a faded and torn first Cavalry patch on the shoulder.

"Been to that party," I said.

"I seen. Can read 'Nam on faces."

"What you see?"

"That shit-upon, fucked-by-fate look."

I offered him a Marlboro, and we smoked. He'd hauled a load of eight-by-tens from Axapomimi Lumber to a building supply house in Midlothian.

I sweated the danger that a police cruiser might be lying in wait at the King County Line, a worry for nothing. We rolled across unchecked. I asked Norman to let me out on an empty stretch of road west of town.

"Thought you was going to the Wharf," he said.

"Got an appointment with a man."

"Sure," he said as he shifted to drive off, "seen that too."

I tried to get my mind settled on what I should do next as I skirted town and hiked the river path to the sycamore, where I changed back into my overalls, soiled shirt, and tennis shoes. I folded my good clothes into the cache.

It was late afternoon, sunlight slanting to the east side of the river. Again I asked myself who profited most from killing John and his family. Maybe Edward was too obvious.

What about John's wife, Eleanor, or somebody in her family? Not much of a shot. She was an only child. Her widower father had been a history professor at Agnes Scott, and while at Leavenworth I'd learned in a letter from my mother he'd drowned in a boating accident off Savannah. According to Walter Frampton her estate had been willed into the trust.

How had my mother managed to take out an insurance policy with my name on it? My father had handled all her business affairs. He doled out the money at Bellerive. Possibly she found a way to hold back nickels and dimes over the years. She would've needed to negotiate with an agent and keep my father from knowing. What agent?

My father got himself killed on a tractor. He loved running bushhogs over Bellerive's fallow fields and often daringly gunned the big International Harvester as if racing phantoms. According to

Edward's note to me in prison, my father at full throttle traversed rather than paralleled a slope in a field of cut sorghum. The low-side tires struck a terrace, the tractor lurched, tumbled, and rolled over him. Though accompanied by a guard I could've again received emergency leave from Leavenworth, I didn't attend the funeral.

I had difficulty envisioning my mother ever deceiving my father. She yielded to what life brought her. The thing I'd seen that Christmas night was the real reason, not my grades or fighting, for my father sending me to Santee Military Academy. He couldn't endure the knowledge and charge in my eyes.

Hunger pains. I scoured for mussels and cattails along the river. I slept on the bank and woke to hear a lynx cry from the woods, a sound that reminded me of Lizard Inlet. The moon shone on water still as silver.

At first light I walked to Jessup's Wharf and the courthouse. Rodger sat in the squad room. He had his booted feet on the table. I signed the legal pad.

"What you doing with yourself?" he asked. He'd been cleaning his Ruger 9-mm automatic, and the room smelled of gun oil. He inserted the clip by bumping it with the heel of his hand.

"Contemplating the sinfulness of man."

"You watch it, buddy," he said, holstered the gun, and made a quick draw aimed at me.

I walked through town to Walter Frampton's office and waited on the steps for him. Wearing his khaki suit and regimental tie, he walked with slow, looping strides along Bridge Street. He carried his attaché case, the weight of it pulling one shoulder lower than the other. His face was set as if he were rassling deep thoughts, and when he raised his eyes, he showed no delight at seeing me.

"Hell of a way to start the day," he said and stepped around me to climb the steps.

I followed. He drew an outsize key from his pocket. When he unlocked the door and entered, I moved in after him. He switched on lights and the wobbly ceiling fan that made a continuous clicking sound.

"Got something of interest," I said.

"What I'd find of interest is a law practice that pays the rent and allows me to replace a heap of bolts that is fatuously called an automobile with a machine that possesses a modicum of dependability."

He crossed to his desk and dropped the attaché case on it.

"You're worried only about wheels," I said. "I'm thinking of skin."

"Is it worth the travail?" he asked and unhinged his angular body to sit. "Your skin I mean?"

"Walt—"

"Did I give you permission to call me Walt?"

"I don't like dealing with you any more than you with me. Happens I don't have much choice, if any."

"But, you see, the fact is I do."

"May be money in this for your wheels."

"How I hate that subjunctive," he said, tilting back. "A man can drown in the possibilities of 'may be.'"

He reached into his shirt pocket for his pack of Winstons. I'd smoke his cigarettes if offered and save the Marlboros I had left. He didn't offer.

"I stopped by Bank of the South's trust department," I said.

"Run that by me one more time."

"The head office."

"You got permission to go to Richmond?"

"Signed off on it to myself," I said and sat without an invitation.

"Real smart. If caught, they'd be dancing do-si-do right now at the courthouse. And I don't want to know anything about what you did."

"I don't care any more for 'if' than you do for 'may,'" I said.

"You stopped by the Bank of the South's refined trust department wearing overalls and raggedy-ass tennis shoes? Must've created quite a sensation."

"I got other clothes."

"Where'd you get other clothes?"

"You don't need that information."

"I repeat I don't need any information about you. Now I'm about to record a deed and make myself fifty or sixty bucks. And who can tell? Some rich old lady might walk in and let me draw up her will, naming myself executor. I could buy a Porsche."

"Maybe you got somebody here with money."

"We're in 'may' country again."

"There's an insurance policy. And I'm the beneficiary."

He drew on his cigarette, held it in his effeminate way, and raised an eyebrow.

"How much?"

"It's accumulated to a hundred twenty-eight thousand or so."

"A policy in your name that you'll collect upon in full, no complications?" he asked and tapped the ash from his Winston into his clam-shell ashtray. It still needed emptying.

"Don't know from nothing about complications."

"Ah."

"A policy my mother took out."

"Your mother named you the beneficiary? Thought you were the black sheep."

"Never with her."

"Why wasn't it paid to you when your mother died?"

"The policy wasn't presented for payment because most likely it wasn't found among her things."

"Whose things?"

"I'm guessing. My mother died before my father from a stroke and massive hemorrhage. At the service the preacher said God loved her so much He couldn't wait to take her. Whom the Lord loveth he killeth, huh?"

"This isn't exactly the moment for a theologically doctrinal discussion."

"My father wouldn't have wanted me to collect the money. Probably discovered and locked the policy in his safety deposit box."

"Shouldn't it have surfaced when he died?" Walt asked, definitely interested now.

"Suppose brother John found it first and stuck it in his box. He wouldn't want me to inherit either. If I turned up dead, he and Edward could cash it as heirs."

"A hell of a charge to bring against your father and brothers."

"We had a great family life."

"What's the bank intend to do with the policy?"

"A trust officer named Bartlett claims everything in John's estate has to be inventoried first and looked over by their accountants and lawyers."

"They'll stall," Walt said and dunked out his cigarette. Back in Sailors Cove I'd pick up smaller butts. "They'll want to make absolutely sure they don't get burned."

"You could help me."

He stretched his arms and flexed his long fingers.

"Question. Why would your mother take out a special policy on you rather than name you in her will?"

"My father wouldn't have allowed her to name me in a will."

"She bought the policy on the sly?"

"Had to. I been trying to think of what agent she'd use. I remember old Mr. Daughtrey Baskerville, a vestryman at Christ Church."

"Daughtrey Baskerville, an independent agent, died last year," Walt said. "He was eighty-eight."

"Wouldn't somebody have his files and records?"

"Possibly. I might look into it, but I'll have to give it more thought."

"I realize I'm not your favorite client," I said and stood.

"Understatement of the year. I liked your brother John, his wife, Eleanor, and the son, Paul, whom I saw each Sunday at services. I think of them dead and the bloody way they died."

"Everybody seemed to like John."

"A fine and generous man. He couldn't walk down River Street without people stopping him to talk. They didn't want anything usually. They simply liked being in his presence."

"An experience I never experienced."

"He knew I needed work and saw to it I helped with his various land transactions. I was invited to Bellerive for the Christmas party. I find it hard to believe he'd hide an insurance policy."

"It was in his safety deposit box."

"So you claim."

"Check with the bank. You don't have to like me to get what's mine and a fee for yourself."

"What would you do with the money other than pay me if you're ever allowed to spend it?"

"Montana."

"Why Montana?"

"Space," I said.

15

I **WORKED** **DOWN** to the river and the sycamore cache, where I changed into my khakis and blue denim shirt but not John's brogans—I still had blisters from my Richmond trip.

I climbed to the paved road but stood back from it till a Ford double-axle hauling a harrow chained to the bed rattled toward me. I stepped out into sunlight and raised my thumb. The truck slowed.

"Going King's Tavern way?" I called to the driver, a scrawny teenager wearing a John Deere cap and Levi's. His was a field tan.

"Get in this buggy," he said.

I opened the cab door and stepped up beside him. A tape played with a banjo lead, and a deep bass voice sang, "The light in her eyes caused the darkness in mine."

The youth, grinning over snaggled teeth, joined the chorus, his voice high-pitched and whiny. He glanced at my tennis shoes.

"Feet bothering me," I said.

"No hoof, no horse," he said. "Don't believe man was ever meant to wear shoes. You from King's Tavern?"

"Looking for a job but work hard to come by these days."

"Who you mean to see?" he asked, his question direct in the manner of country people. They were polite but felt if you passed through their bailiwick they had a right to know.

"The Gaffreys," I said. People Rajab Ishmael had told me were brother John's special friends. Maybe I could learn something from them about what brother John had been into.

"Ain't no real work at that fancy farm. If you can operate a tractor, I'll put you on haying."

"Looking for something steady."

"Good luck finding it at King's Tavern," he said, and his eyes measured me. "I ain't seen you around."

"I been away. The military."

If that's what you could call Leavenworth, the place I'd killed my second man. The first was in the Mekong Delta, where Charlie raised his head slowly and obliquely to peer from elephant grass. His skull exploded, and blood spurted from his nose, ears, and eyes.

"We pass the Gaffreys' entrance," the driver said. "I'll drop you off."

He stopped the Ford before an aluminum gate closed across a lane. A sign hanging by chains from an arm of a wooden post read FOX HAVEN. I thanked him, stepped down, and unlatched the gate to let myself through. He drove off, leaving a wake of exhaust fumes and bluegrass.

I walked the lane between a series of creosoted plank fences. Mares and foals, their coats lustrous, raised their heads to watch warily. Three louvered white steeples topped the stable. A grove of hackberries dropped a pale shade over a one-story brick-and-glass house that appeared too modern to exist in rural King County. The lawn had just been mowed, and clippings stuck to my shoes.

A yellow Lab loped toward me. I stood still and let him circle and sniff my hand. The woman appeared next from the side of the house. She had long brown hair and wore a black-and-yellow vertically striped bathing suit. She held a pool skimmer.

"You didn't drive up," she said. She was maybe forty, thin and shapely. The dog stayed between us.

"I walked in to see Mr. Gaffrey."

"You selling Bibles?" she asked and fingered hair behind an ear.

"No'm, just hoped to talk a second."

"Come on around," she said and looked at my shoes.

Around was a turquoise swimming pool. Dead crickets lay in wet spots where she'd dipped and emptied the skimmer onto the concrete apron. The house was larger than it appeared from the front, the glass tinted a faint purple, several sliding doors open but screened. Flowers bloomed from large Mexican clay pots. Chairs and chaises had been placed about. A green hose lay coiled.

"What's your name?" she asked in a way that made me know she was used to being served.

"Watkins. Jeff Watkins."

"I'll get my husband," she said and leaned the skimmer against a redwood shower stall before walking to the house.

She might be a fine piece of female flesh, but I felt no desire. I'd finally gotten control of that. I'd not had a woman since Kansas City, Missouri, where on the day after my Leavenworth release I'd gotten drunk, lain with a coffee-colored whore, had my wallet stolen, and caught the clap.

As I waited I looked out across the fenced paddocks to kennels holding black-and-tan hounds that bayed in trembling, sorrowful voices. Naturally brother John would've been friends with horse people. He'd often jumped his bay over a five-foot pasture gate and been so completely joined to the heavy gelding, so synchronized to its surging leap, that I'd pictured the centaurs that Mr. Longworth had described while teaching us mythology.

I knew this land. There'd once been a two-story frame house here owned by a family named Honeycutt. I'd bird-hunted across the lespedeza fields with Grandfather LeBlanc, who shot classic style, his left arm fully extended along the Parker's barrel, appearing leisurely in the few seconds he had to bring down a partridge. He'd taught me to shoot with both eyes open.

The woman returned from the house with Gaffrey, a short, strongly built man at least a dozen years older. He wore baggy red shorts and leather sandals. His chest hairs were sun-bleached. He held a computer printout.

"You a stable hand?" he asked. His speech wasn't the leisurely draw of King County but clipped Yankee. He, too, looked at my shoes.

"Mucked a million," I said.

"Vicky," he said to the woman, who'd again taken hold of the skimmer, "I'm expecting a call from Michael. He's running Cal's Cannon in a claiming race at Aqueduct."

"The splint doesn't worry him?" she asked.

"They've fired it," he said and turned to me. "You got references?"

He padded to a white metal table from the center of which stuck a red-and-yellow fringed umbrella. He laid the printout on the table and weighed it down with an empty highball glass. Blood horses and their lineages.

Vicky levered her skimmer into the pool and dipped up a dead insect. She reversed the skimmer and banged the frame against a painted green barrel to dump the wasp. The action firmed her body so that muscles in her thighs and stomach became clearly defined. A light skim of oil gave off a sheen.

"Mr. Gaffrey, truth is I didn't come here to talk job but to ask you about John LeBlanc and what happened out at Bellerive."

He'd telescoped open the umbrella and been about to sit but checked himself to stare at me.

"Watkins, just exactly who do you represent?"

"I guess I represent myself. I was close to John once and been trying to put together what happened out at Bellerive."

"You maybe hoping for a reward huh?"

Vicky had been listening as she dipped the skimmer. She propped it against the shower stall and crooked her finger at Gaffrey. He crossed toward her, and his leather sandals slapped the pool's apron.

"If you were close to John, you know about the black sheep brother," Gaffrey said as he returned to me.

"I know," I said. Vicky moved around to the far side of the pool.

"Caused his family great distress. The police believe he's responsible. So do I."

"Maybe the police are desperate to lay it on somebody," I said.

Vicky slid open a screen door of the house and faded into shadows.

"Bad seed," Gaffrey said. "Dishonorably discharged from the service. A jailbird. Thought he could get money or did it out of meanness. Damn fine people gone."

"You think of any explanation except the brother?" I asked and wondered about Vicky.

"Funny thing. One minute you talk country, the next up a level. You're no rube."

"I've traveled."

"I notice speech since Vicky and I came down here to King County six years ago to escape the New Jersey rat race. Nobody was nicer to us than John and Eleanor LeBlanc. They opened doors, took us in, showed us the real Southern hospitality, treated us like family. It had to be the younger brother. He was army and taught to kill."

Vicky walked from the house. A black maid in a white uniform followed and began sweeping among the pool furniture but kept looking at me. She spoke to Vicky.

"Harry, a word with you?" Vicky called.

Harry walked around the edge of the pool to confer with Vicky and the maid. They entered the house.

I didn't know the maid, but most local blacks would recognize a LeBlanc. As I thought about escape, Harry stepped from house shadows carrying a Parker twelve-gauge side-by-side, the same antiquated model shotgun used by my father and grandfather for bird hunting, a Southern gentleman's upland game sporting weapon. Automatics were for meat hunters.

"I'm leaving," I said and raised my hands.

"You sonofabitch, you're no Watkins, and I ought to separate you from your balls," Harry said.

"Just let me go," I said and started toward the front of the house. Vicky could be dialing the sheriff.

"I hope they strap you in the chair. I could drop you right now. Tell Rutledge you came here to rob us. He'd be glad I did."

"On my way," I said and felt my back's exposure as I walked from the pool and around the house to the lawn and lane. The yellow Lab no longer wagged its tail but growled. It was all I could do to keep from running.

Soon as I reached the road, I cut into woods on the far side and lay in deep pine shade. When Rutledge and Cole arrived, they sped past. The silver Oldsmobile 88 turned in at Fox Haven. The hounds bayed.

Maybe not just the call from Vicky. Falkoner and Rutledge had possibly learned by now about me breaking my promise by my visit to Richmond. When the Oldsmobile left Fox Haven, the sheriff and Cole drove slowly along the road. They squinted into woods. I pressed down, my nose deep in pine tags. Crackling tires receded over hot asphalt.

Time to leave King County.

16

RUTLEDGE AND HIS deputies patrolled roads during the afternoon and evening. I stayed low in the woods. Toward the west, lightning streaks and thunder. A fine drizzle rode in on a strengthening breeze.

Rain fell harder, the cooling drops at first feeling good as they rolled down my neck. Then the chill as the thunderhead's downdraft swooped earthward. I hunched against it. I thought of hiking to Bellerive's barn, but the law might've discovered I'd used it and be waiting.

Lightning ghouled the land. The squall stung and I bowed into it. A glint among darkness. I crouched. Another lightning flash bared a car carcass abandoned at the center of a wind-whipped field.

I crossed through broomstraw brushing against my legs. I tried to open doors of a rusting 1974 Plymouth Fury sedan. Lying on my bunk at Leavenworth I'd studied auto magazines. I'd pictured myself driving into vast, unpopulated areas of sunny, unfenced freedom.

The Fury's doors were stoved in and wouldn't give. I walked around to the other side and by tugging freed the rear right door enough to squeeze inside. The windows had been smashed, but by squirming down on the floor and pushing my back to the slant of rain, I protected myself from the squall's full force. Heavy drops slammed the exposed flank.

I drew my body tight and shivered. At Lizard Inlet I could've battened down and lit a fire in the stove I'd rigged from an oil drum. I'd been able to make my shack snug. Here water sprayed over me and collected on the floor. "Goddamn you!" I shouted. "Goddamn everybody on this whole fucking earth!"

Lightning struck fast, just seconds between strokes, changing the world to a land of the living dead. Thunder shook the ground. Thoughts of Montana grew larger. Let the pricks try to catch me on grassy plains big as oceans.

I thought of Edward. He gained from John's death, yet had no material needs. And he'd never liked blood. When I'd knifed open game to dress it and stuck my fingers in cavities to scoop out guts, livers, and hearts, he'd paled and turned away. He was too fastidious to kill. Could he have hired someone?

The rain stopped abruptly. Tossing trees quieted but continued to drip. Thunder rolled eastward and became faint. Toads croaked in celebration of wetness. I felt stiff and unkinked myself from the car. I was a soaked rag. As I pushed through clinging broomstraw, I slapped at mosquitoes who scented my blood's warmth. My tennis shoes squished.

I again stalked the road's edge as clouds slid from the moon. Headlights. I ran among pines. The Sheriff Department's Galaxie cruised past, its tires hissing. They were using a spotlight to sweep each side of the road. Red taillights wound into darkness.

More rain. I passed unlit farmhouses and the black silhouette of a shed set back from the road—a swayback curing barn. I splashed through puddles, stooped inside, and found a dry corner to let myself down. The smell of hickory smoke and tobacco still resided in clay-chinked logs. I toppled over and slept, my face settling into damp, cold ashes.

Sunlight woke me, and I scouted the terrain before I crawled outside. I was still wet, coated with the ashes, hungry. My sopping

Marlboro fell apart in my palm. I cleaned my face best I could in ditch water.

As yet no patrol cars, but I was still a good distance from the river. Through gaps of pines I spotted a building, a white-frame country church, the Beautiful Plains Baptist. It appeared closed up, no cars in the lot. There could be a kitchen and maybe food.

I ran to the rear of the church. As I started up steps, the door opened, and there stood a young matron, her hair chestnut, her lips small, a dimple in her chin. Lacquered sand-dollar earrings. She held a bunch of wilted flowers—black-eyed Susans.

For a second I didn't recognize Laurie. She wore a sleeveless pink dress, and a brassiere strap had partly escaped an armhole. She was groomed, fresh, and terrified.

"It's me, Laurie. Charley LeBlanc."

"Charley?" she asked, her voice and the black-eyed Susans shaking. Her choked-back scream ridged muscles of her throat.

I'd dated her my freshman year in high school—before my father sent me to Santee Military Academy down Georgia way. In the front seat of my rebuilt Corvair she'd allowed me to bare her breasts and suck her nipples. She'd not permitted a hand under her perfumed skirt.

We'd made noises and claimed we loved each other. When I drove her home, clothes disarranged, hair frazzled, her mother never again allowed Laurie to go out with me. Another entry into the local book of my bad reputation. But for a couple of hot minutes I'd really believed I'd die for her.

"Oh you scared me!" she said and drew a breath like a person bobbing up from underwater. "Heard you were in town."

She was trying to be brave. To her I appeared dirty, dangerous, threatening. Where were her wheels? Approaching, I'd seen three sides of the church. The car had to be on the fourth.

"I won't hurt you, Laurie."

"I believe that, Charley," she said, trying to. She swallowed and held up the black-eyed Susans. "Throwing these away. Should've been done after the service Sunday."

"Didn't know whether you still lived around Jessup's Wharf or what."

"I'm married now," she said and showed me her diamond. Her nails were rose-tipped. "Lester Apperson. You remember. He played halfback for the Herons."

The Herons were King County's high school team, and I'd fought Lester behind the bleachers. He outweighed me thirty pounds, but I'd danced around and nicked at him till he punched himself out. He claimed I fought dirty. Because of my reputation, people believed it. My father had.

"We have a house and two daughters," she said. "Lester runs the Exxon distributorship. Gasoline, heating oil, lubricating products."

She was clean and attractive, yet, like with Vicky Gaffrey at Fox Haven, I felt more ache than desire.

"Happy for you," I said.

"I hope things turn out okay for you. Well, have to be going. Dancing lessons for my daughters."

I stood aside for her to walk around me. She threw the dry black-eyed Susans into a galvanized trash can. I held the door of the red Honda Civic open for her. She was careful to keep her legs covered as she slid across the seat.

"Good to see you, Charley."

"Same," I said, and Laurie looked as if she might cry. She backed the Civic, straightened it, and as she left raised a hand, at the end of which were those rose-tipped nails.

17

I **WORKED DOWN** through woods till I heard the Axapomimi running full after the rain. I located the sycamore, knelt, and stuck my hand into my cache for John's brogans. Nothing. I shoved higher. All clothes, the scissors, the razor, gone.

That fucking Cole. They must've made a sweep along the river. I scooped up mussel shells and hurled them into the rising water. Filthy as I was and without a shave and better clothes I'd never make it far from King County.

I found pokeweed growing along a cleared strip of land under a power line. I picked the small leaves and swallowed them, but they didn't dull my hunger's edge.

I hoped Laurie wouldn't report having seen me to Rutledge. I remembered dances, girls in crisp scented dresses, the Christmas parties I as a LeBlanc had been invited to. I'd owned a tuxedo, dancing slippers, a maroon cummerbund. I braved my first French kiss on a planter's daughter named Lucy May. She taught me about blowing into and licking ears.

I felt the sun's heat. At least I was drying out. The tennis shoes chafed my blisters. Again I kept to road edges, moving west away from Jessup's Wharf till I reached a junction called Carter's Fork where the pavement intersected two dirt roads, one locally and unofficially named Poor Folk after the farmhouse the destitute were sent to during tight times in the days before welfare. It'd burned.

I passed fields of corn, soybeans, and tobacco—crops rising from the weight of last night's thunderstorm to unfold to the sun's warmth, property mostly owned by what my father once while drinking had called the King County peasantry—men and women who scratched out livings from a sullen soil.

That soil had been winning even during my boyhood, the scratchers forced to work in the mills and billet woods to put food on the table. My father bought up their bled land at bottom dollar and sweetened it with lime as well as enriched it with fertilizer to produce bountiful yields.

The small brown bungalow stood back among a stand of Kentucky coffee trees. A Ford station wagon that had a flat tire was parked down a graveled lane. Clothes hung on a line strung between wooden posts at the rear. I used the woods to skirt the house before I lowered to my knees and crept forward. I pushed aside prickly sweet gum branches. Pinned to the wire clothesline were a man's white shirt, underwear, a pair of outsize dark gray polyester trousers.

I watched and waited. No smoke from the chimney, no lights, no sound of a radio or TV, though the roof sprouted an antenna. At the center of the yard, a millstone had been planted, and petunias grew from its center. Water lilies bloomed in a rocky fish pond. No telephone line stretched from the power pole at the road.

I ran from the woods, grabbed clothes, and wheeled to flee.

"You're welcome to my undershorts too," a voice called.

The man stood at the bungalow's doorway. He was a blimp wearing loose-fitting pajamas and hairless as a skinned rabbit.

"Why not come on in and join me for a cup of coffee?" he asked.

His offer could be a trick, a means of delay till he alerted the sheriff's office, yet how would he unless his phone cable had been buried underground—a thing not very likely in rural King County.

"About to fry up eggs and sausage," he said.

Just the words *eggs and sausage* caused my stomach to clench. Unless the blimp pulled a gun, I could handle him. As I righted myself and moved toward the bungalow, he stepped inside and held the screen door for me. I smelled tobacco. He'd have cigarettes.

I entered a small, neat kitchen that had flowered curtains at the window. On walls hung paintings of a moldboard plow lying overturned in a weedy furrow, a mule standing by a split-rail fence, and a sagging wind-honed barn.

"Sit yourself," he said as he drew a chair from a square, speckled Formica-topped table. He clicked switches of an electric stove and set an iron skillet on a front eye, a coffeepot on a back one. From a refrigerator he lifted a plate of sausage patties and a bowl of brown eggs.

I still held the clothes I'd taken from the line. I looked down a short hallway to a room that had books piled on chairs, the mantel, the floor. A clock ticked, and a calico cat lay curled in sunshine of a windowsill.

"Those garments won't fit a lean man like you," he said as he faced the stove. "I have others no longer useful. You can take what you want. No offense, but perhaps you'd like to bathe?"

Yeah, and have deputies swarm out here while I was naked and defenseless.

"I won't summon authorities," he said. He had a precise way of talking, a fully pronounced and unhurried utterance of each word. "If you want to steal from me, help yourself. You'll find no money and very little of anything else."

He dropped sausage patties into the skillet, and smoke curled around him. The scent made me lightheaded. I tipped from the chair and reached to the table to right myself.

He set a mug of coffee before me. He did have eyebrows, but the color was so closely matched to the lightness of his skin that they were hardly visible. I laid the clothes on a second chair before reaching to the mug. Using both hands, I lifted it.

"Sugar or canned milk?" he asked.

I shook my head, swallowed, and felt the hot jolt all the way down. While whistling an aimless tune, he cracked eggs into the skillet. He used a spatula to turn the sausage patties and flip grease over the eggs.

"Why you doing this for me?" I asked.

"You're Charles LeBlanc," he said.

I set the coffee down quick and gathered my feet to stand.

"Was in town yesterday," he said. "There's considerable talk about you. Troopers driving up and down the roads. You have the LeBlanc chin. I deduced you must be he."

Deduced. A fancy word. All the books lying around.

"You a professor?" I asked and reached for the mug.

"I'm a retired salesman. Also an amateur painter and self-professed local historian. The name's Arthur Moss. I can recite your forebears back to Jean Maupin LeBlanc."

"Why give a damn?" I asked. The smell of sizzling meat caused me to bend forward to ease my hurt for food.

"A habit developed wherever I hung my hat."

He was older than I first reckoned, the smoothness of his skin belying his age.

"I studied history at the University of Tennessee," he said. "Taught high school a year in Memphis. The intricacies of life's patterns have always interested me. They possess the complex weavings of Oriental carpets. You can never be certain where strands will lead."

He turned the eggs and dropped slices of bread into a toaster. He set a stick of butter, a paper napkin, a knife and fork before me.

He served me a plate with two eggs over easy, two sausage patties, two slices of toast. On a lazy Susan he set a glass of dark jelly alongside salt and pepper. With quivering fingers, I buttered toast and spread the jelly thick. It was damson, like Juno had made at Bellerive.

I peppered the eggs, used the fork to puncture the yolks, and smeared sausage chunks. Oh Christ, the hot sweet taste was a rush like coming. I closed my eyes at the goodness. Arthur watched and smiled as I wolfed down the meal and rubbed the second slice of toast around the plate until it shone clean.

"More?"

I nodded, and he did it over again, eggs, sausage, toast, the damson. I tried to eat more slowly but bent low over the food. He refilled my mug.

"Actually we've met," he said as I laid down my fork, wiped my face, and leaned back.

"Sorry, I don't remember."

"You couldn't be expected to," he said and carried my plate to the sink where he ran water over it. "You were an infant. I was riding the C&O back from Hinton, West Virginia, after a business trip."

I shrugged.

"I sold clothing to miners. Measured and fitted them in company stores, which marked up my price to earn their profit. For years it was a good living. Your mother was returning from the mountains. She had a private compartment on the Sportsman and held you in her arms."

My father had used High Moor coal money to restore Bellerive, and though he continued to operate the mine, he installed my mother, my older bothers, and me at the house long before he returned from the mountains to live with us.

"I'd make three trips a year to the region and always stopped by High Moor," Arthur said. "Oh how those miners loved to spend their pay. Made drunken sailors seem like Scots by comparison. Silk shirts, vested suits, fine leather shoes. I knew your father and mother only by sight. I spoke to her on the train, but she was greatly occupied. You had colic and were crying."

"I'll ask again, why you doing this for me?"

"Your mother was a lovely lady. I think of her holding you on that train, the care, the devotion. You were so tiny, miserable, help- less, she so beautiful."

"Will you let me wash up?"

He showed me the bathroom, which was clean and painted white. No shower. When I turned on the water, I felt a well pump switch on. I cracked the door and stepped quietly into the hall to see whether Arthur meant to run for the sheriff. He stood at the sink rinsing dishes.

I filled the tub to my chest. I made it as hot as I could take it. When I sat up, I used both hands to cup water over my hair before soaping all the way down. I slid under. The bathroom steamed.

I dried myself, wiped the mirror, and used Arthur's safety razor to make long shiny swaths down my face. I patted on his stinging Lilac Vegetal.

When he tapped on the door, I wrapped the towel around my hips. He handed me clean underwear and backed off. No way the underwear could be his, for it almost fit me.

"Here," Arthur called when I stepped into the hallway. What must've been intended to be a bedroom was filled with dressers, boxes upon boxes, trunks, racks of clothes. He drew out a drawer that held shirts still wrapped in cellophane.

"Never been able to throw anything away," he said. "Leftovers from my life on the road. As is your underwear. Just help yourself."

I buttoned on a brown shirt that wouldn't show dirt bad. He opened a closet door. Suits hung on hangers, and shoes lined the floor. He eyed me for size and lifted a beige gabardine.

"My assessment is you wear a forty long," he said. "Try this Monarch Ready-Made. After all these years, the cut's a bit out of fashion, but who's to notice?"

The pants were the right length, though the waist felt loose. From a hook on the closet door he selected a brown leather belt. I cinched it tight. He held the jacket for me. The sleeves and drop around the shoulders were okay.

Lastly he brought out a pair of blue socks and brown leather shoes. The oxfords felt narrow, but a second pair fit. He handed me a blue tie, and my fingers fumbled on the knot. They'd forgotten how.

I checked myself in the mirror tacked to the door. Because of my shaggy haircut, I didn't look quite respectable, yet almost.

"I suppose I'll never be able to give up a haberdasher's ways," he said. He tugged at the rear of my jacket. "Let's have more coffee."

I followed to the kitchen. The shoes were stiff, but the socks padded and eased my blisters. He refilled my mug.

"I also knew your mother's father," he said. "Angus MacKay opened the first mine in Wandering River Gorge and attempted to develop the Shawnee seam at High Moor."

Grandfather MacKay, a man from Allegheny County, Virginia, who speculated in mineral leases and drilled for oil. I had no memory of him other than the curled photographs in a floppy album— photographs of the stern, mustached men wearing derbies and dark unpressed suits posed stiffly before mine mouths, steam-driven machinery, and timber shays, one with the name Shawnee Land & Lumber Co. painted on its side. Two mongrel dogs had managed to get themselves in several of the pictures.

"He was a visionary," Arthur said. "The first man to see the possibility of mining coal in that forbidding region of West Virginia. Persuaded the railroad to lay tracks into the gorge. Talked about a river of coal that would pour out wealth. He'd never been to college but was an educated man. Always appeared to be seeing farther than at what he was looking."

"He went busted out there," I said. We carried coffee into his front room. Arthur cleared books off two chairs. I made out Plutarch's *Lives* on top of a stack. The calico cat didn't rouse.

"Not at first," he said. "For a time there was great demand for coking coal in Virginia's iron industry, up through Bath and Allegheny Counties. He signed contracts with the biggest producers and built himself a fine house on the mountain. But Virginia iron went under while Pittsburgh triumphed. He held on awhile and was exploring that Shawnee seam when a roof fall crushed him. Without him all development ceased."

During my youth I'd detected in my father a certain disregard for the MacKays—the inbred Tidewater attitude toward people of western Virginia. My father had said the mountain had finally gotten Grandfather MacKay.

I eyed the glass humidor of cigars on a card table Arthur used for his desk. He noticed, stood, and lifted the top off the humidor before offering it to me. He reached for barn matches on the mantel. We lit up twenty-five-cent King Edwards, the working man's best smoke.

"Your mother was the child of his old age," Arthur said.

"So I heard," I said. Grandfather MacKay had taken care of my mother as if she were a princess. Her mother had been a younger woman, his third wife, and died of diphtheria. It was told in the family that while Grandfather MacKay lived, my mother's feet hardly ever touched the ground.

He'd sent her to Sweet Briar, and I'd seen her diploma and old yearbooks. In an oval senior-year photograph she looked dreamy and mistily unreal, her picture surrounded by a chain of entwined roses.

"Your grandfather lived for her," Arthur said. "She wore white dresses and shoes in a coal camp. Miners took off their caps to her. At Christmas your grandfather let her hand out silver dimes to the High Moor children."

She'd done it at Bellerive, too, though it went up to fifty cents, and then to a dollar.

She'd met my father at Sweet Briar while he was a university undergraduate. He drove over from Charlottesville in his De Soto convertible to date her. When they first married, he'd tried to make a go of farming at Bellerive, failed with the general collapse of commodity prices, and in a desperate effort to save the family bet all on an attempt to resurrect coal operations at High Moor.

By then Grandfather MacKay's mountainside house had been vandalized and stripped. My parents had lived in a Jenny Lind little more than a shack, but World War II saved the business. The demand for coal became ravenous, and my father sold every chunk his High Moor miners produced.

I finished the coffee and drew on the cigar as I thought about him as a young man leaving decaying Bellerive for the alien mountains, a story that became a legend within the family and around King County. Until **my** sight of him that night after Judge Pechiney's party, I'd believed him the greatest man alive.

"Wild and woolly times back then," Arthur said.

"For my father too?"

"Well, yes, union troubles, shootings, tipples blown up. Like frontier days."

Shootings and tipples blown up? Some festering connection between what happened at High Moor long ago and the blast at Bellerive?

"You knew my brother John and his family?"

"Everybody knew John. I talked with him several times about

LeBlanc history. He always received me graciously. We worshiped at Christ Church."

Christ Church, where I was baptized, a shuttered brick structure of classical symmetry built before the American Revolution. The pews had small wooden doors, and the leaded glass windows distorted shapes of the cemetery's moldering tombstones.

"I didn't blow up the portico," I said.

"I don't pass judgment," Arthur said. He'd crossed his legs and leaned back in his chair. A bedroom slipper dangled away from the toe of his chubby foot.

"Who could've hated enough to kill wholesale like that?"

"No idea. Never heard a bad word spoken against John or his family."

"But you have against me."

"I admit that's so."

"They're getting the rope," I said and again thought about how the killing must've been done. People around King County would know a little something about explosives. Farmers might use dynamite to clear tree stumps and blow up beaver dams flooding low grounds. But how could anybody have laid and detonated a massive charge under the portico without being seen?

"You'd be doing me a big favor if you let me stay till dark," I said.

"Done."

"If they find how you've helped me, you won't be popular with the courthouse crowd."

"I'll simply tell them that I believed you a person in need, which is a truth. Moreover I've never considered popularity a gift of the Spirit."

18

I STRETCHED MY legs, sprawled, and snoozed in Arthur's easy chair during the afternoon. I'd surface to hear him moving about softly in the bungalow. Once I sprang up to cross to a back window. He stood in his yard painting a canvas propped on an easel, his subject billowing cumulus clouds sliding over the Kentucky coffee trees.

I again lounged on the chair, closed my eyes, and thought of my need for money and the insurance policy. The company might balk. Throw attorneys back-to-back against me and eat up time I didn't have, as well as sap the policy's surrender value through legal fees —an old game with lawyers.

My brother John had kept the policy in his safe deposit box since my father's death. The Commonwealth might claim I'd learned of it, furnishing additional motive for me taking vengeance against a family that'd disowned me.

I'd been in the army and did know something about explosives, particularly the mining of perimeters with claymores. Falkoner could contend I'd demonstrated a pattern of violence. He'd milk the death of John, Eleanor, and their son. A great courtroom crier, Falkoner would have the jury simultaneously weeping and thirsting for blood.

I thought of High Moor, the union troubles out in West Virginia, my father's legacy there as spoken of by Rajab Ishmael. Whether I'd learn anything of use or not, the state offered what I needed most—a place to run.

I sat forward. Something changed—the crows had stopped quarreling, and no birds sang. I looked out the window. Arthur still stood before his easel but gazed toward the road.

I grabbed my jacket, ran out the back door into the woods, threw myself on the ground under a thicket of Scotch broom. A county cruiser balled down the road, skidded, and swerved into Arthur's lane. Yellow and blue lights flashed.

Cole, Rodger, a black deputy, and Rutledge bailed out. Rodger and the deputy moved toward the front, while Cole took off for the rear. All had pistols drawn. Rutledge stopped before Arthur.

"We'll need to search your house, Arthur," Rutledge said. "We're in pursuit of a fugitive in the area."

"Well I don't know," Arthur answered and glanced about uncertainly.

"We have a legal right. He's wanted for questioning and believed dangerous." Rutledge waved the deputies on.

Cole jerked open the screen door and blitzed inside. They banged through the bungalow searching and exited together at the rear to gather around Arthur, who still held a raised brush.

I crawled deeper into the woods before standing and running. I heard shouts back at the bungalow. I thought of hounds tracking, and when I reached a shallow branch I shucked off my shoes and socks and jerked my pants above my knees to splash upstream and kill scent.

I slowed to rest. The sun had lowered, but the day was still bright. If I reached the Axapomimi I had a chance. I circled through the woods to the paved road where I knelt watching. Like deer hunters, deputies might be parked at straight stretches waiting for me to cross. I dashed over and ran among pines.

I stopped to listen for sounds of pursuit before zigzagging to the river where I collapsed heaving on damp spongy soil under looping willow branches. My breathing quieted. Only the Axapomimi's whisper and a kingfisher's cry.

Dusk seeped among trees. A fish jumped, doves fluttered, and fireflies glowed above the still, darkening water. As I stood, mosquitoes spiraled around my face. I wiped leaf mold off my clothes and set out toward Jessup's Wharf.

I kept close to the sloping bank and stopped at hundred-step intervals to listen. Night filled the woods, and under heavy foliage I held my arms in front of me as fenders. The river became a shiny blackness.

Ahead were lighted windows, a dog barked, and wind chimes tinkled. On screened porches people sat and conversed. Matches flared as cigarettes were lit.

I crouched and heard a hull nudging a private dock and, when I squinted, made out the shape of a skiff. I moved onto the dock and knelt to the stern. Oars lay inside. I looked up through a tangle of birch limbs to the house. People were playing cards.

I loosened the painter, stepped into the skiff, and shoved off. Slowly the current took hold and curved the boat downstream. I lay across the thwarts till I'd floated past the cottages, and as I took up oars heard a distant siren.

I rowed gently and steadily. With the current's lazy push I figured I ought to be able to reach Salt's Landing seventeen miles downstream by morning. If the skiff's theft weren't discovered early, I'd try to ride my thumb westward to High Moor.

I kept the skiff centered in the river till I floated past a campground. The radiance of lanterns lit tent fabric, a guitar twanged, a woman squealed, and smoke from grills drifted among spectral sycamores.

A cabin cruiser, its hull white, motored upriver, the engine richly subdued. Red and green bow lights reflected in the black water. As it passed, people partying on the aft deck came into view. Ice clinked, and whisky-lubricated hilarity erupted.

"How's the fishing?" a voice hollered, and a spotlight flashed and picked me up in its blinding beam.

"Nothing 'cept skeeters biting," I answered.

"What kind of bait you using?"

"Shiners."

"Luck to you," the voice said, and the spotlight died. Leaving a shimmering wake, the boat moved on.

A large fish splashed beside the skiff. Drops of water struck my arm. No sharks in the low salinity of tidal water this far upstream, yet I pictured dark shapes sliding under the surface in wait for me.

Hunger and fear were aches in my belly, the accustomed diet. Black emptiness along the banks. I closed my eyes, thinking that to lie back and give up would be easy. The skiff bumped a tree that erosion had felled into the river. I pushed off and rowed.

The river widened. Ahead a gleam in the sky, not sunrise but an industrial plant where yellow bulbs burned on a silver superstructure reared high into the night. The arm of a crane swung in and out of darkness.

Sulfuric odors of a paper mill. Whitish smoke twisted upward from a stack, machinery clanked, steam hissed, and shadowy figures worked on barges moored along a pier.

I drifted past on the opposite side. The boat spun in a lazy circle. Herons squawked and flushed, their wings batting wind.

I rowed till my arms gave out. My hands were tough from life at Lizard Inlet, yet I felt the burn of blisters. I slumped, my chin against my chest, and gave myself to the current.

An osprey's cry woke me. I blinked into a false dawn. Downstream, navigation lights of the drawbridge at what had to be Salt's Landing. I paddled to the western bank, ran the skiff aground, and used the painter to pull it high among the shedding birches.

I climbed to level ground where trees gave way to a picked, ragged cornfield soft underfoot. The stalks' leaves slashed at me as I jogged till I reached a two-lane paved road that led into Salt's Landing. The town emerged from morning haze, and soil knocked loose from my shoes.

Salt's Landing had been only a post office and a general store during my youth. Now it had a motel, a factory that made golf carts, a truck stop. A restaurant fan exhausted the smell of bacon frying. My knees felt rubbery, and I steadied myself by holding to the guy wire of a power pole.

I dusted off and straightened my clothes before walking among the rigs. A driver swung down from the cab of a shiny green Peterbilt hitched to a moving van. He smoked a pipe and wore a cap that had an embroidered silver largemouth bass leaping after a purple dragonfly. He was stout, needed a shave, and wore steel-frame glasses.

"Feed me breakfast and I'll help with your load," I said.

He looked me over, those eyes a steady gun-metal blue honed hard and sharp by thousands of concrete miles. To him I had to appear questionable even in the suit Arthur had furnished me.

"Where you headed?"

"Working my way to Nashville," I said, the first city that rose to mind. "My mother's bad sick."

"Where you coming from?"

"Newport News. Been laid off at the shipyard and had a run of bad luck."

"Well, hell, I reckon I can dig deep enough to find some pancake money for a hungry man. I been there myself. Name's Lester."

He walked swinging his legs wide like a man who'd been long in the saddle. Truckers had filled the counter stools of the noisy restaurant, and Lester called to them as we passed to the men's room to wash up. With blistered, wet palms I smoothed back my hair.

We sat at a booth by the window, and like all the other truckers, Lester didn't take off his cap. That way they never lost them.

The middle-aged waitress, her expression that of a woman who'd heard it all, drew her order pad from her orange uniform pocket.

"Two orders of tire patches with ham and grits," Lester said, not asking me. "And the coffee better melt lug nuts."

"Nothing melt crap like you, Lester," she said and prissed off. Lester eyed her legs.

"You heard my name," he said. "What's yours?"

"George."

"Well, George, I'm headed out Roanoke way, then on to Bluefield to pick up a load. Far west as I go."

"It'll do," I said, trying to visualize roads.

"What's wrong with your mother?" he asked and took out a clasp knife to begin clearing his squared-off nails.

"Stroke. She's part paralyzed and can't talk or feed herself."

"Tough throw. My mother's eighty-six and still mows grass."

A blue-and-gray Crown Victoria pulled into the lot. The trooper stepped out, his uniform neat, his campaign hat tipped slightly forward. I was beyond King County, but Rutledge could have a statewide want out on me by this time. I looked for a back door.

The trooper didn't enter the restaurant but talked to a trucker, checked his papers, and drove off. I realized Lester was watching me, that he'd seen the blisters I'd been trying to hide.

"They tough on thumb riders," I said.

"Let me tell you something," he said. "In my cab I carry a hogleg Colt forty-five and a tire iron. Before I let you ride an inch with me, I gonna search you. You even think of trying to do me bad, I'll leave you bleeding in a ditch. Got it?"

"Got it."

The waitress brought the pancakes. I asked for extra butter and spread it thick between the three layers. I poured on syrup, not caring that it ran over the ham, and drank three cups of black coffee. Just the fear left in my belly.

Trucks pulled in and out of the concrete parking area, bells ringing each time tires rolled over the black pneumatic hose. Lester looked at the plastic digital watch on his thick, strong wrist.

"Let's get aboard," he said.

He paid, called his good-byes, and we left. Before he unlocked the Peterbilt, he patted me down. He fingered my Old Timer but let me keep it. I climbed up to the cab, which had the feel of domesticity: radios, a compass, bucket seats, carpeting, a color picture of a chubby laughing woman with her hands on the heads of two brawny boys.

Lester shifted the diesel's gears and edged onto the highway. He cut on the CB to pick up trucker chatter and police alerts. Seven miles down the road we swung onto Interstate 64 West.

I asked permission to study maps that he kept in an accordion file wedged between the seats. I couldn't find High Moor but I did Cliffside, a name often heard from my father.

Lester slid in a Hank Snow tape. I loosened my shoelaces. The roar of the big engine and thumping of tires against road joints merged with Hank's deep, lulling voice and my weariness.

I slept.

19

AT RICHMOND, I woke hoping Lester'd stop so I could again phone Edward's house and attempt to speak to Juno. He didn't.

"You sawed a pile of logs," he said and glanced at me.

"You drive a first-class bedroom."

"Best on the road," he said.

He had cigarettes. We smoked and listened to tapes. He told me he'd served twenty years in the navy, retired as a chief petty officer, and received a pension. He owned the truck, and his Portsmouth duplex was paid for.

"Ever in the service?" he asked.

"Couple of years," I said. Nothing more, and he didn't pick up on it.

We reached Roanoke early afternoon, stopped by a McDonald's for burgers he paid for, and unloaded furniture at a brick rancher in a development so new not all the streets had been paved or grass planted on lawns.

I took off my gabardine jacket and shirt to keep myself cool and them from getting any dirtier. The young wife followed us around, fearful that we'd break her wedding china. When we finished at three, Lester handed me a twenty-dollar bill.

"You stronger than you look," he said. "Don't reckon you interested in regular work?"

"Got to see my mother."

"Okay, on to Bluefield."

"Just let me off at Princeton."

"That the best way to Nashville?"

"Yeah I'll drop down on 77 and pick up 40."

"Your call," he said. "And by the way I ain't believed two seconds the story about your mother."

Ahead mountains, the Appalachians a high dark barrier that blocked entrance to West Virginia. The road grade steepened. From an overlook I glimpsed green forested combers spread all the way to the horizon.

When Lester stopped in Princeton at the ramp up to Interstate 77, we shook hands. I watched him drive off. If I hadn't fooled Lester, no chance I could lie my way past pros who might detain and question me.

The day was still sunny and soggy. Down the road I spotted a sign in a strip mall advertising a Waffle House. I didn't know where my next meal'd be coming from, so I'd lay on fat while I could.

I used the john, washed up good, and stroked my hair with a comb somebody had left on the sink. My face had again darkened with beard stubble, but the gabardine suit didn't look too bad from the jacket up.

I ate the Pecan Special with bacon and coffee and bought a pack of Camels before heading back to the ramp, meaning to travel north, not south. From studying Lester's maps I knew I had to reach Beckley before Cliffside. I carried no memory of the town, but my father had said it was the only civilization near High Moor, site where my grandfather Angus MacKay had opened his mine in the Wandering River Gorge and the LeBlanc downfall had been reversed. I figured there was little chance that Benson Falkoner or Lewis Rutledge back in King County would think of me fleeing through the region.

The first pickup I raised my thumb to, a mud-scabbed Toyota, slowed for me. The bed held chain saws and gasoline cans. A wad of tobacco bulged the bearded driver's cheek, and a .303-caliber Enfield was racked across the rear window.

"Never know when a West Virginia rabbit's gonna attack," he said and paid the turnpike toll.

"Rabbit?"

"What we call deer 'round here," he said.

He drove hunched over the wheel, the accelerator stomped down hard, and the pickup shook so badly chunks of mud fell off and broke bouncing after us.

We were in Beckley by nine-thirty. The driver let me off at the intersection of State Route 709, which he told me led northeast to Cliffside. He was, he said, making for home, to a place called Slab Fork.

"Watch out for them rabbit attacks," he called.

I walked the road, a thumb raised. My head hung heavy, my feet dragging pavement. I felt a blister bust and water run between my toes. Only a few cars passed, and none stopped.

I thought of Zeke Webb. We'd been in 'Nam together, and he'd talked about Beckley. Maybe a chance I could find his name in the book and call him. No, keep it simple and leave no trail.

I reached a low rock wall around a cemetery, the tombstones lying white up the slope. A black iron gate had been closed and locked. I climbed the wall, worked off my shoes, peeled my socks, and pissed under a rustling juniper.

I let myself down on the grass between two mounds to join the dead. The night was still warm. I couldn't read names in the dark, but I made out the silhouette of a winged stone angel against a lowering sky.

I WOKE WITH dew wet and cold on my face and stared into a shredded mist. A spread flock of starlings flew over. I heard sounds of trucks. As I sat up, my bones ached, and I pushed back my hair. My gabardine suit was damply grass-stained. I rubbed my sore feet gently before fitting on my socks and shoes.

I limped along the road's shoulder. A construction gang of a dozen booted and hardhatted men gathered in a paved lot before a heavy machinery dealership that had fences around bulldozers, forklifts, and mining equipment. Each picked up a shovel from a pile.

What had once been a yellow school bus turned into the lot, the county's name masked by a swipe of black paint.

"Go near Cliffside?" I asked the last man in the line.

"Go through her," he said.

I lifted a shovel and stepped on the bus. The driver said nothing. I sat by myself on a torn seat at the rear as the bus revved up and lurched forward.

The road twisted and climbed. The driver had to gear down, and the engine strained. We kept winding higher. This was different terrain from the turnpike, less tamed, the grade radical, narrow ribbed hollows, hardwoods clinging to rocky ledges.

Men sat silently, resigned to whatever work they'd do. No magazines or newspapers. Their bodies counter-shifted against the road's snaking turns. They smoked, and gazed at what? The way became so steep the driver shifted to bulldog till the bus at last gained the top of the ridge and began a run down the other side. I smelled overheated brake linings.

We looped around the mountain and leveled at a rusty metal sign announcing CLIFFSIDE, ELEV. 3190. It'd been punctured by bullets. Humble frame houses, some covered by artificial brick siding. We passed a stone Victorian courthouse with turrets and a Chinese tile roof.

Across from the courthouse, a food market, a hardware store, a barber shop, all with second stories whose windows were empty eye sockets. Red-and-yellow whirligigs spun on wires strung over a used-car lot.

I stood, left my shovel, and walked forward.

"Let me off," I said to the driver, who had tangled long blond hair and a horseshoe nail worn as a ring.

He shrugged, braked in front of a garage, and opened the door. Soon as my feet touched ground, he yanked it shut, and the bus jerked away, the stoic faces gawking down at me.

At the garage a mechanic lying on a creeper worked under a jacked-up begrimed Mack dump truck. I stooped to ask about High Moor as he pounded a wrench to loosen a bolt in the differential casing.

"Three mile," he said, his face grease-smeared. "Down the road and follow it till you reach where Bear Creek spills over. You got to look close to find the trail on the high side of the creek. It's mostly growed up."

In the Shawnee Food Market I bought myself two cans of Bea-nee Weenees, a slab of rat cheese, a box of saltines, and two Baby Ruths. Matches were free.

I set out along the descending street where houses needed paint and FOR SALE signs stuck from lawns. Within a hundred yards the town gave out, and there were no more dwellings—just a narrow mountain road spiraling down a forested descent.

As I walked, I ate a Baby Ruth. Stagnant water had collected in drainage ditches. The sun stood at high noon, yet the air held a clean freshness. I believed I'd missed Bear Creek till I saw water ripple across the pavement. Entrance to the trail lay in a parting of thickly growing laurel.

The trail almost disappeared under accumulated leaf fall and tangles of hawthorn. At a turn, I looked down and saw the river far below, its surface broken by the lacy whiteness of rapids. A brook splashed from a cave among huge, pale boulders, and the battered water caused a dazzling spectrum in a shaft of sunlight. The brook poured coolness. I pulled off my shoes and socks and rolled up my pants to wade across. The water was so cold it sent sharp aches up my ankles and legs but also relieved the blister pains. I slipped on rocks slickened by green slime and held my sack of provisions high.

Again shod, I met the first signs of human enterprise: rusted pieces of broken machinery lying among weeds. Then, in the face of the mountain, a stone portal covered by a welded iron grillwork like a portcullis.

I approached the thick bars and peered inside. Dark water covered the crushed slate floor. Like shark fins, slabs jutted from the surface. There was dripping deep in the mountain, and I thought of entering that blackness and having the weight of those great boulders over me.

I hiked on. Broad yellow leaves plastered across the trail. Around a bend trees thinned, and I walked onto a sunny bench of land cut into the mountain. Ahead were stone buildings, the windows broken. Behind them dark entries, again iron-protected, and leading from them, rusted rails grown up with an ashen wild grass that had found root among crushed coal.

Wheelless buggies lay overturned. Crows flew from a cross beam of a wireless power pole. Kudzu everywhere, climbing trees, dislodging stones, and claiming the land.

Below, an abandoned settlement where miners must've once lived: uniform rows of board-and-batten houses on both sides of unpaved roads. At the far end two wrecked buildings—possibly a school and company store. A third structure I identified as a burned church, for vine-tangled gravestones were terraced behind it. I wondered how anyone could've made a life in this wild goddamn place.

Slate steps led downward above crumbling moss-covered coke ovens and the tipple where half a dozen tracks curved beneath black spidery piling.

The town street was cindered, the houses flanking it the same—each one-story, a chimney, front porch, a privy in the rear. Most had drooped, rotted, or collapsed. Wind and weather had scoured away all paint. I remembered a phrase I'd heard from a radio preacher in Georgia: *Desolation upon desolation.*

The sun was lowering to the high western ridge. I found a house that still had a roof and appeared stable enough to hang together awhile longer. At the front, a fallen picket fence and a birdhouse atop a slanted post. When I stepped on the porch and pushed the door, it fell over, spuming dust.

Three small rooms and a kitchen, all fixtures torn out. Small animals, maybe rats, scurried under the mushy floor. I found a child's plastic rattle, the handle snapped off. Swallows' mud-dried nests everywhere.

From the walls, yellowed sheets of newspaper that'd been tacked up for insulation had now peeled down. I lifted a piece of the Cliffside *Advertiser* dated July 4, 1967, and the headline read HIGH MOOR LAID LOW.

I sat on moldering wood of the porch and watched a deep crisp shadow fill the gorge and climb the eastern slope before I cleaned out the chimney coal grate, then levered a board from the side of the house and stomped it for kindling.

I lit paper under the kindling, hoping that swifts hadn't stopped up the flu. I laid on more wood, some so soft it shredded in my fingers. The fire caught and burned quickly. I popped a can of Beanee Weenees and set it at the flame's edge. I cut slabs of cheese, placed them on crackers, and covered them with hot beans. For dessert I ate the other Baby Ruth.

I needed water and worked down through sumac and across the tracks to the river. I cupped my palms. The water had a gritty taste from the rapids' pummeling boulders, which in the dusk resembled elephants gathered to drink.

With the side of my foot I scraped a sleeping space among debris just inside the doorway. I slipped off my shoes and hoped snakes wouldn't seek my body heat during the night. The mountain throbbed with insects heard despite the pounding rapids. I listened to a train pass, and its horn sounded the bugled tattoo of lonely men everywhere. The muted clack of wheels became lost in the river's din.

My fire died. I smoked and drifted off but woke suddenly and sat up. I felt addled, unsure where I was. I glimpsed a slice of moon above the high ridge and heard the crunch of cinders. I rose on my hands and knees to crawl to the porch and look out along the line of ghostly houses. A shape moved, not so much walking as seeming to glide. I reached for my Old Timer and clamped the blade in my teeth to open it as I gathered myself to spring forward, strike, escape.

The shape fused with gaps between the houses, then reappeared like a figure in a ceremonial procession, a moon-silvered form flowing slowly through night to become reabsorbed by blackness.

I waited, crouched. Gradually I let down but kept the knife open and set my back against the door frame.

20

I LAY ON my side and watched the dawn seep through mist rising from a wild river that was nothing like the serene, domesticated Axapomimi. Through the night I'd smoked my Camels, and feeling stiff and raw-eyed, I held to the door frame as I pulled myself up.

I looked both ways along the row of houses. The heavy mist slowly circled, and tar paper flapped on roofs. I stepped to the weedy yard, glanced at the birdhouse, and found painted on it faded miniature windows and a door, yet it had no real entrance. Instead the top unlatched and lifted off. How were the birds supposed to get inside?

I checked the footprints along the cindered street but could make out none except my own. I knew damn well I hadn't dreamed the shape's passing.

I ate crackers and the second can of Beanee Weenees cold. The last of the cheese I stuck in my jacket pocket as I left. Ready with my knife, I checked the open doorway of every forlorn house I passed and turned to see that nothing stalked me from the mist.

As I hurried past the coke ovens, wet kudzu grasped at my pants legs. The black tipple formed up before me, and I climbed the slate steps till I heard somebody below whistling "Amazing Grace."

I slowly moved back down toward the tracks. Out of mist emerged a figure walking on rail ties. He wore a fisherman's vest and a canvas hat hooked with artificial bait. Over his shoulders he'd slung waders. He carried a rod and tackle box. I stood very still so he wouldn't see me.

Still whistling, he turned off the tracks and sidled down the bank toward the river where he walked onto a boulder that poked into the flow. He set the waders and tackle box down and laid the rod across them before baiting his line with a golden spinner worked free from his hat.

He lifted his rod, flexed it, and cast into white water. His retrieve was rapid and jerky. Maybe he'd have cigarettes. I slipped down the bank to the boulder. I thought of taking him. It'd be easy to jump him before he could react, use a choke hold, lift his wallet, shove him into the river.

Dumb, because if the bastard survived he'd go to the law, and they'd be hot after me. Tie me in with a want from King County. He was a happy man out for a day's fishing, and I both envied and liked the proficient way he handled the rod.

"They biting?" I asked.

He pivoted, startled—neat, lightly built, forty-five or so. Never taking his eyes off me, he reeled in.

"There's a record smallmouth down there just past that outcropping," he said and pointed using an elbow. "Waits in an eddy for his meals to float by. I had Old Pete on the line last fall, the big daddy of these parts. Like to get hold of him one more time. Not for my table. He's too grand to be mere food for a table. Just land him, kiss his lips, and turn him loose. My name's Givens. Frank Givens."

The golden spinner snapped tight to the rod tip. He knew he stood at the boulder's edge and had no way around me.

"Ben Dawes," I said, the name of a cellmate at Leavenworth convicted as a deserter. He'd taught me how to shave and palm dice and had thrown the switch to the mess hall's washers and dryers the night I gave Whitlow the steam.

"You a fisherman?" Frank asked.

"Been known to wet a line."

"I come here every summer. Live up in Ohio, Akron, where I work for Mr. Goodrich, but I take my vacations in the gorge. Got a camper parked down the tracks near the bridge crossing. Charge up my battery for life's next onslaughts. You from around here, Ben?"

"Just passing by," I said. He was afraid, and I'd use his fear to get tobacco off him if he had any. "Got a smoke?"

"Sure 'nuff," he said and reached inside his vest pocket. He offered his Kents. "Take them. And if you're meaning to rob me, I'll give you my money without a fight. I'd appreciate it if you'd leave me my credit cards and driver's license."

"Just an ever'day nicotine habit, Frank."

I spilled cigarettes into my palm and fitted them in my shirt pocket before returning the pack. He thumbed a Zippo with the Ducks Unlimited insignia on it to provide fire. He very definitely wished to please me and glanced up the mountain where mist lifted in hope of help.

"High Moor's a remarkable place," he said. "For a while one of the great mines in the Appalachian coal fields. Advanced methods of extraction and transport. Remarkable men opened these diggings."

"You a native?" I asked. I'd detected traces of a nasal hillbilly accent.

"My father was the carpenter who built the company store. Sold everything from chewing tobacco to Chanel No. 5. At its height High Moor poured more tons of low-sulphur coal out of this gorge than any other colliery on the line. The Secretary of Commerce made a trip here to present a presidential award. Night and day you heard the drags and banging of hopper cars. Lights burned up and down the slope like the mountain was burning."

He cast but watched me with side glances. The lure worked through a sluice of heaving water. I looked up at the lifting mist along the ridge—a high wall of stone devoid of growth.

"How'd people and equipment get down here?"

"They were lowered over the top from a hoist house," he said and pointed. "The mancar, a kind of wooden wagon with iron wheels that ran on tracks, the seats set at a forty-five-degree angle and lowered by a drum and cable. Held sixteen men. During the descent the seats leveled out. You could walk it too if you had the strength. Steps all the way. Many a drunk broke an arm or leg trying."

"The place's dead now."

"But it was a boomer once," he said and cast again. "Took trucks and machinery apart up top and reassembled them down here. Built two towns to accommodate over three hundred men and their families, one up top for the native white miners. Foreigners and blacks lived here in the gorge. Had their own churches and schools. It was all segregated even to the time the mine closed in the sixties. Nobody ever heard of civil rights then back in these mountains."

His rod bowed, and he raised it high and fast to set the hook, but no fish. He reeled in and checked the spinner. The triple hooks were bent.

"That wasn't Old Pete," he said and laughed. From his hat he unsnagged another spinner, this one silver. He attached it to the swivel. "Horsed the fish instead of being patient. Old Pete'd've taken my rod too."

He cast, and I tried to picture my mother in this setting. I couldn't reconcile it. The image seemed as jarring as immaculate white-gloved hands bearing black chunks of coal.

"Rough country," I said.

"I love it. Was born in Cliffside and always feel it's where I belong. Lived up top a few years when a boy. Played baseball and shot hoops. I travel back, and my genes tell me I'm in the right place."

I finished the cigarette and stepped on it. Mist strung out, letting more sun through and lightening the river to a wan green except where it beat white against rocks and flung up spray.

"You come in along the tracks?" he asked.

"The trail," I said.

"The bench level. The mine portals, haulways, ventilation entries. Also the maintenance shop, an office, and powder house. During the early days each miner bought his own powder to shoot his coal. If a man worked hard and saved money, he could buy himself a Model A and drive his family to Atlantic City. Course he had to keep his car up top."

Powder, I thought. Explosives.

"The Shawnee seam, coal taller than a big man, some of the most beautiful bituminous ever mined, true black diamonds," Frank said. "It was dangerous, but the miners liked the work. Same cool temperature all year long underground, you were your own boss, and it was manly labor with enough danger to keep it from becoming boring. Not like bookkeeping or banking."

He cast and reeled in the spinner into the swirling flow.

"Not for me," I said.

"Men get coal in their blood. Like Angus MacKay. Experts told him the gorge was too rough, not suited to mining. He went bust trying. His ideas were sound, but his timing was bad."

I thought of finishing my slab of cheese but didn't want to share it.

"Then John LeBlanc moved in for a try. War started up. Steel needs coal and coke, and the Shawnee seam provided the best. LeBlanc was a brilliant man. Developed the know-how to extract, clean, and market the coal."

"I heard about him."

"Took guts for him to come here and reopen the seam. Place was overgrown and deserted. Guts and plenty of mechanical and engineering smarts."

"You know him?"

"Not up close. I was a kid. The LeBlancs had a house up top with a tennis court, and Mrs. LeBlanc helped at the school. He might've been a high-born Virginian but he got right down to it and worked with the men. Went into the mountain and came out grimy as any coal grubber."

"The house still there?"

"Not much left. For a while squatters used it, then there was a fire."

"Hard to believe anybody could live around here," I said and again looked to the wall of stone, moist with mist.

"Once High Moor was a thriving place though, men working underground for good pay, wives hanging out the wash, the kids throwing balls. Big strong men, brave pretty women, everybody dreaming dreams. Not how most people see a coal camp."

"Heard there was union troubles, shooting, blowing up tipples."

"Plenty of that early on. John LeBlanc got fanned."

"Fanned?"

"Shot close to. Bullet just missed his ear."

"Who did it?"

"Just a happening. Nobody caught. Lots of miners owned rifles. Pistols too."

"Anybody left around here now?" I asked and thought of the shape moving through darkness of the company street.

"Not that I know of," he said, again reeling in. "Nothing to hold them."

When he cast, the spinner hit the water behind the rock, and the rod bowed almost to his feet. He hollered. The reel shrieked, and the fish ran line into tumbling rapids. Pressure not only from Old Pete, but also the current's force.

Frank held the rod's butt in his belly. He tried to loosen the drag, but the line sang out, grew taut, snapped, and whipped back at him. He reeled in, his spinner gone, yet he smiled.

"Old Pete's smart. Smarter than me. He's learned to cut into the strongest flow, circle back to get a second of slack, and power on. Uses the river. I'll never land him, but we have a relationship."

He laid the rod across his tackle box and pulled out the Kents.

"Yeah, for years I thought the river ran black," he said. "Now I carry it green and clean when I go back up to Akron. I'll be leaving tomorrow, but I got the river in here."

He pointed at his head.

21

I LEFT HIM fishing. I crossed the tracks to the slate risers. My calves ached from yesterday's climb down, and I counted steps and stopped at seventy to rest. I brought out my cheese and ate thin slices off my knife blade. I watched a diminished Frank Givens cast to the river. He reeled in and set his rod down as if he meant to stop fishing but looked up and saw me. He waved and lifted his rod.

I climbed. At the bench level I leaned against a coal buggy that lay tilted outside a barred portal. Letters chiseled into the concrete keystone had filled with grime. I squinted: SHAWNEE NO. 1.

I stopped by the windowless stone building that had an iron door. The powder house, I guessed—the safe place to keep explosives. No way to climb to the door as the wooden steps had decayed. A black, empty keyhole and latch I couldn't reach.

Blasting powder. The charge that had smashed Bellerive's portico had to come from somewhere. Not possible. My father had left these mountains some twenty-three years ago when the Shawnee seam gave out.

Again I climbed. Broken lengths of track lay among hairy, glistening poison ivy vines—maybe once used for what Frank called the mancar.

As I rested, I pictured miners during cold, killing winters lowering by cable down the mountainside through sleet and snow, the wind ripping at them. Hardy men they had to be to endure the weather's assault and troop daily into deep cavities of darkness.

A plane flew over, high, a silver glint in the colorless sky. Risers were missing, and I grabbed at scrub growth to pull myself upward. More ruins—rusted iron girders, sheeting, what looked like a blown steam boiler.

Sore, out of breath, I made it to a concrete platform and the iron drum that'd been used to wind and release the cable controlling the mancar. Scraps from a broken donkey engine lay scattered among weeds. My knees pushed through briars to level ground. Abandoned structures still stood, sidings and roofs gone. Kudzu wound high on corroded legs of what had been a windmill or water tank.

All that remained of the large house on the highest ground were a half-fallen chimney, blackened timbers, stone of a foundation, and a charred clawfoot bathtub filled with plaster and black water.

I thought of my father coming to this brutal land, he with his University of Virginia fraternity-boy background, the contrast between this pitiless gorge and Bellerive's benign acres. I pictured my small, quiet mother as she must've fought coal dust and mountain blasts to keep house and rear children. How had she abided it?

Among weeds I found what'd been the tennis court, the surface made of fire brick, a bent pipe that'd held one end of a net entwined by bloomless morning glories. Had my father and his player friends worn correct whites and used spotless balls in a coal-smudged land?

The street had become broken asphalt chunks, and thistles grew from fissures. I followed it to a paved county road. As I walked I looked for a route marker and found none. No traffic passed.

The earth soaked heat from the fully emerged sun, causing locusts to tune up. I trudged on till I sighted a white clapboard building that had two gasoline pumps in front shaded by a tin-roof over-hang that needed paint. Three men sat outside on a wooden bench beside the door, all elderly, wearing caps, overalls, high-top shoes. Years had leeched their faces like eroded land. I noted an arm missing from a shoulder. Jaws worked tobacco with the methodical cudding of cattle, and ancient eyes of judgment followed me.

"Day warming," I said.

They didn't answer or acknowledge my greeting but continued to stare as if I'd spoken in a foreign tongue.

I opened a screen door and walked inside. Long wooden shelves stretched into dimness. An unlit barrel-shaped coal stove sat in sand at the center of the room. From walls mounted deer heads looked down, their accusing eyes impaired by dust. A single un-shaded bulb burned from a tattered yellow cord, and beneath it a scrawny white-haired clerk stood with his hands on the counter. He wore a checkered sport shirt and a brown apron. His skin appeared thin as parchment.

"Hep you?" he asked, a scratchy voice.

"Wet my whistle," I said and crossed to the soft-drink cooler. I lifted the lid and picked up a can of Nehi grape soda. I thought of Rajab Ishmael.

"Ain't seen you before," he said.

"Ain't been here before," I said and also slid from a shelf a can of hot Louisiana sardines as well as another package of soda crackers.

Wood of the counter was grooved by coins dragged over it. The cash register's scrolled metal ornamentation flaked gilt paint. The clerk wound a handle to open its drawer, and a bell sounded like a prizefight gong.

"You don't look like no fisherman," he said, "and if you hunting work you come to the wrong place. We shut down around here. Keep this store open out of habit."

Once my eyes adjusted I saw shelves lay mostly bare. I bought a pack of Camels. I still had five Kents I'd bummed off Frank Givens.

"You musta been plenty busy in the old days," I said and popped the Nehi.

"Sure, when High Moor was booming. Had three clerks working for me. Drove a Packard automobile and bought my wife a sheared beaver fur coat. We took trips to Cincinnati to see the Reds play."

"You knew the LeBlancs?" I asked as I took change from his veined hand.

"Everybody knew the LeBlancs. For a time saved this place. Long gone. Nothing left around here but coons, crows, and cockroaches."

"What kind of people were they?"

"First thing Mr. LeBlanc he fixed the clock."

"What clock?"

"When he come up from Virginia, he carried keys and unlocked the old mine office where the clock hung on the wall behind the desk. He took it down and got it running before he started hiring men to put the mine back in operation."

He sniffed and wiped a bony finger under his nose.

"One big bastard of a job, but he fixed that clock first. Stopped by here once in a while. Spoke soft and polite. Made hisself a trainload of money and hauled it to Virginia when he pulled out. Never came back."

I pictured my father repairing the clock. He'd always liked fooling with machinery and farm equipment.

"Just like the rest of them," the storekeeper said. "Come into the coal fields, take all the money they can dig up, and hightail it. After they gone, nothing left. Not that I give a shit any longer. Got enough to keep going. A roof and a bed. My burial insurance paid up. When I die, just let the damn place fall in on me."

22

I WALKED THE lonesome road till I passed a glen shaded by drooping honey locusts. Tired and sweat-slick, I turned in and let down on the wild grass. I shucked off my shoes, lay back, and looked skyward to see buzzards circling high, wobbling, their wings dipping. Not yet, you bastards, I thought, and closed my eyes.

I slept, and when I woke, the sun slanted toward the western ridge, and I sat up thirsty. I heard water running. I walked under locust shade to a stream winding through the grass and knelt to drink. The water had a sulphur taste. Mine drainage? I ate my sardines and crackers, used the empty Nehi can to drink from.

I pissed, took off my jacket and shirt, and gave myself an upstream soapless wash. My socks were tattered, and I threw them away before I put on my shoes and limped back to the road. A strip of mountain shadow now lay across it.

Thunder. A swollen cumulonimbus slid like a zeppelin over the ridge. As I stepped faster along the road, a forked streak of lightning and more thunder. The first drops hit hard as ice pellets.

Lights ahead—a blinking, splayed redness. Closer, I saw it was a one-story, tar-papered tonk, the windows framed in jittery multicolored tubing. Over the doorway a red neon miner's pick and a blue sign that read THE PIT. Grimy pickups parked on the gravel apron. Music thumped the flimsy siding.

Though rain fell harder and the drops had a biting edge, I hesitated before entering. I told myself there was little or no chance that word from Jessup's Wharf about me had reached Shawnee County. Nobody in these mountains knew my face. As for police, I hadn't seen a uniform since I entered the state.

I opened the roadhouse's door and stepped into smoky, agitated light. Rough-looking trade sat on stools along the counter. Four booted men played pool at the single table, and a bejeweled jukebox pounded away on a platform made from raw lumber. Wooden booths held drinking couples. Maybe this was payday, or more likely the day welfare checks arrived.

Eyes rifled me as I shut the door. The place smelled of tobacco, perfume, sweat, coal. Smoke had settled into a stratum at the level of electric lights shaped like kerosene lanterns that hung from hooks screwed into unpainted rafters.

I shook rain off myself. It'd been a long time since I'd drunk a beer in a roadhouse and given myself to the music of lonely humankind. One brew for the road wouldn't kill. Get me through till the storm stopped. I found a stool at the end of the counter near a cubicle that served as a kitchen. Eyes still followed. Chunky, bearded men drinking here, some with the mascara-like darkness around their eyes—coal dust over the years ground into skin. The man sitting to my left had rough-grained hands that made the Blatz bottle he gripped seem diminutive.

The short, thin woman tending bar wore a pink patch over her right eye. Below the patch a scar ran straight down along a cheekbone to her chin. The good eye was black, as was her short hair. She wore black jeans, a thick black belt that had a large Mexican silver buckle shaped like a bucking mustang, and a white cowgirl shirt embroidered with curlicues of black thread. Her complexion was dark—Italian, I guessed, or Greek.

"You look like the dog that's done drowned," she said, her accent pure hillbilly. She'd painted her small mouth scarlet and from her ears hung looped golden earrings. Her clipped nails were done in alternating reds, whites, and blues.

"Reckon you could fetch a thirsty fellow a beer?" I asked.

"It ain't beyond the impossible," she said. From among chunks of ice in a fifty-gallon oil drum she offered me a Blatz, no glass. Her small, lean fingers decorated with costume rings didn't let go of the bottle. "Be seventy-five cents."

I laid a dollar on the counter. She dug out change from her jeans. She didn't carry my bill to the cash register but folded it into her shirt pocket. Screw the IRS and Uncle Sam. She moved away to serve customers calling her name. Blackie. She wore black-and-white diamond-patterned cowboy boots with high heels that caused her tail to stick out.

Men, their elbows propped forward on the bar, still watched me. The Pit was not a place that cared for strangers, and nobody appeared to be having much fun either. Women sitting in booths acted aggrieved. Only one couple danced, heavy-footed, more duty than pleasure. Faces were fixed, as if drinking were serious business a man had to set his mind to.

I avoided eyes. Johnny Cash sounded mournful and lost. I lit one of Frank Givens's Kents before tasting the beer. I wanted to take my time and savor the moment. I'd been in a thousand tonks, worked a bar in Everglade City, felt my blood beat to the country music and stomping heels, but never with the feeling of so little gaiety as here in the Pit—sullen men and women drinking with grim persistence.

"Any luck, Kermit?" Blackie asked the man next to me. His heavy forearms lay crossed. She collected three empty Blatz bottles and tossed them into a second oil drum already filled to the top with discards.

"Clearing the hell out," Kermit answered. "Shoulda done it long ago."

"Something'll turn up," Blackie said. She worked fast and sure behind the counter, which was made of half-inch stained plywood. I thought of the Bellerive's covered broken windows and front door.

"Yeah, me dead," Kermit said. He hadn't lifted his face to talk but peered at her from the tops of his eye sockets.

"The drowned dog's looking better," Blackie said, facing me. "Ain't seen you before."

"First time in Shawnee County," I said and then wished I'd told her nothing.

"Once you get in you never get out," Kermit said.

"You not a Sharp?" Blackie asked. She had a way of narrowing her good left eye to focus. "You look like you got Sharp blood."

"Nope."

She moved off. I inhaled the good smoke deep and lifted the Blatz. Jesus, there were few things better than the first cold brew after a bad day. The beer washed across my tongue and brought its promise of release down my throat to my belly where the old water-logged fear resided. Trouble was, all bottles had bottoms.

"Another?" Blackie asked. She threw my empty in the drum, where it clanked.

I didn't mean to have a second but felt the need. Rain beat the roof, and I was beginning to feel comfortable on the stool. Through a window hung with canary yellow paper curtains, I glimpsed heavy drops disturbing red puddles. Blackie set the bottle before me. I again lit a cigarette.

"Watch you damn elbow," Kermit said. He wore an Orioles base-ball cap and sweatshirt. His biceps had been tattooed with a coiled rattlesnake that held a lily clamped between fangs.

"Sorry."

"Sorry don't buy shit," he said.

There was a time I'd have swung my bottle into his mouth. My nose had been broken twice, and the cartilage in the knuckles of my left hand still ached during cold, damp weather, a result of the fight with Whitlow at Leavenworth. No more. I'd learned to accept insult and abuse. And brawls drew police.

Kermit wiped a forearm across his lips, stood, and clomped out into the rain. His pickup's tires splashed the red water. Trouble avoided.

As I lifted my beer, I realized a man was peering at me from the other end of the counter. Bearded, his cap pushed back over greasy locks of brown hair, his skin pale except around the eyes, a short thick neck, shoulders massed—a cross between a bear and an ox. Without shifting his eyes off me, he blew into his Blatz bottle, causing a fluting tone.

"Seen you coming down the road," Blackie said, her voice husky and deep for such a small woman. "Got no wheels?"

"Walking for my health."

"You're full of it too," she said.

The jukebox fell silent. Nobody fed it. The bear-ox watched her and me and scowled. He kept blowing over the bottle to create a low, doleful sound.

"Where you hail from?" Blackie asked as she wiped up Kermit's mess. Knives had cut initials into the counter.

"Maryland," I said, as good a state as any.

"You a long way from home. Another?"

I shook my head. The bear-ox narrowed his eyes. Rain or not, I'd leave. As I pushed off the stool, he set down his bottle, stood, and hiked up his big-ass Levi's. I walked to the john—more plywood. Initials carved into its walls beside penciled messages, one of which read "Prepare to Meet Thy Breaker." I locked the door and watched the knob.

It turned. No window to escape through. No weapon except my

Old Timer—like using a toothpick against a bull. I'd have to feint past him and make for the exit. Where once I fought, I now fled.

I gathered myself, opened the door, and stepped out fast. The bear-ox waited, the broadness of his body taking up more space than any human being had a right to. I started to his right, ducked left, and got around him to race for the door. I'd have made it except bear-ox's buddy at the counter hooked out a boot toe and sent me sprawling. The bear-ox was on top me and dragged me by my belt to my feet. He banged me against the wall. I felt its give. He straightened my gabardine jacket and brushed grit off its sleeves.

"You in a big hurry, brother?"

"Don't want trouble."

"Thing is trouble might could take a liking to you."

The place quieted, and the faces became gravely intent at the scent of blood.

"Didn't mean no harm," I said. The bear-ox's reddish brown eyes were set close.

"You come in here fooling with another man's woman," he said, his breath smelling like beer, plug tobacco, and rotted meat. Tobacco had stained his lips brown at the corners.

"Junior, I ain't your woman and never have been," Blackie called from behind the counter.

"Yeah you is. You just ain't let the idea settle good into your brain."

"The hell with you, and I don't want my place busted up," she said. "I'm calling the sheriff."

"Everthing'll be taken care of before the sheriff can clip on his badge," Junior said.

"Let me buy you a beer," I said to Junior.

I turned toward the counter and the line of faces. They could've been worshiping devoutly in church pews.

"You don't belong 'round here and I'm particular who I drink with," Junior said. His tangled chest hair grew over the collar of his sweatshirt, which had BEAT THE PANTHERS printed on it.

"Just let me walk out the door," I said and then to Blackie, "Serve him a Blatz on me."

"Oh you leaving," Junior said. "You might go out the door air mail unless you do us a little dance. I bet you a fancy stepper. Entertain the troops."

He stuck a paw into his pocket and came up with a quarter. He tossed it to the rat-faced runt who'd tripped me.

"Slug 'Up on the Mountain,'" Junior ordered.

Ratface crossed to the jukebox and fed in the quarter. The machine clicked. Whine of a steel guitar, beat of a drum, the song through the nose of a woman who sounded in pain:

I was walking the valley
To pick me a rose,
But when I reached out my hand
I stuck me a thorn

"Dance," Junior said. He stood with his paws on his hips and bellied me toward the booths.

I'd learned fighting. The man who struck first generally prevailed. I started a shuffling two-step. Grins broke faces around the room. Somebody hee-hawed, onlookers clapped, and a woman wearing a Stetson giggled.

I caught sight of Blackie lifting the receiver of the wall pay phone. I could abide humiliation but not the sheriff.

I danced to the pool table, snatched up balls, and threw them at the bear-ox's head. He shielded his face with his forearms. The balls deflected and banged to the floor. I grabbed a cue stick and whacked him with the butt end. It snapped.

I kicked his shin. He acted more surprised than hurt. He hopped on one foot and pulled up his pants leg to peek at the harm done. I caught a handful of greasy cap and hair and yanked down hard as I kneed upward. Three times I slammed my knee into his face. When I let go, he still stood, his arms hanging loose, his nose pulsing blood into his open mouth, his expression stupefied.

As I cut around him to the door, he reached out and caught me by the collar. My jacket ripped, and my feet ran out under me. I dove at him low, jamming my shoulder into his belly, which looked all gut but was like oak. He grabbed my hips, upended me, and tossed me across the dance floor.

I rolled as customers hollered and scattered. The bear-ox lumbered toward me. He licked at blood. Blackie ran around the counter and started beating him with a soup ladle. She cussed him. The grieving singer was still picking thorns. There had to be a rear door behind the kitchen. I climbed the counter.

Junior dragged me back. He held me by the neck with one hand and fended Blackie off with the other. My fingers found a ketchup bottle. I tried to bash it against his face, but he bowed his head, and the bottle broke against the top of his skull. Ketchup splattered over him.

He grunted and flung me across the room. The singer sang "you was the thorn." I slid back up against the wall. The bear-ox pushed Blackie away as he plodded toward me. Customers were escaping. I lunged around Junior and clambered over a booth. When I stepped on a table and knocked bottles to the floor, a woman screamed.

Bear-ox caught me by my pants waist. It tore. Jesus, his strength! I hit him with a right hook. Ketchup-blood streaked his face. I hadn't hurt him. He laughed at Blackie clawing and pounding him with the ladle. I banged my head against his chin, kneed his balls, and smashed a foot down against his arch.

He paused. I broke loose and grabbed a chair set at the end of a booth. He raised an arm over his head. I felt the jar of the blow through the chair. Its metal legs had bent, but he didn't go down. He wrenched the chair from me and sidearmed it away.

He lifted Blackie, who'd never stopped cussing or clubbing him with her ladle, set her on a bar stool, then came at me with arms spread. I ran at the window, crashed into it, but the frame held, and glass shattered over me as I fell. The bear-ox lifted and hugged me. The great constrictor. His face grinned inches from mine as he tightened his grip. The jukebox thumped to silence.

I couldn't move my clamped arms. Blatz squeezed up from my stomach and ran from my mouth. The bear-ox's heaving breath bubbled through blood and ketchup. Again the stink of rotted meat. My joints cracked. Vomit oozed from me like paste from a tube. I puked into his face.

23

A DRIFT UPWARD to a slowly spinning light. Christ I hurt. I blinked through a swirling haze to make out the spinning blades of a ceiling fan. A red tassel dangled from it and traced a languid oval.

I moved my head. Pain throbbed through it. I focused on a lever-action Winchester .30-30 racked across antlers, a framed diploma, and a kerosene space heater.

I smelled my vomit. I attempted to identify the area of my worst pain. My head, my stomach—hurting was general. When I turned to the other side and groaned, the sound seemed a long distance off—as if coming from a person in another room. I made out a dark blue sofa and fringed yellow pillows. The back of the sofa had a multicolored patch quilt draped over it, and an end table held a lamp and radio. Beyond a curtained window, darkness. Definitely no jail.

I lay on a floor. Feet wearing white moccasins crossed toward me. My eyes worked up along legs enclosed in shiny black slacks to narrow hips, the big silver belt buckle, a maroon short-sleeve shirt, and the scarred face with the pink velvety eye patch.

Blackie looked down at me, her face twisted by contempt and disgust.

"You'll live," she said. "But you sure one damn mess."

I closed my eyes. Pain told me I'd at least partially survived the bear-ox. What about the sheriff and law? I opened my eyes to see Blackie stooping and holding a washrag.

"Don't you move and dirty up my place. I've dealt with hogs that smelled better."

She dabbed at my face with a warm dampness that was part soothing, part sting. She worked the rag under my eyes and around my mouth. Spread under me were plastic garbage bags.

"Not that I give a shit about you after the damage," she said. "But it wont your fault."

"How'd I get here?" I asked in a voice distant to myself.

"Dragged you like a dead dog just ahead the mounties hitting the door."

"Jesus God!" I said as pain shot jagged behind my eyes.

"Jesus and God ain't here. Left this damn country for a better place. Would've got booted out anyhow."

She sat back on her haunches and cupped my chin in her fingers to stare at my face. A lip curled upward. She stood, walked through a doorway, and came back carrying a bottle of rubbing alcohol. As she again stooped to me, she unscrewed the cap and wet a cotton blob. The burning bit deep.

"Drinking always makes Junior jealous," she said. "Which is usually. Can you sit up?"

I positioned my palms flat on the plastic and worked at rising. I was so dizzy I had to brace against the floor. My torn jacket hung from me in strips. My shirt and pants were crusted with dried blood and puke. I tried to stand but toppled. When Blackie reached to me, I shied.

"Don't like nobody touching you huh? I know the feeling. Now let's try getting you in the bathroom, exterminating them rags you're wearing, and cleaning you up. Not your face. I already done that."

Her bathroom was just big enough for a sink, crapper, and metal shower stall. She guided me in and closed the door on my back. Holding to the sink, I looked into the mirror at my misshapen likeness. Scabs were in the process of forming around beard stubble. I wouldn't't've recognized myself if I met me on a street.

I sat on the john to toe off my shoes. I dropped reeking clothes on the floor and stumbled into the confining shower. The metal stall creaked. I was so dizzy I flopped around against the sides.

Managed to get myself washed in slow motion and sagged under the flow. Could've sunk away. When I turned off the faucets and slid the shower curtain aside, I stood dripping. My clothes were gone from the floor.

I dried and wrapped Blackie's blue towel around myself before using her toothbrush and Crest. I scraped away sludge at the roof of my mouth. I spit a clot of blood into the sink. My teeth ached and felt loose.

"Do I come out?" I called.

"There's clothes on the divan. Get dressed. I'll be up front."

When I opened the bathroom door, she'd left. I stared at the clothes laid out for me—twill fatigue pants with baggy pockets, skivvies, a handkerchief, all were olive-drab GI issue except for a shirt that was tourist Hawaiian. My shoes were set on the floor, and they'd been wiped clean.

My wallet, change, and Old Timer lay on the end table. I checked the wallet and found no money gone. As I dressed and babied my pains, I eyed a large color photograph in an elaborate brass frame set under the table lamp—a girlish Blackie wearing a white dress and pillbox hat and holding a bouquet of red roses. No scar or eye patch. Standing beside her, a grinning army sergeant, his face full and rugged, his body heavy from army chow, the sleeve of his uniform jacket bearing chevrons and two three-year service stripes.

She'd provided GI socks, too. I carefully lowered myself to the sofa—what she'd called the *di*-van—to pull them on. The shirt and fatigue pants hung loose around me, yet the fabrics felt cool and softly comforting. I thought of this being the second time in recent days I'd been bathed and clothed by a stranger.

I crossed to the window. Darkness lifting. Behind the Pit land sloped to woods, and leaves glistened from rain. I turned to the framed diploma under the Winchester. Blackie's official name was Marguerite Pearl Spurlock, and she'd graduated from Shawnee High School. Date 1978. If she were eighteen then, it would make her now about thirty.

I heard tapping and cracked the door to the front. Blackie leaned forward to tack pieces of cardboard over broken window panes. She slipped from a booth and laid down the hammer to reach for a broom to sweep up glass.

"You still ain't no movie star."

"Never knew I had so many parts that could hurt."

"You running from something, ain't you?" she asked and leaned on the broom.

"From getting killed by Junior."

"More than that. You was running when you came in. You got flighty eyes. Be in the jailhouse right now if it wont for me."

"I owe you," I said. Shards of glass and the smashed chair had been collected before the jukebox, the lights of which still dazzled as bubbles drifted up through the liquid colors of garish plexiglas tubing.

"You talk different from 'round here," she said. "Just don't try putting your hands on me. I'd as soon ventilate your ribs with my Winchester as swat a fly."

"I appreciate the clothes," I said, righting the splintered back of a booth that lay askew. "You army?"

"Do I look like them clothes would fit me?" she asked and again started sweeping. She used the broom angrily.

"No you don't. Allow me to help?"

"You in great shape to help," she said. Her lips drew in, and she glanced at me. "Though you fought Junior pretty good. You been in fights before."

On a wall behind the counter hung a circular electric clock advertising Blatz Beer. It had a red neon ring around the face, which read 5:57. I worked my jaw and again felt dizzy. She saw me steady myself on the counter.

"Use some coffee?" she asked.

"Might save my life."

"Reckon you're worth it?" she asked and leaned the broom against a booth. She switched on a fluorescent ceiling light in the cubicle used for a kitchen. A refrigerator door opened and closed. Ice cubes rattled. She set a Dixie cup filled with ice and tomato juice before me.

The cold juice caused my teeth to ache. I reached for a cigarette before I remembered what I wore weren't my clothes.

"Yours was flattened," she said and drew an opened pack of Luckies from beside the cash register. She tossed it to the counter, struck a match for me, and lit up herself. She allowed her cigarette to dangle from her mouth as she drew on rubber gloves to work at the sink. I finished the juice.

"Want to pay for a pack," I said and drew my wallet.

"Glory be and I'll need a wheelbarrow to haul the money to the bank. What you really doing 'round here?"

"Made the mistake of passing through," I said and laid two dollars on the counter. When I inhaled, my ribs hurt. I touched at them.

"Nobody just passes through Shawnee County. Ain't nothing but roads to nowhere. Why the hell I'm still hanging out trying to earn my beans I don't know."

"You own the place?"

She stripped off the gloves, slapped them into the sink, and walked to the kitchen. She came back holding two white, heavy mugs of coffee.

"Can't get shut of it," she said, and her small mouth shot smoke. She stood across from me, an elbow on the counter, sipping coffee with one hand, the fingers of the other cupped around her cigarette like a man. She'd removed last night's costume jewelry and wore no makeup.

"'Lessen I torch it," she said. "Seems I been trying to get away most of my life. Borned down the road about ten mile and the farthest I ever been is Hinton. My daddy worked the Shawnee seam 'long with most every other able-bodied man in the territory. I got an uncle dead in that mountain. Fire damp. Had to seal up the entry to stop the burning. Some grave."

Maybe her face had a Spanish cast instead of Italian or Greek. Immigrant, possibly just a generation or two off the boat. I'd heard my father talk about how the coal companies shipped trainloads of foreigners in from the Northern ports, and blacks from the South.

"You know any LeBlancs?"

"I seen Boss John and Lupi from a distance when I was knee-high," she said and reached under the counter for a box of sugared doughnuts. She set two on a plate, stuck them in an electric oven, and switched it on, then set a timer.

"Boss John?" I asked. They'd called my father that?

"He the owner."

"And Lupi?"

"Followed Boss John around like a pet. Ugliest man who ever lived, yet nice. Carried lemon drops in his pockets for the kids. They all begged him."

"What's happened to him?"

"What happens to everybody around here," she said and laid paper napkins on the counter. "In the ground. What you care?"

"I been hearing about the LeBlancs, their union trouble and all."

"Always union trouble in this state. My daddy said Boss John was smart. Made his pile and cut out. Wish I could. Never want to see a mountain again."

"Where would you go?" I asked as the timer buzzed. She lifted the doughnuts from the oven and set them between us.

"Florida. I'd open up an orange-juice stand way down south where it's flat and steamy. Sit under palm trees and sell it ice-cold. If you're just passing through, where you mean to end up?"

"California," I said.

"Sounds good. Anywheres warm and flat. Just holding on here in the Pit, or was till you and Junior 'bout broke up the place. I'd sell in ten seconds if I'd find anybody dumb enough to buy."

"Your daddy tell you anything else about Boss John and the LeBlancs?" I asked. I dunked a doughnut in my black coffee.

"Daddy said Boss John never looked like he belonged in a coal camp. Talked too much like a gentleman. Some called him and Lupi Mutt and Jeff."

"Anybody left in Lupi's family?"

"Lupi never had no family. Who'd marry an ugly? Had lots of friends though. Anything needed fixing, people'd holler his name. Aunt Jessie Arbuckle'd remember him best."

"Your aunt?" I asked. Unlike people in Tidewater, Virginia, she'd pronounced *aunt* like *ant*.

"What everybody around here calls her. Esmeralda knew him too, but she won't talk to nobody even if you find her."

"Why not?"

"Funny upstairs," Blackie said and tapped her temple before re-filling my mug. "Roams nights wanting food. People 'round here,

Aunt Jessie 'specially, keep her fed but don't never see more than a shadow and slip of her."

I thought of the shape I'd seen moving along the dark street among High Moor's ghostly desolation. And the name: Esmeralda.

"Aunt Jessie live around here?"

"Down the road the other side of Persimmon Creek and a path up the holler," she said. She dunked out her cigarette in the sink. "Now I got work."

"I'll be pushing on," I said as I wiped my mouth. "What about the clothes? I can pay something."

"Yours. They no use to me. And keep them cigarettes and your two dollars."

"You been good to me, Blackie. I thank you."

"I always help kicked dogs," she said. "Don't send me no post-card from California. I won't be here."

24

I LEFT THE Pit, my back bowed as if carrying the
weight of years. I felt fragile, brittle, and my head still throbbed,
each breath continuing to stab my ribs.

I stepped around puddles. The day lightened, the air washed
fresh. Rivulets ran unseen. I smelled the invigorated forest. It was
half a mile to a one-lane chipped concrete bridge over a branch I as-
sumed was Persimmon Creek. The path on the other side trailed up
beside the flow. It ran fast and clear, grassy strands like long green
hair stringing beneath the current. Despite wetness, the worn
ground felt hard under my sore feet. It jarred my pain. The path
turned from the creek and crisscrossed the slope as if laid by a
drunk. The crookedness might've been intentional, a means to lessen
the pull of direct steepness, a modified switchback.

Sumac, laurel, and black haw bushes covered the slope. I
passed outcroppings of lichen-splotched limestone. The path pitch
lessened to cleared land, a semi-vertical farmstead contained within
split-rail fences. A pasture held a Holstein cow standing in shade of
a hickory tree. Water flowed from beneath a plank hut, which I
figured to be a spring house, and red apples flourished in a slanted
orchard.

The southern lee of the mountain protected the log cabin,

which had a cedar shingle roof and a fieldstone chimney giving out a coil of lazy, thin white smoke. Dominickers and guineas pecked about the yard.

A scythe leaned against a persimmon tree, and an iron pot sat on a circular bed of rocks—maybe used for making soap, apple butter, stews.

The dog ran barking toward me, a spotted mongrel that looked like a cross between a German shepherd and a collie. He circled and growled as the guineas raised a fuss.

I knocked at a screen door, causing flies to spiral. A horseshoe large enough for a Belgian or Percheron had been nailed over the entrance. No answer. I shaded my eyes to peer inside and made out a rude table, an oil lamp, and a fireplace where coals still pulsed. I smelled onions, cured meat, baked bread.

Somebody hollered from the rear of the cabin. I walked around and saw a woman working a garden. She hunkered along a row of snaps, picking and dropping them into a galvanized bucket. She wore a poke bonnet of a kind I didn't know could be bought in this day and time, and her plain brown dress appeared homespun and also from another age.

Her body curved to her work. She was ancient, her face weathered, the wrinkles in so deep they shadowed themselves. Her skin appeared tough as saddle leather. Her hands were gnarled and clawlike, yet she gripped pods with a deliberate tenderness as she pulled them from the vines.

Despite the dog's barking, she hadn't glanced at me. When I spoke, she raised her face and cocked her head as if uncertain what she'd heard. Her creased eyelids fluttered. She lifted a hand to shield the emerging sun, and her blue eyes located me.

"Who beat you up?" she asked, her voice raspy. The blue eyes were alert and as startling as if seen in a terrapin.

"Stumbled into a buzz saw," I said.

"That buzz saw have a name?" she asked. She again picked. "Junior."

"I know Junior Bartow. Knowed his father and granddaddy. All them Bartows rather fight than eat. You got a name?"

"Drake. Lionel Drake."

"Ain't no Drakes 'round here," she said and scuffled sideways in her hunkered position to reach the next snaps. She wore boxy high-top shoes that lacked laces. The soles had collected mud.

"Heard tell you knew people from High Moor days," I said.

"What's it to you?" she asked. Pods plunked softly into the bucket. More than years had twisted her hands. Arthritis.

"Just always wondered how men could leave the good sunshine and find nerve enough to go into the blackness of mountains to dig their livelihoods."

"Always huh? Long time. Livelihood not our kind of word either. You too banged up to help?"

My body ached so bad I hated stooping. As I did, I swallowed a grunt. Mud squished beneath my shoes. I reached to dangling pods and waited for her to speak. She didn't but humped on along the row.

I worked opposite her and thought of the women who each spring came to Bellerive to pick strawberries. They wore colorful kerchiefs, pulled up their skirts, gossiped, and laughed. I'd carried them water.

"You lived at High Moor?" I asked.

"Borned there," she said without looking at me. She'd twisted her skirt around her legs so it wouldn't drag the ground. "My husband Prater died there. Had seven children, all gone and spread to the four winds. The last I heard from was Jacob, the youngest. Lives in Seattle and sent me a Christmas present, a GE toaster, and I got no electric. You chew?"

"'Fraid not."

"Nothing to be afraid of. Dip snuff?"

"No'm."

"So far you ain't much use."

"I got cigarettes," I said and slid the Luckies from my shirt pocket.

"It's a poor man or woman either without 'bacce," she said.

Still hunkered, she drew the cigarette from the pack and allowed me to light it.

"Cigarette ain't much of a smoke," she said as we worked. "Me and Prater grew our own leaf. So strong we never needed no worming."

When we reached the row's end, her bucket was half filled. She pushed down against it to stand. Straightening was difficult for her and me. She tongued out her cigarette and twisted a heel on it. I did the same as the dog watched.

She was a wizened thing, not five feet high, and her back stayed curved. I reached to the bucket to carry it for her, but she pulled it from my grasp.

"I ain't crippled," she said.

She let her skirt slide down to her ankles and walked toward the cabin. The dog started barking.

"Rattler, shut your yapping mouth 'fore I stomp you!" she yelled. "Been off chasing rabbits."

The dog quieted but continued to circle. I followed Aunt Jessie's slow rocking gait, her **buck**et swinging outward with every other step. She set it down before kicking off her shoes, entering the cabin barefoot, and letting the door slam. Flies resettled on the screen.

As I waited outside, shadows crossed the land—a flight of buzzards gliding over. Aunt Jessie came back holding a twist of dried brown tobacco that crinkled in her fingers. She broke an end chunk and fingered it into her mouth. She offered the rest of the twist to me.

"Carry it along if you like," she said. "I still got me a little patch."

I thanked her, took the twist, and gnawed myself a piece to stuff in my jaw. I fitted what was left into a fatigue pocket. She watched, maybe waiting for me to gag and my eyes to water, yet raw leaf was nothing new to me. In 'Nam I'd chewed worse.

"You all right," she said and smiled before spitting.

My jaw bulged, and I spat too. She sat on a bench that was a log split down the center and set on four legs, and indicated I could join her. The bench was so low my knees jutted up. Her bare toes just touched the ground. The Dominickers pecked around us and a cider press. Rattler let down in shade of the persimmon tree.

She set the bucket between us and pouched her skirt before reaching for a pod, snapping it twice, and dropping the pieces into her lap.

"My people been living 'round here two hundred year," she said. "Fought Indians and killed bears. I never been anywheres else and never thought about trying. Ran the beauty parlor at High Moor. All the women came to me for prettying up. Worked ten hours a day."

"You musta heard lots of chatter," I said. She smelled of earth and tobacco.

"Hear that everywhere," she said, tonguing her chaw. "Even wind talks."

"You know the mine owner?" I asked. The tobacco was strong and burned the inside of my cheek, but it was a good burn that seemed to draw pain from the rest of my body.

"Everybody knew Boss John. He pass, men took off their hats. His wife come to my shop. She could've got herself driven to Cliffside but stayed faithful to Jessie's. Nice, spoke kindly, acted like you was doing a favor taking her money. Played the piano at Mt. Laurel Church. Bought it for the church. All lady."

"I heard about Boss John fixing the clock."

Those blue eyes lifted from bean snapping to me. She turned her face away and spit a good three feet out onto trampled grass. The Dominickers investigated.

"He a man," she said. "Tells it all."

"Don't think much of men?" I asked and also spat, my spit arching short of hers.

"Men gets the glory, but it's women who hold up the world," she said.

"I don't disagree."

"Everybody talks about how Boss John come from Virginia and hiked into High Moor one day, unlocked that old office, and first thing took the clock down off the wall to fix it. Truth is, he tried to, had parts all over the desk, but it was Lupi who figured out how to put it back together."

"I've heard tell of Lupi too."

She shot another look at me, those clean blue eyes under the ancient lids sharp and penetrating. Her jaw stilled.

"Everybody 'round here heard of him. Boss John and High Moor wouldn't've lasted no time without Lupi. He figured how to lay the headhouse tram, the sizing shake, pump water to the tank. Boss John had the ideas, but Lupi worked them out."

"He an engineer?"

"Went to no college but could see things mechanical," she said and juiced her chaw. "Boss John never took a step without Lupi."

"How'd he get to High Moor?"

"Was here when Boss John came. Lupi's father worked the Shawnee seam under Mr. Angus MacKay. Whole load of I-talians come in by train. Lupi hadn't growed right. Never to full size. Short bandy legs, big head and thick lips."

She and I spat.

"Yet just look at a machine and tell you what ailed it. Pick up a pencil or piece of charcoal and draw your picture too in less time than it took you to set your face."

Her hands never stopped snapping pods.

"All gone now," she said. "High Moor empty. Dust to dust."

"Somebody out there the other night," I said.

She stopped snapping and stared.

"What you doing there at night?"

"Got caught at dark and no motel around. Somebody walking the street."

"You from the state people in Charleston, ain't you?" she asked. "Come up here to fetch Esmeralda. Just put your foot on the path and get on away!"

"Swear I'm not."

"Swearing don't prove nothing any longer," she said. Those blue eyes flayed me. "You'd be powerful unwelcome 'round here if you even thinking of taking her off. Junior Bartow be no more than a skeeter bite."

"I have no way of taking her. Just curious because of what Blackie told me down at the Pit."

"Blackie told you huh?" she asked and finally shifted those eyes off me. She gripped her skirt to hold the snaps, stood, and entered the cabin. Rattler watched me. A lip rose over wet fangs.

Aunt Jessie ambled back holding a brown paper shopping bag that had twine handles. Her crooked fingers drew out a piece of gray cardboard, the kind used to stiffen a new shirt. It was covered by tissue paper. She uncovered a crayon portrait of a young girl.

The girl appeared twelve or thirteen, her brown eyes enormous in a small, thin face, her expression not so much frightened as wildly alert—a vigilant faun. Her dark hair hung past her shoulders to the bottom edge of the cardboard. A hollow cheek was smudged, whether by smeared crayon or a realistic attempt to depict soiled skin.

"Esmeralda," Aunt Jessie said, sitting and holding the portrait so I could see but not offering it for me to take in my hands. "A child first spotted wearing rags, filthy, and hiding behind trees above High Moor."

"What'd happened to her?"

"People believe she'd had parents up some holler, they likely killed by a flood or rock slide. She snuck into camp to steal scraps of food. Like a dog that never knew man. Ran back into the woods if anybody tried to talk or get close to her."

Aunt Jessie gazed down the slope at an area of burned-over land. A few trees stood leafless, their trunks blackened and gaunt.

"Well, Lupi did what taming Esmeralda ever got," she said. "Nights when he fixed his supper, he cooked up an extra portion and left it in a bowl for her hung on a locust limb high enough to keep coons from reaching. He planted a post in his yard and nailed a box shaped like a little house on top. You could lift off the roof, and he'd stick food in the box for her. She'd sneak to it, eat, and clean her bowl in the river before putting it back."

I was still looking at the wary childish face. The eyes swallowed me.

"Lupi'd sit off a distance from the little house on the post and watch her snatch food from it. He spoke to her like you would a puppy or kitten. Took lots of time and patience. Tossed her lemon drops. The state people from Charleston heard and came to grab her. Wanted to stick her in an institution but couldn't catch her. Sent troopers with bloodhounds and never picked up a scent."

Aunt Jessie spat, then tenderly rewrapped the portrait in tissue paper before fitting it back into the shopping bag. She held it as if fearful it might break.

"One night when Esmeralda come to get her bowl, she was sick with fever. Too weak to run, tottering and about to fall out. Lupi carried her inside his house. She didn't weigh nothing."

She reworked her chaw. No use trying to rush words out of her. She had her own timing.

"He laid her on his bed and cooled her off with wet rags. He ran after Doc MacSwain in Cliffside. Lupi and the doc kept her secret. Lupi fed her medicine and food. The third day when Lupi got home from work, she was gone."

Aunt Jessie smacked a fly lighting on her snap bucket.

"She a full woman now. Lives in the woods, empty camp houses, or caves along the high wall. Hear her sometimes, but nobody could get close as Lupi."

"How'd she get the name Esmeralda?"

"I don't know, maybe Lupi."

A family name, or taken from Dumas's heroine in *The Hunchback of Notre Dame*? Lupi a reader of books?

"She became special around High Moor," Aunt Jessie said. "Brought luck is what people thought because coal became good again and the mine was hiring. But she wouldn't fool with nobody except Lupi. He bought her clothes at the company store. She'd bring him pawpaws, sassafras bark, and wild grapes. He helped keep her hid from the state people."

"You ever see her?"

"Just catch a glimpse of her face in the laurel. Folks allow her to raid they gardens and leave food and clothes hanging on tree limbs. An outsider like you'll never lay eyes on her, but she'll see you. Them eyes see everything."

"What happened to Lupi?"

"Died at High Moor three years ago come January. He the last one in camp. Everything closed up. Kept to hisself and hiked to Cliffside for needings. Section foreman for the railroad found him at the company office. It'd been snowing, and Lupi sat in the cold, the stove fire gone out, snow piled up to the windows, just sitting and frozen at Boss John's old desk like there was coal to be dug, the fixed clock still ticking on the wall."

25

I THANKED AUNT Jessie and started down the winding path. When I looked back, she was moving in her rocking gait toward her garden. She held a hoe, the handle of which she used like a staff.

I walked the road toward Cliffside. I didn't know which way to turn next, but I was hungry and thinking maybe I could find a real meal—steak, potatoes, hot beef gravy. When I stepped among a stand of beech trees to unzip my pants and piss, I heard the car moving slow. I backed deeper among shadows. The brown-and-tan Cougar slid past, two mounties watching both sides of the road. Hold the panic, I told myself. They didn't have to be after me, yet Frank Givens, the fisherman from Akron, could've spread the word about seeing me, or maybe they were out searching as a result of the brawl at the Pit.

I worked cautiously along the road to Cliffside and paused at the outskirts to eye Main Street. Mountain people seemed to be going about their lives and business in normal fashion. An empty coal truck rattled past, the whirligigs strung over the used-car lot fluttered, an aproned woman swept the walk before the Shawnee Food Market.

I heard what first sounded like a church bell. The gonging

came from the tower of the bastardized Victorian courthouse. Law day. Cars and pickups had parked along the curb in front and at the sides. The pigeons were restless atop the Chinese tile roof. Men stood on the front steps talking, smoking, waiting to be heard and judged.

I knew to skirt the front of the courthouse where the sheriff's men were bound to be in attendance. I cut behind to a street named Saw Lick lined with empty, ramshackle buildings that once must've held going businesses. All were boarded up except a machine shop, where a welder worked under a tin overhang. His torch flared yellow before he adjusted it to blue, the flame reflecting in goggles he pulled down over his eyes. He flipped them up to look at me.

I gave him a wave, but he didn't respond. I didn't feel right about it. I glanced back to see him still watching, the torch extinguished. I was an outlander, plus my beat-up face and my clothes could be making him curious. Again I looked back. The welder walked into his shop.

I decided I'd better forget food for the time being and ease away from town. I crossed around the rear of the courthouse and up to the main drag where I passed a cinderblock two-bay volunteer fire station. A face looked from a dusty window.

As I walked on, heading out of Cliffside, I heard a car with big horses accelerating. Only police would be allowed to drive that fast through town on law day. I turned to a one-story frame building with a painted sign over the door announcing itself as THE TRUE CHURCH OF GOD. I tried the door, and it opened. I slipped inside, closing it as the car sped past. Definitely a souped-up engine. I cracked the door and saw the tail end of the Cougar—deputies not necessarily after me but possibly following routine procedures of delivering court summonses.

The church was bare-bones—no narthex, a few torn hymnals,

lumber benches, and an altar table and pulpit dotted with exposed nailheads. Scrawled in white paint across the wall behind the pulpit the verse THE WAGES OF SIN IS DEATH. So, I thought, are the wages of life.

I tried to lock the door, but it had no bolt. I walked down the single aisle and sat in a pew, listening to sporadic traffic outside and occasional distant sounds of chain saws. The church's arched, dirty windowpanes clouded sunlight. Outside, an ailanthus tree looked thin and pale. Lying back on the pew, its boards smoothed by asses of many worshipers, I looked at the ceiling where clods of dirt-dauber nests bonded to trusses.

I closed my eyes. I'd wait till things quieted before moving on. I thought of Montana, the Great Plains, a sea of grass with a breeze blowing through it, myself riding a pinto horse western-style beside a river where water ran clean, fast, and sweet.

In the reddish darkness beneath my eyelids I sensed a difference and sat up slowly. A tall, gaunt black man stood at the end of the row watching me. He wore a dark suit, green shirt, black tie, and his skull had been shaved.

"Just a pilgrim needing a little prayer time," I said as I wiped back my hair.

"'Thou shalt not oppress a stranger,'" he said, his voice mournful. He lifted a long, narrow hand. "Peace be with you, brother."

"And with you also," I said.

He walked to the pulpit and behind it. I listened to his footsteps fade. A back door opened and closed.

I stood, tiptoed to the rear, and peeked out. He was gone. Mid-afternoon, the sun high and hot. I wanted to wait for the cover of darkness, but the preacher might already be telling a tale. I stepped out the door and ran down the bank to woods where I sidehilled it below the highway till I was out of breath. Holding to a maple tree,

I rested. A hawk flew over, and its flight silenced birds that'd been singing among branches.

I worked along the bank. When I'd gone what I estimated to be half a mile, I climbed to the highway and parted laurel. Ahead either the same Cougar or another. Deputies stood at the center of the road stopping cars and asking for driver's licenses. Could be only a routine traffic check, yet too much risk to hold course. If they knew about me at all, they'd figure I'd be heading west. Best to backtrack and hike down from Cliffside into the gorge where I'd outflank them by following rails north.

Again I sidehilled it, and by the time I passed below Cliffside and reached the steep pitch of the gorge, more blisters had burst on my feet, and I stumbled. Rocky soil, mostly shale, crumbled underfoot and splattered beside me along the incline. Gravity got a hold on me and dragged me too fast. I sat and slid to a sprawled stop.

The land had become partially shaded, the sun again blocked by the ridge, the gorge filling with shadows. I continued down and rested twice before I spotted the glimmer of rails I'd begun to believe I'd never reach. As I gathered to jump to the roadbed, a dog barked behind me. I dug in my heels and looked back up the mountain. I saw nothing except woods and outcroppings of shale.

I heard what sounded like a gasoline lawnmower. I flattened my body against the ground and peered through weeds. Two men on a yellow motorized handcar rolled along the track. They were uniformed deputies holding rifles and staring up at the mountain. One spoke into a walkie-talkie, and the other pointed at the slope. The handcar putted on.

Sweat dropped off me, and greenies attacked my neck, face, and eyelids. I couldn't use the tracks. I sucked air and climbed higher. I needed to find a place where I could hide awhile, wait for the cover of night, review the options.

I heard distant shouts and laughter, and around a bend of the river a black raft bobbed into view—white-water riders, colorful in red life jackets and helmets. Their excited voices seemed wrong in this place. No one had a right to be happy here.

I climbed till I became so weak I grabbed at anything I could reach to pull myself up. I became blocked by a vertical face of boulders, stones of giants, prehistoric rock formations heaved up from the earth's fiery intestines. I didn't have strength to attempt a traverse.

I clawed at thin, pebbly soil and looked down to the rails and river, the plunging water darkening in shadows. I thought of release and letting gravity have me. A simple free fall, and after a trivial span of fear and pain, maybe a forever rest. I closed my eyes and felt the grip seeping from my fingers.

"You in one hell of a shape, ain't you?" a voice asked.

When I slowly raised my face, I saw a man watching from a boulder. He appeared seven feet tall, skinny, his beard silver, his bushy eyebrows black. He had on no shirt and wore a gray fedora and brown corduroys held up by suspenders. He carried a hemp rope coiled over a shoulder. He hunkered and crossed his arms on top his knees.

"Not able to hold much longer," I said.

"It's a fact," he said.

"Help me?"

"You got money?"

"A few dollars."

"Could just wait, let you drop on down, and taken it offen you when you busted up and can't wiggle."

"I don't much care."

He continued watching, as if a spectator and entertained. I believed that's what he meant to do—let me maim or kill myself and rob me afterward. He stood and stepped back out of sight. I pressed against stone. My fingers gave, and I began slipping.

"Grab ahold," the man called.

The rope uncoiled when he tossed it and fell heavily across my back. He'd fixed a knotted loop in the end. With my left hand I clutched at the mountain and with my right worked the loop over my head and under an arm. Then I let go and held to the rope with both hands. I slid till it jerked tight.

"You some kind of fish to haul in," he called.

I struggled to work my feet under me as he drew line. He heaved upward with slow, steady strength. My knees bumped the boulder. He stopped, spat, and his spit curved past. He loosened his grip and allowed me to slide back a little.

I stopped breathing and waited.

"Never liked fish anyhow," he said and tightened up on the rope. As he pulled, I dug the sides of my feet at the boulder. I banged stone and scraped my knees and elbows. Pebbles and flakes of lichen fell on my face. All the while he tugged on the rope in the leisurely fashion of a man drawing a bucket from a well.

At the top I reached for his legs, but he stepped away, keeping the rope taut. I wormed over the edge, rolled to my back, and lay gasping.

"I done my part," he said and dropped the rope. "Now it's your'n. Don't try nothing 'less you want a third eye."

From his hip pocket he drew a pistol, a Luger he pointed at my forehead. I rolled to my side for my wallet, and he wrenched it from my hand.

"This all you got?" he asked, pulling out the dollar bills, counting, and jamming them into a hip pocket. He patted me down to feel for and take my change, Old Timer, Luckies, and tobacco twist. "Hell, you wont worth hauling in."

He pocketed his plunder and the Luger, and tossed my empty wallet back. As he coiled the rope, he moved off with long, gangly strides to a fissure between boulders. He hooked a foot into it and climbed to a higher level.

"You can come along, lie, or die," he said with a glance back at me.

I pushed to my knees, rubbed dirt from my face, and stood. He watched me struggle to find footing in the fissure but offered no help. When I wedged upward to his level, he climbed another course of boulders. Exhausted, unsteady, I tried to keep pace. His strides swung unhurriedly, yet carried him far ahead.

"You sure God kicked up a hornets' nest," he said when he stopped to allow me to catch him. "And me, I hate them damned hornets worse than rattlers in my bed."

He kept on and led me through a canyon of boulders. A black-jack oak had tried to grow from a thin pall of soil but failed. Its bare limbs and trunk had been honed pearl by ceaseless wind.

He drew a red bandanna from his pocket, twirled it, and ordered me to turn before tying it over my eyes. He guided me forward by touching me on one shoulder or the other. The rocky ground caused me to lurch, and I thought of the long fall if I misstepped. When I tottered, he gripped me by my elbows from the rear and set me right. I heard pebbles dropping away.

After time and stumbles past counting he halted me to remove the bandanna. His rope looped over his shoulder, he backed down a gap and partly around a boulder while hugging it. His feet found purchase on a strip of ledge.

"Less'n you can fly, watch it, bud," he said as he sidled along. "And don't think I can't catch you if you try to run."

The railroad tracks were so far below they looked made for a toy train, and the rapids were only a fleeting whiteness in the winding river. As I worked backward down the gap, I slewed my feet to keep them on the ledge and pressed a cheek to the boulder.

He was gone. I thought he must've slipped and fallen away into the draw of space.

"You coming or ain't you?" his voice asked.

On his knees he waited inside a cave's low entrance. I let myself down shakily, and as I crawled inside, he pulled back from the light.

The cavern felt moistly cool, and the roof was high enough for him to stand. As my eyes adjusted, I made out a blanket roll, lantern, a wood supply, cooking utensils, and blackened rocks of a circular fireplace with a spit rigged above it. Lengths of heavy chain lay about, and stacked along walls were bound rolls of what looked like copper cable.

"You can flop till morning," he said, pitching the rope to the floor and gesturing me to proceed him. I could just make out a passage till we reached a fault in the overhead rock that admitted an intense streak of sunlight. Water spread along a mossy side of the cavern and sluiced away through a breach among stones. He lifted a dented dipper from a driven nail and held it canted to the flow before offering it to me. The cold water tasted of moss, and I gulped so fast it ran over my chin.

"Let's get things settled 'tween you and me," he said and touched the Luger in his hip pocket. "You mess 'round with this ole boy, you end up in the gorge. All I got to do is drop you down on the tracks for a train to run over. Mounties think it an accident."

"All I want's to rest."

"You pick you a spot," he said and again motioned me ahead of him.

At the front of the cavern I allowed my legs to give and settled my back against a wall. My chin sank, my mouth hung open.

He laid twigs onto dry leaves piled in his fireplace and lit a match under them. The flames created a flickering light. He added wood, and the cavern brightened. From a bucket he lifted two wet and skinned rodent-shaped carcasses. Squirrels. I was hungry enough to eat rats. He impaled them on the iron spit, used a railroad spike to poke the fire, and set the meat over it. The shiny gray flesh first smoked and then began to sizzle quietly.

"Courtesy Appalachian Power," he said when he caught me looking at the rolls of copper cable. "They my employer." He squinted across flames at me. "What you want 'round here?"

"To get the hell away," I said. I slipped off my shoes and worked the socks loose from blisters.

"Everybody wants to get out of Shawnee County," he said. "Hard to do when you was born under a lump of coal." He turned the meat by twisting an angle bent into his spit. "You a LeBlanc, ain't you?"

"My name's Marlowe," I said.

"Sure, sure. Good to see a LeBlanc grubbing it for once. My daddy tried to organize a union out at High Moor. LeBlancs growing rich off miners' blood. Guards threw him out the camp. Pitched my mama's furniture and mattresses on the ground. I was a chap watching and hearing her cry."

"Meaning you too hate LeBlancs."

"Who don't?"

"Do I look rich?"

"You look like a piece of poor sheep shit," he said, and his pink gums and the squirrel flesh glistened from firelight.

"What makes you think I'm a LeBlanc?"

"You getting famous. Talk about you on the radio. I figured you'd be carrying a couple of hundred anyhow."

"You got a radio?"

"I got ways of getting to one."

Fat dripped and flared. A natural draft created by the waterfall drew smoke along the roof.

"You knew Boss John?" I asked.

"Never got introduced."

"What about Lupi?"

"Sure. Funny little fart, talked wop, and had a face ugly enough to scare hants. Took care of Esmeralda."

"I heard."

"I come on her once while she was picking cress along the creek. She run so fast I couldn't catch her. Got eyes they no end to."

He crossed to the cavern's entrance where he knelt and looked out.

"Yellow bug still searching," he said.

I crawled over, and he moved aside for me to see. The handcar slid along the tracks and around the bend.

"Don't know your name," I said.

"Names don't mean nothing."

He lifted the squirrels from the fire, laid them on a slab of plank, and held them with his knife to pull out the spit. He used the single-blade frog-sticker to spear and pick up the larger carcass. He hung it in front of his face and gummed at the breast.

"'Bout right," he said. "Since you company, you welcome to the other."

I crawled to and fingered it cautiously. I palmed it from one hand to the other and blew before I licked. The flesh burned my tongue, but, Jesus, no wild meat ever tasted more succulent. I bit deep into the breast, ate every shred of flesh, sucked the bones, and chewed the smaller ones into bits I could swallow.

"Reckon that'll hold your belly to morning," he said.

"Can I get another drink?"

"Ain't charging for water today. Toss your leavings on the fire and scrub my cutting board."

I moved back into the cave and the waterfall, where I scrapped gravel from the breach drain to rub on my hands and the board before running them under the flow to clean off grease. My fingers had cuts on them. I drank from the dipper and hung it on the wet nail.

"Reckon I can share a cigarette with you," the man said and grinned as I returned and let down.

"Nice of you since they mine."

We lit Luckies by drawing brands from the fire. He was careful not to get close and kept touching the Luger to let me know he kept it handy.

"Just a friend of man," he said and cackled.

We sat across from each other smoking. Darkness was claiming the fire.

"Piss call," he said and tossed his butt on the coals. "Out the door. You first."

I took a last pull on the cigarette before kneeing through the entrance to the ledge. I again felt the pull of gravity and stood with my back hard against the boulder.

"Make room," he ordered.

I sidestepped, he joined me on the ledge, and we arced our water into space. No light burned along the gorge. It seemed to emit rather than receive the night blackness.

"Got one blanket," he said when we crawled inside. "No mattress. Travel light."

The coals pulsed, and I couldn't see him on the other side of the cavern. I lay on the floor, so tired its rock hardness felt good. I listened to him stretch out.

"Don't be thinking nothing," he said and cocked the Luger.

26

DURING FIRST SOMBER light of morning, the friend of man unwrapped himself from his tattered Indian blanket, set on his fedora, and again laid a fire. He handed me a gallon can that likely once held fruit or vegetables. The top was cut off.

"Fill it to half," he said.

I felt my way to the waterfall and carried back the can. He set it on the fire.

"Sorry we got no hog and hominy," he said. From a .30-caliber army-issue ammunition case he brought out a plastic pouch and tapped seeds from it into the can. "Chicory weed, the poor man's coffee."

He had a second smaller soup can to use for a cup, and we shared it. The bitter mustard-colored brew scoured my mouth.

"You got man, woman, or dog who cares about you 'round here?" he asked.

"No."

"Then you in tough titty city," he said and stood. He thumbed off his suspenders to pull on a brown short-sleeve shirt. He re-hooked the suspenders over bony shoulders. "All right, let's get at it. You first."

He made the Luger snug in his pocket. I fitted on my socks and shoes. I crawled out onto the ledge, and when I straightened, I felt rusted and seized up.

He emerged and motioned me ahead of him. I sidestepped to the gap that led up among boulders. We climbed. Mist like a deep white lake filled the gorge.

"Hold it," he said when we reached the top.

From his pocket he drew the red bandanna and again twirled it into a blindfold before stepping behind me and tying it tight.

"What you doing to me?"

"Don't want you trying to find your way back. Or telling the law how neither. You do, I got ways of making you sorry unto dying. Stick your hands behind you."

He bound my wrists with turns of what felt like stove wire. I still sensed the pull of the gorge behind me. I pictured myself spiraling to the tracks.

He nudged me forward. Afraid I'd trip, I lifted my feet high. He again tapped me on one shoulder or the other to change course. He directed me when to step long or crouch. For a time the footing remained hard and uneven. Then stones gave way to soil, and I smelled hemlocks. He balanced me when I slipped.

He allowed me to rest. The wire hurt my wrists, and I felt blood pumping in my fingers. He checked the bandanna. I wondered whether he could mean to turn me over to the law. No, he hated the hornets and likely had reason to. I heard jays screeching and sounds of a distant chopper. Would Shawnee County have equipment so advanced to search for me? They could've called in the Feds.

I got shoved against a tree trunk till the chopper flew over. Again we hiked.

He stopped, loosened the blindfold, untwisted the wire, and stepped back as I blinked. We stood among red oaks bordering a paved road. He slipped something in my pocket. My Old Timer.

"Don't go looking after me," he said. "Count to five hundred slow before you even think of moving."

"Don't know where I am."

"Ain't that the American way, bud?"

I didn't hear him slip off. He could still be watching. I counted, yet not slow. At five hundred, I hesitated before turning. He'd gone.

I looked in both directions along the road. The mist diffused sunlight. I heard a truck and retreated into the woods. It was a beat-up Autocar semi hauling logs. Bark blew from them and scattered. Diesel fumes hung heavy in moist air.

I tried to make out the sun's position. As I walked, my shadow gradually formed before me. Good, I was moving west.

I sensed eyes and kept turning to stare behind me. Maybe the friend of man followed. Or some timberhick. Not the law. They'd have grabbed me. I again turned into the woods, doubled back, and squatted. Nobody passed.

Like the stem of a T, the road fed into a junction. Now I had to decide north or south. I turned south. Occasional traffic and more hiding for me. Something familiar about the road. I rounded a curve. Ahead was the Pit, its neon switched off, the black tar-paper shiny wet.

A Metro van idled in front, its side decorated with the picture of a yellow-haired little girl eating a slice of buttered white bread. I sat in the woods to wait. When I heard the van leave, I approached the tonk from the rear and heard a faint music. I climbed the three wooden steps, listened, and tapped on the door.

Blackie opened it. She wore denim shorts, a red tank top, and a blue eye patch. She'd tied a white cleaning cloth around her hair. She was barefoot and held a dust mop.

"Damn if I'm letting a thing like you in here," she said and lifted the mop handle across her chest like a rifle held at port arms.

"I'm in bad need of your phone, Blackie."

"Looks to me you need more than a phone. Half the county after you."

"Let me use the phone and I'm gone."

"How I know that? Look at you, a damned sorry-ass jailbird LeBlanc and 'bout ruined the clothes I made the mistake of giving you."

She closed the door and locked it. I heard a car and ran back down into the woods till it passed. I returned to the steps. When I knocked, she looked out the window before opening the door. She held the lever-action Winchester.

"Could turn you in," she said. "Might be a reward."

"You could also help an innocent man."

"Hell, ain't nobody's innocent. Ought to throw that word out the language. You're one sorry mess. If I let you come in here, I'm watching you every inch of the way."

She moved aside reluctantly, and I walked past her and through her apartment into the front. The only lights switched on were from the jukebox and red neon around the Blatz clock behind the counter. The time was 8:37. I lifted the receiver from the wall phone as I read the instructions. To reach the operator, I needed a quarter, which would be returned.

"I been emptied like a bag turned upside down," I said. "Would you be kind enough to allow me the temporary use of a coin?"

Expression disgusted, the Winchester pointed at me, she crossed to the cash register, rang open the drawer, and fingered out a quarter. She flipped it to me off her blue-painted thumbnail.

As I raised the coin to the slot, tires crunched over gravel. Out the window a Pepsi truck. I pinched back the quarter, ducked into her apartment, and shut the door.

She might give me up. She had not only the rifle but the help of the driver. I was in no shape to fight or run. I stood with my forehead against the plasterboard wall and heard them talking.

"Doing all right, Cale?" Blackie asked.

"Get any tighter I got to get me a smaller skin," he said.

Sounds of him wheeling a dolly and rattling crates. Unless she was winking at him or was using a hand signal, she hadn't set me up for the law.

Her small radio played hillbilly on the end table by the sofa. It also held a *People* magazine and the framed color photograph of her and her sergeant, she young and wearing the white dress, the white pillbox hat, holding the roses, behind them a palm tree.

When the Pepsi man drove off, she opened the apartment door.

"Make your call and get out," she said. She held the Winchester.

I dropped the quarter in the slot and dialed Information. The operator gave me Walter Frampton's number in Jessup's Wharf, and I used a stub of a pencil dangling from a nail to write it among others scrawled on the wall. When I hung up, my coin didn't clink back. I hammered the phone with my fist.

Her lips curled, Blackie drew a second quarter from the cash register and flipped it to me. I deposited it, and the instrument clanged. I asked the operator to dial Walter's office number collect. He answered on the first ring.

"Where the hell are you?" he asked. "Your brother's posting money for your hide. And what makes you think you can call me collect?"

"What about the insurance?"

"Tracked the policy down in old files of the deceased agent Daughtrey Baskerville, they stored in the basement of his nephew's house right here at Jessup's Wharf. The nephew's a jackleg electrician."

"At the moment I'm not greatly interested in old Daughtrey's nephew."

"The policy was purchased by your mother a few months before her death while you were at Leavenworth. The proceeds aren't yours yet, if they'll ever be. There's the immediate complication of your birth certificate, which is not on record here in King County."

"My brothers and I were born in the mountains," I said. "It'll be at the Cliffside courthouse, Shawnee County, West Virginia, or maybe a city or adjoining county close around."

"Means I'll need to phone or write to locate it and request a duplicate while I grow poorer waiting payment. No more collect calls. I won't accept them."

"Walt—"

"Walter's my name."

"But you'll stick with me on the insurance?"

A pause. I feared he'd cut me off, and I slumped against the wall. Blackie watched, her Winchester still raised.

"You got a Social Security number?"

"A couple," I said and gave him the first, which my father brought home to me in turn as he had to John and Edward before me when each was old enough to earn wages for farm work he required of us at Bellerive.

"All right, I'll push it a little farther," Walter said. "Now I'm signing off. You're costing me money I may never get back."

"I need a hundred dollars."

"Boy, you do have gall. I'm not about to aid and abet a fugitive from justice, and my legal advice is for you to turn yourself in, the quicker the better. My last word, this conversation's finished."

He hung up. I set the receiver on the hook.

"That's it," Blackie said, jabbing the rifle at me. "Hit the road."

"I've run out of road."

"I ain't losing my license over you. Had hard enough time getting it. Move."

I nodded and walked through the doorway to her apartment. My knees gave, and I sank as if punctured into a heap on the rag rug centered on the checkered two-tone green linoleum floor.

"That ain't gonna work," she said. "I'm telling you to get to your feet and outa here or I'm phoning the sheriff!"

I had no control over it. I drew up my knees, clenched my eyes, and grieved loud and long.

"Well, goddammit, what's next?" Blackie asked.

27

I SAT BOWED forward, my knees spread. I no longer cared whether I was caught, and I was so tired all I wanted was to lie down forever.

"What I gonna do with a poor thing like you?" Blackie asked, edging around me.

I had no answer. The radio still played, not hillbilly now but the nine o'clock news from Beckley. The world continued to turn and go to hell. She switched it off and stood pinching her chin. The Winchester barrel lowered. I looked at her bare feet. They were toughened, yet the nails had been painted the same red, white, and blue as her fingers. The soles made a soft swish on the linoleum.

"No way I can keep you 'round here," she said. "You been on that radio. Don't want no kin-killer in this place anyhow. I ain't crazy."

I had no strength. I'd used it all. Blackie circled.

"If I allow you a spell to get yourself together, you promise to git?"

I flopped to my back. Let 'em come and carry me off.

"You stay there on my floor and rest," Blackie said. "I sure as hell don't want your mess on my divan. Now I got work up front. I'll be listening every second, this rifle close."

She moved off into the front, and I heard a clatter of dishes. I slowly spun into a drifting sleep. Forms moved through its darkness—like being under a current and glimpsing a murky surface. I never again wanted to reach that surface.

Thumping music reached down and brought me up, not Blackie's radio but the jukebox. I turned my head. She'd closed the door. Talking, laughter, the hiss of bottles being opened. A ticking windup alarm clock set on her dresser read 11:53. The lunch crowd.

I stood, swayed, and staggered into her bathroom. My scabbed, stubbled face was less misshapen. I washed it and combed my hair. I lay back on the floor and waited. I gazed at the photograph of her and her sergeant. She looked about sixteen, maybe younger.

"Been hoping you gone," she said when she stuck her head in.

"You know a man who lives in caves? Tall, silver beard, bushy black eyebrows, toothless. Lots of wire around."

"Cornstalk Skagg," she said.

"Told me he worked for Appalachian Power."

"He works them all right. Steals the lines for the copper. Shorts them out by throwing chain across them, then uses a bolt cutter. Strips the copper, rolls it up, and hauls it off to sell. Caused blackouts all over the county and worn out two or three jails."

"You spare me a coffee?"

"You hungry, I got a slab of beef liver and cornbread left from the special. Eat 'em and leave."

"Got a hole in me that was once a stomach."

"Drag it out front," she said.

I pushed up and followed. The place had emptied. She'd leaned the Winchester against the cooler. She set a plate and a glass of iced tea on the counter. The liver was smothered in onions and gravy, the cornbread buttered, the iced tea sweet.

"On your way," she said when I sopped up gravy on the last bite of cornbread.

"Let me stay till dark," I said and wiped my mouth with a paper napkin. "Please. I promise I'll cause no trouble."

"Who ever got his hand on a promise? Can't pick one up, stick it in a drawer, or eat it with a spoon. Bank won't lend you a dime on it."

"I'll just stretch out again on the floor," I said as I stood from the stool without waiting for an answer.

"You come on back here," she called after me.

I walked into her apartment and settled on the rag rug. She'd have to tow me out. I waited for her to fuss and threaten, but she didn't.

I dozed, waking briefly each time she entered the room. I heard her lock the bathroom door. She was showering and fixing herself up. When she came out, I smelled perfume. She had on her cowboy boots, black jeans, long-sleeve white Western shirt threaded with black curlicues, and a black eye patch. Her lips were painted scarlet, her looped golden earrings swung abruptly. She only glanced at me as she strode past and slammed the door.

Customers were arriving. The jukebox thumped to life. For men the workday had ended, bringing beer time. I pushed up and crossed to the window. Still too much light to risk leaving. The juke-box became silent. I sensed a quieting out front and moved to the door to crack it. Two mounties stood talking with Blackie at the counter.

I hid in her bathroom till the jukebox revived, bottles again clinked, and a voice hee-hawed. I sat with my back against the door.

"You here anywheres?" I heard her call.

I stood and stepped out.

"It's dark, get going," she said. She held a bar towel.

"What chance I got with mounties all over the road?"

"I supposed to care about your chances?" she asked, her dark eye shiny and hard.

"You have so far."

"I'm tired of kicked dogs. And I ain't letting you stay another night so you can rob and kill me."

"Never killed anybody except to keep from getting it myself," I said, almost the truth.

Customers hollered for her, and she left. I thought of Whitlow, the body-building, grinning ex-Marine. He'd been leader of the Leavenworth kitchen crew who'd ganged me. Seven days later I trapped him alone among the drum kettles. I washed him down with the steam hose, and against the wall he did a howling, flinging dance. Spinning, pounding, grinding clamor from the battery of mechanical dishwashers covered his screams.

I left the hose cut on, and it thrashed around like a frenzied snake. The billowing steam confused the guards and prevented them from identifying me or anyone. Along the cell rows the word went round, and from then on when I walked the yard, other prisoners made way.

The Pit hushed as customers left. Their pickups' engines roared, the tires hurled gravel. The jukebox played out, sounds of Blackie cleaning up, a few remarks to last drinkers. I heard her call good night.

Without speaking, she walked into the room and opened the hideaway bed. She held the Winchester. From under a pillow she brought out a pair of yellow pajamas and carried them to the bathroom. I listened to her flush the john, brush her teeth, and gargle. She came out still holding the rifle.

"I'll use it," she said and laid the rifle beside the hideaway. "Move one damn inch in my direction and you dead. I've given up men. I don't want none the rest of my life."

She switched out the lamp. I listened to her settle in and sigh. The Pit was quiet except for the sound of the cooler's motor.

"What was you in prison for?" she asked in the dark.

"I hit an army officer."

"Why'd you do that?"

"He had an obnoxious personality."

Lieutenant Philip Poindexter from Mobile, Alabama, who tried to hide his fear behind chickenshit. He'd been riding me because under mortar rounds I'd seen him break, sob, and foul his pants. He made me point man through a delta sweep where I scented Cong as a bird dog would quail.

I told him we ought to pull back and approach from another angle of attack. "Move it," he ordered. It didn't feel right, and I hung back. "You disobeying me?" he asked. His courage came from a bottle and pills swiped from a medical supply.

The shit erupted from the other side of an earthen dike. The platoon dove into scummy, stinking paddy water, the sun scorching, flies feasting on blood of the half-floating wounded and dead. Poindexter shouted wild crazy fucking orders to rush the dike in the face of direct fire. When nobody obeyed, he really went ape. He crawled splashing to my side, kicked me, and jerked at my ammo belt to force me forward. I jammed the butt of my M-16 into his chin and broke his jaw.

I'd saved his life, my own, most of the platoon's, but it didn't count. That night after we dragged out of the paddy and back to firebase, MPs jeeped me cuffed and shackled to Saigon, where three days later I was court-martialed. Flew me to Fort Benning for a verdict review, then on to Leavenworth. Lieutenant Poindexter was reassigned to the Quartermaster Corp's Graves Registration.

"I been in the hole," Blackie said. "Three years."

"For what?"

"Killed a man. He was army too. Cut me with a broken liquor bottle."

Her scar, the loss of an eye, the sergeant in the color photograph on the end table?

"Turned out he had another wife," she said. "In Carolina. Big fight when I found out. We was both half drunk. He had the bottle, me the carving knife. It was Thanksgiving."

"Bad day."

"Yeah, 'cause I loved him," she said.

28

AT FIRST SALLOW light Blackie roused. She switched on the table lamp and her radio. She'd taken off the eye patch, and her face appeared not so much damaged as unfinished.

"Guess you ain't so dangerous after all," she said and set the Winchester on the wall antlers. She used the bathroom. She came out still wearing her pajamas and strode barefooted into the front.

I used her razor, only a partial shaving job because of scabs. When I joined her, she was setting out orange juice, scrambled eggs, and toast. She had on a zebra-striped eye patch. We ate across from each other, drank coffee, smoked Luckies.

"Can't keep you no longer," she said. "Don't want no more bad with the law." She crossed to her cash register and drew out a ten-dollar bill. She laid it before me. "Best I can do."

"It's a lot."

"You ain't going to get far looking like a hobo."

From her closet she brought out a pair of brown polyester slacks. In a bottom dresser drawer she located a blue-and-white striped shirt with a button-down collar. I didn't know whether I owed her sergeant or another man till I tried on the pants. They were too short. Not the sergeant's. I zipped up and left the shirt open at the neck. I had a belt and shoes. She provided another pair of GI socks. When I shook her hand, she pulled her fingers away quick.

I left through the backdoor, thankful for the mist. I walked fast, my soles sibilant along wet asphalt. At the one-lane bridge over Persimmon Creek, I turned onto the winding path up to Aunt Jessie's. Before I cut out of Shawnee County, I had a few last questions for her.

Plaintive cries from the mountain. Not crows, ravens. They lived, my mother had said, along the highest ridges, lonely, furtive, fog-shrouded birds.

I was out of breath by the time Aunt Jessie's cabin took shape. Moisture glistened on plants of her garden. The Holstein stood at the fence, and its side-slipping jaw stilled as I passed.

Rattler barked before I reached the door. When Aunt Jessie opened it, she looked at me with no change of expression. She wore her bonnet, an apron, the homespun dress. What other clothes would she have?

"Thought you'd flew the coop," she said and shushed Rattler to let me in. "Sit yourself."

The chair had a woven reed seat, the legs heavy and crudely formed, perhaps by Miss Jessie herself or her husband, or maybe it was a frontier piece passed down through generations. The table looked as if sliced from the butt end of an oak, the wood never shellacked or stained, having taken on the scrubbed ivory tint of lye soap and age. A mason jar held a spray of wildflowers that resembled bluebells. They matched Aunt Jessie's eyes.

The room was warmly cozy from her fireplace. An iron pot hung on a crane that could be swung over the flames. She was frying something in a three-legged skillet set among coals.

"Buckwheats stick to your bones," she said and pulled on a leather glove to lift the skillet by its handle. She used a wooden spatula to slide two outsize pancakes from the skillet onto a tin plate. Before I could refuse, she laid them and a fork before me. She set on the table a dish of country butter and an earthen pot that had a small wooden spoon sticking from it. I knew I'd better eat or risk offending her. Moreover, the road had taught me never to turn down food. I buttered the pancakes and lifted the wooden spoon from the pot to drip honey on and between the buckwheats. I lifted a hot, mealy bite.

"My honey," she said. "Sourwood. My buckwheat too. Grind it for bread. Give you a loaf to carry along."

She still had an intense way of watching me with those young eyes as if she were trying to do more than just see. Without explaining why, she left the cabin. I smelled burning wood as well as onions that hung by their stalks from wall pegs. In the other room was a bed covered with a red-and-white patch quilt. A ladder led to a loft where what looked like an ox yoke lay at the head. On a shelf opposite the fireplace a candlestick I stood to lift. Though tarnished, it was silver. I turned it upside down and found an English benchmark. Maybe a piece brought long ago across the sea.

She entered holding a clay jar, its sides wet. She'd carried it from her spring house. She set a glass on the table and filled it with milk so rich that the cream rose to and layered at the top.

"You lied to me about your name," she said.

"I didn't want to," I said, surprised but not alarmed. My father'd told me mountain people had little use for the written law. They were their own law.

"A man on the run's got his reasons. Think I wouldn't find out? Everybody in Shawnee County's heard 'bout you by now. You favor your father. Got the LeBlanc chin."

"I been told that," I said as I finished the buckwheats and drank the milk. "You heard why I'm wanted?"

"I heard," she said and crossed to her sink, which had a pitcher pump to supply water. Alternately she ran one hand under the flow while cranking with the other. She dried using a towel draped over a nail.

"You believe it?"

"Ain't my business to believe," she said and from a curtained shelf brought out a clean square board she laid on the table.

"You remember when I was born?" I asked.

"I do," she said and again gave me the judging look.

"Here in Shawnee, not another county, right?"

"Sure-fire," she said and scattered flour on the board. She drew down and uncovered a wooden bowl from a cupboard.

Okay, my birth record would definitely be on file in the clerk's office at the county courthouse in Cliffside. I watched her gnarled hands lift out dough and work it over the board.

"Lupi loved your mama and made you a cradle," she said.

I thought of the cradle in a corner of my mother's sewing room at Bellerive.

"People called him ugly, like a dwarf, and he was swarthy, but he wont ugly to anybody who knew him long," Aunt Jessie said, her fingers deep in the dough. "I thought he was when I first seen him, yet when you got to know Lupi he changed before your eyes. Your daddy didn't know coal from crows. Lupi learned him."

She again crossed to the sink, pumped water over her hands, and dried them. She walked to the other room. At the foot of her narrow bed was a wooden trunk bound by iron bands. It could've reached this country by sailing ship and would have brought big money in antique shops. She opened it and returned holding a notebook, the spiral kind children use in schools. She handed it to me and again floured her hands before kneading.

The notebook's brown speckled cover was worn and flimsy, the lined pages yellowed. Across them were drawings of gears, hoists, tracks, pulleys, blocks, diagrams of what looked like engine cutaways as well as mathematical equations, all inked in a fine, even artistic hand. Each was identified beneath by an Italian word: *girella, valvola, congiunzione, elettrizzare, bacchetta . . .*

"Lupi'd take one look at anything and picture it," she said. "See what nobody else could. Had far eyes."

"Where'd you get it?" I asked, still turning pages that felt dryly fragile to my fingers.

"When Lupi died, he didn't have nobody, so I packed up a few of his belongings." She again floured her hands, and the crooked fingers dug into dough. "I seen he got properly buried too. Lupi run things at High Moor while Boss John did the selling. Your daddy had a sweet tongue and knew how to sugar the coal buyers. Rode trains up to Washington and Pittsburgh. Fed and liquored the steel men when they come to High Moor. Children stood along the tracks to sell them chinquapins."

She hit her fists against dough.

"Lord it was a busy place. Working three shifts, floodlights on all night, coal drags rattling out, miners flush and spending. Had our own bank at the store which loaned money to Cliffside to put in running water. You couldn't walk the street without hearing somebody hollering or laughing. Now I can't go back and look. Everything fallen down."

I again studied the beautifully intricate sketches of coke ovens, mule harness, and mine buggies. I made out specifications for a system of great fans to ventilate the mountain. Everything had been drawn to scale, and its economy of line possessed a grace that far surpassed function.

"All these Lupi's ideas?"

"Not all. Your daddy was smart, but Lupi had to care for the details, and the first couple of years Lupi took Boss John by the hand and led him."

My father had loved to reminisce about his mining days, the re-opening of the seam and hardships endured, the eventual triumph over what had appeared failure. He'd described the first load of coal shipped out and the check that came back, a copy of which he framed and hung in Bellerive's library.

As I turned pages I came on something else toward the end of the notebook—a sketch of a scene I immediately recognized, a view of Bellerive complete with portico, as if one stood at the river landing and looked up across the lawn to the house. Lupi's sketch was so detailed I made out the lightning rods, the ironwork around the roof's crown, the weather vane.

I was puzzled. I figured Lupi would've either had to be at Belle-rive or copied a photograph. I asked Aunt Jessie as she used butter to grease her two loaf molds before working dough into them, shaping the tops, and carrying the molds to her oven built into stones above the fireplace. It had an iron door. She slid the pans inside.

"Lupi a couple of times worked for Boss John down in Virginia after High Moor closed up," she said. "When Boss John had troubles nobody else could fix with machinery or the house."

I turned pages to a drawing of the portico detached, its dimensions in curlicued numbers along edges. I squinted at what I initially supposed might be Lupi's name signed at the bottom corner, a small, smudged Italian word—*compire*. I knew no Italian, but it was a romance language, and I tried to think of a Latin equivalent. It'd been too many years since I sat in Bellerive's library to recite Virgil before Mr. Augustus Longworth.

Possibly Lupi had designed the portico or supervised its construction. There was always restoration going on at Bellerive. Each morning workmen drove in, and some lived for weeks using the slave cabins. It was said that in King County while my father was rebuilding, nobody else could find a carpenter, plumber, or electrician. They were all hired out to him.

"Lupi ever mention me?" I asked, thinking of the cradle.

"He did. Told me he'd seen you and Boss John have a bad falling-out."

So Lupi had been among the workmen who'd seen the fight. A third time I studied the drawings. There was one that looked like a flat, pale bean. Under it the word *seme*. Lupi thinking of gardening at the same time he solved problems of mining coal?

"He didn't like going down to Virginia," she said. "Wouldn't go his last years but stayed out at High Moor alone till he give up the ghost."

He had to have been a renaissance type, I thought, a mountain da Vinci able to find beauty in the hoists, pumps, and gears of a primitive West Virginia coal camp about as distant from sunny operatic Italy as man could travel.

29

WHEN I LEFT Aunt Jessie's, she gave me hot bread wrapped in a brown paper sack to carry along, and I remembered the loaf Juno had slipped me after my mother's funeral.

I stopped along the path down the slope. The mist had burned off, denying me cover. I squatted behind witch hazels and wondered what to do next. I hadn't learned anything around Shawnee County that would justify hanging around, yet there was no way I could escape cross country to where—Montana? If I tried riding my thumb, the mounties would nail me before I reached the Kentucky line.

The day's heat was building, there was little breeze, and dragonflies flashed blue in the sunlight as they sped about nettles' purple blooms. I kept picturing Lupi's sketches, particularly ones of the portico. Any possible connection to the explosion? No, Aunt Jessie told me Lupi'd returned permanently to High Moor where he'd lived until found dead on a snowy day three years ago come January.

I again had the sensation of being watched. Maybe this crazy land was doing it to me, the dismal hollers, the deserted camps, a people honed to insularity by the dark Appalachians. A dog barked. I looked behind me up the brightening mountainside. Nothing.

A car passed below, a black unmarked Cherokee. Four men sat

in it. They weren't uniformed but wore hats. FBI? I'd crossed a state line, and I thought about the helicopter that had skimmed over me and Cornstalk Skagg. Even if I found the safety of a cave, I'd not be able to hold out long against resources the Feds could rank against me.

I'd ask one last favor from Blackie. I jumped Persimmon Creek, careful not to snag black haw bushes, and sidehilled the slope above the road till I stood opposite the Pit. No cars parked in front. I listened for traffic before moving down. I ran across the pavement and came up behind her living quarters. I tapped on the door.

"I never took you to raise," Blackie said when she opened the door. "Get the goddamn hell away from here!"

"What I'm trying to do. Brought you some bread."

She slammed the door. I waited. She opened it. She had on the yellow eye patch.

"What you want from me?"

"Get me out of the county."

"Just how'm I supposed to do that? I got no wheels."

"Find me a ride."

She hadn't combed her hair. She laid a hand on a hip of her stone-washed jeans and looked over me toward the woods.

"I been hoping to God I'd never see you again."

"I don't want to be bothering you," I told her and handed her the bread. She took it. "From Aunt Jessie."

"Bother? You a goddamn sight more than bother." She wiped a finger under her nose. "Aunt Jessie sent me this?"

"My gift."

"You think this bread gonna bribe me?"

"Best I can do."

She hesitated and held the loaf in both hands. She shook her head, started to turn back inside, then stepped into the doorway to spit past me.

"Always loved Aunt Jessie's buckwheat bread. Guess she must think you worth helping." She frowned. "Skunk he be stopping by in a while."

"Skunk?"

"Drives a beer truck. Skunk and me go way back. I once pulled him out the river. He can't swim. But he might not do it. Goddamn, you trouble. Come on in here and wait."

She left me sitting on the straight chair while she walked into the front and closed the door. Her hideaway bed hadn't been folded back into a sofa. The sheets were rumpled and smelled of womanly heat.

I looked at the picture of her with the sergeant who'd cut her and she'd killed. How many men had slept in that hideaway since? She came back, walked to the bathroom, and stepped out combing her hair.

"Quit looking at that picture. None of your damn business."

"You're right."

"Damn right I'm right. I tell you one thing, I don't use the word love no more."

"Neither do I."

"Saw that first time I set eyes on you," she said and stroked the comb hard and fast. "Didn't want to be touched."

She turned her head. She'd heard the truck, tossed the comb on the dresser, crooned out front. Somebody entered.

"Never fear, the champ's here," a man called.

"Skunk, you the horseshit champ," Blackie said. "How's Cootie?"

"Worse than you a-witching and a-bitching."

"You a bigger sonofabitch ever'day so she got more to witch and bitch about."

"Hold it," Skunk said, his voice high-pitched and squeaky. "I never argue with a pretty woman. Like trying to swim up a waterfall. What you want this day from the man with a way?"

Blackie gave her order—two kegs and a dozen cases of Blatz.

Whistling, Skunk left and clattered back with a dolly he bumped over the doorsill. He made three trips to the truck. As Blackie settled up at the cash register, she lowered her voice.

"I ain't touching that," Skunk said. "No sir-ee!"

Blackie talked some more.

"Well shee-it," Skunk said. "You wouldn't tell that one on me, would you?"

Blackie walked back into the doorway.

"Come show yourself," she said.

I did and saw Skunk was a burly man with a full face and mottled complexion. He wore blue coveralls and a red cap that had BLATZ stitched in white thread across the crown.

"I don't like doing this one fucking little bit," he said. "If we get stopped, I gonna claim I didn't know you was in the truck, that you musta slipped past me while I delivered suds."

"Agreed," I said.

"I lose my job, Cootie'll kill me," he said. He stared at the scabs on my face. "You vouching for him?" he asked, turning to Blackie.

"I reckon," Blackie said. "Aunt Jessie favors him."

"Don't come out till I signal," he ordered me and as he left again banged the dolly across the sill.

The truck was an International semi, the trailer encased in aluminum. It had double-decker compartments along its sides. Skunk raised accordion doors to shift beer cases and empty a compartment. He looked up and down the road, then waved at me to come on.

"If I get out of this, I'll send your ten dollars back and a dozen roses," I said to Blackie.

"Never cared for roses," she said. "Make it a bottle of Black Jack Daniel's."

I ran to the trailer and squeezed myself in a lower compartment. Skunk slammed down the door. I could only partly lie down or sit up in the dented metal cubicle. The floor felt wet. Beer fumes so thick I tasted Blatz.

"Got to make a couple of stops 'fore I leave the county," Skunk called. "Just sit tight."

When he started, bottles, cans, and kegs rattled and clanged. I felt I was again in solitary. Wheels hit a pothole, the truck yawed, I banged my head.

Cramped and aching, I tried to picture where we were. Too many twists and turns. Skunk stopped. He loaded up the dolly and rolled it away over what sounded like concrete. "Up yours," he called to somebody when he came back.

Two more stops. Beer unloaded, empties retrieved. Skunk had radios in the cab, one a CB, the other FM, Beckley. As we bounced along, a whiny male voice sang, "The long road I've traveled, has done run all over me."

A change in the truck's rhythm, and Skunk slowed among traffic. Repeated stops but no unloading. A horn honked. I figured Cliffside.

Moving again, speeding down an incline. I kept one hand behind my head to pad it against the compartment's jolts and used the other to rub a cramp in my thigh. I straightened the leg as far as I could by shoving it against the door.

A sudden slowing and another stop. I braced myself. The truck shifted forward, paused, jerked, braked. Skunk cut off his radios.

"Guess you done drunk up all the samples," a man's voice said.

"Let you have a case at a discount," Skunk said.

"Hell thirsty as I get standing here I could swallow a keg," the voice said. "Got anybody aboard?"

"Just a whole damn bunch of escaped convicts and two blondes who been snapping they garter belts at me."

"Looks like you ought to share one," the voice said, and I heard the man's footsteps. He walked the long length of the trailer. *Boom!*

I stopped breathing. He'd kicked or hit his billy against the trailer's side. He passed on.

"Maybe what you looking for done gone," Skunk said.

"We'll catch the fucker. Get teeth in his ass."

"Stay happy," Skunk called and geared up the truck. We began climbing, the engine straining, the trailer shaking. Bottles clinked, kegs rumbled. Skunk sang along with the radio, "I dried the last tear I'll cry over you."

We topped a rise. The truck sped downward, and Skunk geared and braked. More traffic. What sounded like the keening of a sawmill, then a woman's laughter. He gunned it along a flat, slowed, stopped, and got out, yet didn't cut the engine. He slid up the compartment door. Sunlight blinded me.

"Highball out of here!" Skunk said, glancing in both directions.

I uncurled myself out to the ground. We stood at the rear of a windowless one-story wooden building. It appeared empty and had a faded sign that read AGRICO MINE & MILL SUPPLY.

"Where are we?"

"Coal Mount and I gone!"

"We over the county line?" I called after him.

"'Bout a spit and a holler," he said, climbed into the International, and laid the pedal to the metal.

Across broken pavement a plank fence surrounded an empty weed-grown lot. I walked in the direction Skunk had taken. The narrow street intersected a two-lane highway. On my side, a Quik-Stop Market and Shell station. Across the highway, a used-car lot where a salesman sat in the doorway of a hut built like a tepee. No mounties or troopers in either direction.

A grimy, fenderless Caprice Classic swerved into the Quik-Stop. Two men wearing billed caps, their faces blackened, sat in front. The driver swung out his legs and entered the convenience store.

He returned carrying a six-pack of Bud in each hand. I walked fast to him as he slid into the Caprice.

"Got room for a man needing a ride bad?"

He was chunky, unshaved, the area around his eyes like ivory goggles. He tapped a grimy hand against the steering wheel to the beat of a Loretta Lynn tape. His unbarbered mustache drooped around corners of his mouth.

"What you think, Percy?" he asked the other man, who sat and positioned the six-packs between them. "We got room?"

They were twins, and even the coal dust that filmed them seemed evenly distributed. Percy ripped open a six-pack and popped a top.

"How you know where we heading?" he asked.

"For me any way'll do."

"I don't know, Edgar," Percy said.

"Hell I've needed rides in my life," Edgar said.

"Put it in the back," Percy said.

I opened the door and bowed in. There was no seat, just a folding metal chair, and I had to make room among balled-up coveralls, wrenches, boots, gloves, canteens, batteries, lamps, helmets, and crushed beer cans.

As they drove from Coal Mount, I looked back through the rear window to the Quik-Stop. The clerk, a woman wearing an orange-colored apron, stood looking after us. So did the car salesman at the tepee hut.

I glanced at the sun and saw we were balling south. A road sign: RED DOG 8 M. Percy popped a beer for Edgar before opening a third he handed to me.

"Tree drop on you?" he asked.

"Fell off a truck."

"Them trucks'll fall you off 'em ever' time," Edgar said.

I looked at a wooden crate filled with tools. Faded black lettering on the side. HER L S and Y A ITE. Also the numbers 30–70.

I'd worked a million crossword puzzles at Leavenworth and studied the letters. *Hercules* had to be the first word. Then the second. Easy. *Dynamite.* I'd had it on my mind.

"Blasting powder and dynamite still used in coal mining?" I asked.

"You from the moon?" Percy answered.

"When I was a itty-bitty baby, my mommy gave me a stick of 'mite to chew on for a sugar tit," Edgar said.

Explosives so plentiful in mining territory. I again tried to make some connection between coal country and what happened at Bellerive.

Edgar stopped at the junction of the highway with a dirt road. He looked over his shoulder at me.

"End of the line," he said. He finished the beer, crushed the can one-handed, and tossed it out the window into a ditch.

"You all got a minute to talk to me about powder and dynamite?"

"You fixing to open up a bank account?" Percy asked.

"Or blow up our damn Republican governor?" Edgar asked. "I'd furnish the powder for that."

"Got an interest in how it's used," I said.

"You ain't got much to be interested in," Edgar said.

"Hell, let him talk to Pa," Percy said.

"I reckon we can find him a bone to chaw on," Edgar said.

He wheeled the rattling Caprice onto the dirt road. The tires splashed through potholes half full of muddy water. As the car bounced, I held to the window frame to keep the chair from toppling.

The road dipped, climbed, and swung left down a lane of basswood trees. The narrow house had two stories, was unpainted, its frame siding weathered a parched brown. Scattered around a yard grown up with crabgrass lay abandoned auto carcasses.

In a lot fenced by logs, pigs stood watching us. An engine block hung by a chain from the limb of a locust tree. The TV antenna had been strapped to a brick chimney that badly needed pointing up.

"Pa can tell you everything about fire in the hole," Percy said.

"He an expert," Edgar said. "Done blew himself up twice to prove it."

A dozen dogs ran barking around the car, big-boned hounds whose ribs showed. Percy and Edgar hollered and kicked at them. As I followed the brothers toward the house, the hounds bayed. Pigs grunted and squealed.

Edgar opened the door, which gave not onto a hallway but a large room, at one end of which was the kitchen. The other held a fireplace and leatherette chairs arranged around a TV set. Ghostly silent pictures fluttered across the screen—spectral forms of what appeared to be galloping horses.

Nails pounded into unpainted board walls held four rifles. The mounted head of a black bear had its features fixed to a perpetual snarl, the fangs yellowed, cobwebs strung between them.

On the floor before the TV, a straggly, white-haired old man sat on a low rectangular platform made from planks, its dimensions maybe three feet square, with wheels cannibalized from a shopping cart or roller skates screwed into the bottom.

He wore only striped pink-and-blue underwear shorts. His beard hung to his navel. He had no arms beyond the elbows, and they as well as stumps of his thighs were covered by riveted leather cups.

"You talk to the man?" he asked Percy and Edgar.

"Told him you was having fits," Edgar said and slung his cap at a hat rack made from cow horns. The cap hooked and spun.

"Told him he better be here by tomorrow to fix the set or you'd eat his gizzard," Percy said.

Pa's expression became fierce, a hawk, I thought, or a feuder like Devil Anse Hatfield. He ducked forward and shoved an arm stump on the bare floor. The platform rolled away from the TV. A yellow cat lying in his path jumped onto a chair.

"He want a call?" the old man asked as he eyed me.

"He don't need no call," Percy said. He and Edgar stood at the sink scrubbing. They sprinkled Dutch Cleanser over their hands and arms.

"Wants to talk about shooting coal," Edgar said.

"We told him you was the expert since you blowed yourself up so good," Percy said.

"You ask if he wants a call?" the old man said.

"Call for what?" I asked.

"Gobblers," he said.

"He invented a turkey call," Percy said.

"Make 'em in our spare time," Edgar said.

"Never had a dissatisfied customer," the old man said. "Show him."

Percy dried his hands and crossed the kitchen to a door that opened into a shed. From a workbench he carried back a six-inch coffin-shaped wooden box. A rubber band held one side in place. He shook the box as you would a carnival rattle. The loose side rasping the box created turkey yelps.

"Made of cedar," the old man said. "Last a lifetime. Just change the rubber band once awhile. Get 'em free at the post office. This model cost you eight-fifty, and we got more."

The caller was good. I didn't tell him I'd seen others like it. Maybe he really believed he invented this one. Trouble was, in a blind you had to lay your gun across your lap and shake the box. Too much movement would spook the gobbler. Best to learn to work off your tongue.

"If I still hunted, I'd want one," I told the old man.

He looked offended and used his stumps to oar himself back toward the TV. The platform's wheels bumped the floor's cracks. Percy laid the caller aside.

Tacked to a wall were unframed photographs of Franklin D. Roosevelt and John L. Lewis, both scissored from magazines. They'd become wrinkled and faded.

"We told him you was best at it," Edgar said, drying his hands and arms at the sink.

"Best at what?" the old man asked.

"Shooting coal," Percy said.

"I could blow the wings off a fly and not mess its hair," the old man said.

"Flies don't have no hair," Edgar said.

"I could set a charge and tell you within a shovelful how much coal would hit the ground."

"One thing about Pa, he don't brag none," Percy said.

"He brag all," Edgar said.

The old man scowled, and they laughed.

"I'm slopping the hogs," Edgar said.

"My night for the stove," Percy said.

Edgar put on his cap and left. Percy banged around at the wood cook stove. He shook down ashes.

"What kind of explosives you use in the mines?" I asked the old man.

"First black powder. Undercut the face with a pick, use a chest auger to drill in above the cut, pour in your powder, tamp her, and set a squib on the lip. That's how come men hollered 'Fire in the hole!'"

"Help yourself to a seat," Percy said.

"No dynamite?" I asked as I sat. The chair's arms had cigarette burns on them.

"It come later," Percy said. "Easier and safer. You could get the combination you needed."

"Combination?"

"To blow coal, you don't want no high explosives," the old man said. "To blast rock, yeah, but in the mine you want a cool flame that heaves the coal off the face rather than smashes it. So you shoot dynamite low in nitro and high in ammonium, sodium, and wood meal to get a slow push which lays the coal down without blowing it all to hell. Safer if fire damp hanging 'round too. Thirty-seventy a good combine."

"No TNT or plastic?" I asked. In 'Nam we'd set cyclonite charges to destroy the little guy's hooches, bunkers, and tunnel complexes.

"TNT fire the whole damn mine," the old man said. "Plastics come after my time. Truth is they don't blow much coal no more. Stripping, they loose up the overburden by blasting, but most of the big seams in drifts use continuous mining machinery or long-wall it. Just chew or slice it right out of the seam and dump it on a conveyor for the ride to the tipple."

"Explosives easy to get hold of?" I asked.

"Not now. Sign your life away, but when I first come along everybody had powder in his toolshed. Hell, you could go to the hardware store and buy dynamite easy as nails. These days, rule for ever'thing except pissing and the government's working on that."

"Lots of hackers still have stuff around," Percy said. "And you can always fit a stick or two of 'mite from a job in your lunch pail to carry home."

"Why'd you do that?" I asked.

"Furnish a little coal for your fireplace from the rathole mine in your backyard," the old man said. "Hell, I got me a can of black powder out in the shed still. Had it since I don't remember when. Best thing about black powder it don't cause headaches like nitro. With 'mite headaches a part of the job."

"They don't deteriorate?"

"Powder some maybe but not bad if you keep it topped tight so it can't draw moisture. Might lose a little bang but still serviceable. Dynamite hold up a long time, but what wont was blasting caps. Detonators. Mostly mercury fulminate. They'd go bad quick. They's other better and longer-lasting caps these days made with lead azide. No longer use squibs or powder fuses. Set off a bang with electric sparks. Safer."

"In his day they called him Gunner," Percy said.

"My charges'd lay down coal so soft it wouldn't ripple coffee in your cup," the old man said. "Got careless one day pulling pillars at Black Eagle Number Two. Stooped over for my canteen to wet my whistle and a packet of caps fell out my pocket, sparked against a chunk of gangue, and blowed. Now I watch the goddamn TV that only half works and sell them turkey calls. Wife left me for a tire salesman. Got two trifling boys, four bony hogs, and that's it. A come-down for the Gunner."

He turned back to phantoms noiselessly sliding across the snowy TV screen.

30

PERCY FED US boiled greens, lumpy applesauce, and cornbread covered with chunks of pork and thick black gravy, all to be washed down with cans of Bud. For dessert we ate peanut butter and cherry jam spread on hard, cold biscuits.

They'd lifted the old man into a chair at the table. Rough as his sons were, they showed a clumsy tenderness by alternately spooning food to his mouth and wiping his lips with a paper towel. When we finished, Percy lit a cigar and set it between his father's teeth. The old man clamped down on it.

"We going to Beckley," Edgar said to me. "You coming?"

I smoked the plastic-tipped Hav-A-Tampa Jewel they offered as I looked to a window and darkness. I told them I'd ride along, used their outhouse, and washed at the sink. The sons changed into slacks and sport shirts. When I thanked the old man, I almost reached to shake a hand he didn't have.

"Don't go busting no caps," he said to me. He wheeled his platform to the TV and breathed through his mouth around the cigar. Percy placed an empty beer can on the floor before him. The old man bent to it and knocked off ash.

"Don't go causing no fire," Percy said.

"I got two of the best fire stompers right here," the old man said and banged floorboards on either side of him with his leather-capped arm stumps.

I sat on the folding chair in the back of the Caprice. Hounds ran barking around us and followed to the paved road. I was again thinking about explosives and a timed charge. The fact that whoever planted them would've had to be familiar with Bellerive's annual celebration didn't narrow things down much. Everybody in King County knew about the LeBlanc's August 16 commemoration of themselves.

I still couldn't see who'd profit from blowing up the portico except brother Edward. Though violence didn't fit him, he could've hired somebody to do the job and might've set up the timing belt delay to arrive at the side door seconds after the explosion. But what would've motivated the act? Possibly he'd gotten himself into a financial pinch and John refused to help. Maybe greed, blackmail, or a woman. And the bastard had put out a money bounty for me.

I had to get back to Jessup's Wharf. There were answers I needed to find—or have found for me. I'd lean on Walter Frampton.

The Caprice climbed. We topped a rise, and lights of Beckley spread under the cool night sky. Percy drove into the city past shopping centers, eateries, banks, and new cars gleaming in rows of showrooms.

"Where you want off?" Edgar asked. "We going to the skating rink."

"Where gals go 'round and 'round," Percy said. "Tight shorts or them little red skirts."

"Good a place as any," I said.

"Better than most," Edgar said.

An organ played at the Mountaintop Rink, a long galvanized building fronted by a sparkling marquee. Percy parked and opened the Caprice's trunk for him and Edgar to lift out skates—coal miners owning custom pairs of inliners.

"Some of 'em gals got long white legs they's no end to," Percy said.

"Them little skirts fly high," Edgar said.

"Wish I could repay you," I said.

"Shoot, you made Pap feel good," Percy said.

"Made him think he was laying coal on the ground again," Edgar said.

We shook hands. They walked to the floodlit ticket window. When the door opened, a swirl of color spilled out and gliding shapes passed as the organ boomed out a rock beat tangible as wind.

I stood in shadows at outer fringes of the parking lot. I had Blackie's ten dollars in my pocket, enough to do little more than buy a couple of cheeseburgers and another pack of cigarettes. No bus ticket or ride on Amtrak, which were too dangerous anyhow.

I considered hot-wiring a vehicle. I knew how to engineer it. The year I ran off from Bellerive I'd stolen a Pontiac Firebird in Miami, used it three days, and left it before a Fort Meyers's high school. I'd cleaned out the owner's ashtray for him.

I checked cars and pickups in the lot. I might be able to gain an hour or two lead before the theft was discovered. On the other hand I could find myself with only a five or ten minute margin and troopers'd be on me almost before I got good in gear. Yet without wheels my last recourse was again to ride my thumb, an act even more perilous the closer I traveled to Virginia.

I watched people enter and leave the rink. Mug a man and force him to drive me. Sure and, if caught, add kidnapping to everything else.

I rejected a recent-model LeSabre. With my need of a shave,

scabby face, trashy clothes, I wouldn't look as if I belonged in such a respectable vehicle. I decided on a F-150 pickup, wheels a miner or laborer might drive. It was mud-splattered and had a CB antenna. I'd be able to monitor the truckers who kept each other informed of bears.

As I reached to the Ford's door handle, a man and woman carrying skates walked from the rink toward the F-150. When they saw me, they stopped dead.

"What the hell you think you doing?" the man called. He wore a cowboy hat.

"Got mixed up is all," I answered and moved away among other vehicles and along a darkened fringe of the lot. I jumped a culvert to the parking area before a Kroger's store. At a side of the entrance I spotted the clam-shaped hood of a public phone.

Zeke Webb, I thought. He'd been platoon radio man in 'Nam—short, heavyset, capable of carrying loads, a good soldier who'd understood just surviving was the art of war. We'd kidded him about his hillbilly accent. He'd played a mean, whining harmonica, and the last I'd seen he was being air-vacced with mortar iron in a leg. He'd showed the wound to everybody while shouting, "I've seen the fucking light!"

Using the chain-bound phone book, I ran my finger along the *W*s. No chance I thought. Probably dead. What was his real first name. Not Zeke. I couldn't remember. The finger stopped. There it was: Clifford E. Webb, CPA, 720 Wildwood Lane.

CPA? We'd had to teach Zeke not to piss upwind.

For change I walked into Kroger's and bought a pack of Camels. The girl in the fast-lane checkout eyed me. Back outside at the phone, I shoved in the quarter and dialed.

"Zeke?" I asked when a man answered.

"Who's this?"

"Fire Base Seven requesting artillery cover to withdraw troops to Saigon Sally's whorehouse."

A moment's pause before he spoke.

"Jesus, a ghost."

"The LeBlanc express. At Kroger's near the roller rink. Can you come over?"

"I don't know that's a great idea. I been reading and hearing about you."

"Zeke, I need you bad. I'll be watching near the public phone."

I hung up before he could refuse. He might not arrive. Yeah he would as he always had when the shit flew.

I stood in shadows at the side of the store to watch cars enter and leave. Maybe fifteen minutes before the black Jaguar with white sidewalls turned in. It circled the lot and stopped a distance from the phone.

When the driver opened the door, he put only one foot on the ground and scouted the terrain. He shaded his eyes against the glare from Kroger's entrance. Had to be Zeke. I moved around a parked van and up behind him.

"Got your harmonica?" I asked.

He pivoted, an arm half raised, instincts still intact. He'd been a bitching, foul-smelling grunt, but now he drove a British car, had blown-dry dark brown wavy hair, and verged on the stylish in a soccer shirt, blue shorts, running shoes.

"Zeke, you look laid away."

"I don't like this a damn bit," he said and squinted toward Kroger's as if up on the perimeter.

"Don't go ballistic. I don't mean trouble for you. Just need a little money."

"Just? How much?"

"Fifty ought to do it. I'll do my best to pay it back."

He hesitated and kept looking around as if fearing encirclement. From the roller rink strains of a rockabilly waltz. Lights of the Kroger sign tinted his face reddish yellow. He'd filled out even more, meaning he was eating well.

"Get in the car," he said. "Let's make it quick."

I sat beside him as he drove to a closed bank that had an illuminated ATM. He left the Jag's engine running, crossed fast to the machine, slipped in his card, punched buttons. Back into the car, he handed me two clean fifty-dollar bills.

"You doing well," I said.

"Yeah, went up to the university and studied accounting, got my CPA. Nothing exciting, but pays the bills. Been hard on my eyes though."

"You were the man in 'Nam, Zeke."

"Different time, different world. Hard to believe now it happened. You really punched out the lieutenant. Lifted him clean off the ground. Hope Leavenworth wasn't too rough."

"Pretty much the same," I said, not quite true, but beasts in both places.

"Look, where can I let you off?" He gunned the engine.

"Zeke, I need wheels."

"Hell, Charley, can't help you there."

"I won't get you involved."

"I'm already involved."

"I promise I'll cover you."

"Jesus, I don't know," he said and ran a hand over his hair.

"If I get caught I'll swear I stole the car. Give me twenty-four hours and report it. Your insurance would pay the loss."

"You really putting heat to me."

"For me the stuff's incoming and I got no bunker."

A second time he ran his palm over his hair.

"Got an old Jeep I used to take grouse hunting," he said. "If it'll start. Guess it'll hold together. But hell fire!"

We drove away from the city and through a tree-lined suburban district. Zeke turned in at the driveway of a brick house that had white shutters. Lights had been switched on over a three-bay garage. He used a remote control to slide up the doors. Headlights shone on the Jeep, a surplus relic that had a patched canvas top and torn side curtains. Parked in a second bay was a new Chevy station wagon.

A woman looked out a screen-door entrance that connected the house to the garage. She was a suntanned blonde who wore a yellow pantsuit and black high heels. She held a shish kebab skewer. "Who's with you?" she called and stared at me.

"Fellow wants to see the Jeep you been after me to sell," Zeke answered.

A little girl squeezed out beside her mother and ran to Zeke. She had the woman's blond hair gathered at the back by a pink ribbon. She held to his leg.

"My youngest," Zeke said. "Suzy Q. Alice Faye and I got two."

"You come on in here," the woman said to the girl.

"I want to watch," Suzy Q. answered.

"Come on in here or I get the hairbrush," the woman threatened.

Suzy Q. released Zeke's leg and slouched into the house.

He used jumper cables connected to the Chevy to jump-start the Jeep. Though the vehicle was battered, the tags hadn't expired.

"Hell of a reunion," Zeke said. "Look, I don't want 'em mixed in anything bad. Sometimes I wake nights in my house nice and safe, my wife beside me, my kids in their rooms, and I can't believe the old stuff ever happened. Oh fuck it. Take it away."

I backed out. He stood looking after me.

Returning along Wildwood to town I kept to the speed limit. I picked up and followed the turnpike sign. I had no driver's license and meant to give nobody reason to pull me over. I wondered how

Zeke would explain to Alice Faye I hadn't paid for the Jeep. Maybe he'd say I was trying it out.

The seats were ripped, the ride stiff, no radio. When I got up to fifty miles an hour, the Jeep vibrated bad and pulled left. Headlights agitated blackened pavement, and everything on the road passed me.

Crossing into Virginia, I felt like a door had clanked shut behind. I gassed up in Charlottesville, circled Richmond on 264, and stopped short of King County at a 7-Eleven. I bought two hot dogs and a Styrofoam cup of coffee.

When I used the pay phone to call Walter Frampton, it was three in the morning.

"What makes you think you have any right to rouse me at this hour?"

"Get in your car and meet me somewhere outside the county."

"Not on your life. And don't even tell me where you are."

"It is my life, and if you won't come to me, I'll try to reach you."

"You do, and I'll have to turn you in."

"All right, be a lawyer prick, but at least chase down an answer for me."

"Answer to what?"

"Get hold of the police report and find out what sort of explosive was used at Bellerive. I'll call back when I can. Now what about the birth certificate and insurance?"

"I contacted the Shawnee County clerk's office. They have no record. Neither do the counties of Fayette and Raleigh."

"Try the West Virginia Bureau of Vital Statistics at the state capitol in Charleston."

"I mean to do so, but at the moment the ever-genial insurance folks are in a position to claim that officially you were never born and don't exist. Except in the eyes of the law, you're presently a non-person."

31

SOUTH OF NEW Kent I found a county road and a fire trail among evenly spaced loblollies that according to a POSTED sign belonged to the Pamunkey Paper Co. I four-wheeled it over uneven soft ground, parked, and lifted out the torn seat to use as a pillow. I lay on pine tags, so much tree cover over me I couldn't see the sky.

My mind kept switching back to High Moor. Mountain folks were feuders. Somebody like Cornstalk Skagg, whose father'd been thrown out of camp, could've still held a grudge against Boss John. But why kill massively, and after all these years how many people like Cornstalk remained to do it?

Again I tried to figure how it was done. Not by somebody lighting a fuse and running. Too much chance of being seen and caught. Nor was it likely the killer hid in the woods bordering Bellerive and used a plunger or other hand-operated electrical detonator. It made more sense to set a delayed charge and provide time for escape and an alibi.

I slipped into a short sleep before crows woke me. They flitted squawking among pine boughs. It hadn't rained, but dew had wet trees, causing dripping. I found a spring in a sink of land and cupped my hands under the shallow pool to drink. The water tasted of pine tags.

I'd have to give Walter time, assuming he'd try to get the police report. Hungry, I drove from the woods and along Route 60 to Bottom's Bridge. At a Texaco station I bought a carton of orange juice, doughnuts, and a pack of Luckies. I hoped the clerk who looked me over would believe I was a local and cut billets for a timber company.

I drank juice, ate the doughnuts, and smoked as I returned toward Richmond. I again wanted to reach Juno. I passed the James River Community College sign and slowed. Disreputable as I appeared, I'd be taking a big chance, yet I made a U-turn and entered the rural campus.

Plenty of space in a yellow-lined parking area. A student with a book bag slung over his shoulder legged by, a lanky kid who looked as if he carried the weight of the world on his brow. He'd learn about real weight if he lived long enough.

"They teach physics here?" I asked.

"They try to," he said.

"What's the professor's name?"

"Bingham," he said. He pointed at a one-story white stucco building. "First floor."

I didn't use the main entrance. Instead I drove to the far end of the building and pulled alongside a line of dumpsters. I watched an exit door that had no outside knob. A bell rang for a class change, and I stepped fast to the building. When a student pushed out, I reached for the door and held it before it closed and relocked.

I faced a shiny gray corridor that was emptying. Notices and announcements tacked to bulletin boards. I walked reading names on doors. A printed card: DR. ALEXANDER B. BINGHAM, OFFICE HOURS: 9 A.M.–4 P.M.

I quietly opened the door. He sat at a desk, his back to me. Beyond him a laboratory and set on counters physics paraphernalia—

pulleys, an inclined plane, a bell jar. Dr. Bingham slashed at papers with a red pencil. He grimaced at them. I pulled the door closed before knocking.

"Drown yourself!" he shouted.

I waited and knocked a second time.

"Better be a good reason for disturbing me!" he hollered.

I opened the door. He'd not turned.

"Even if your mother's gone blind and your father's dying I'm not changing your grade or giving a reexam."

"Like to ask a few questions," I said.

"Everybody likes—" he said, swiveling in his chair. When he focused on me, his mouth closed, and he swallowed. "Do I know you?"

"No, sir, you don't, but you'd be doing me a big favor if you let me pick your brain ten seconds."

He was a young man, thin, scholarly, wearing a polka-dot bow tie and a white lab smock that appeared natty on him. Pens and pencils stuck from the smock's pocket. His glasses had thick black rims.

"You've been in an accident?" he asked. I stood between him and the door, and he was nervous.

"Couple," I said.

"I'm busy grading the test papers of imbeciles. If you want to make an appointment, I'll check my calendar."

"It's important to me we talk right now," I said. On a shelf among books he'd inserted a hi-fi set. From the ceiling light fixture hung a mobile made of test tubes filled with colored liquids. The office had a geometrical feel—everything in its place and squared away.

"I've a schedule to meet," he said and looked at the watch on his thin wrist before half turning to set the red pencil on his desk. He positioned it in line with the top edge of the paper he'd been grading. "Please be quick."

"A couple of questions about explosives and timing devices and I'm gone."

"Hold it," he said and held up a small, clean hand, the nails precisely pared. "Those are not areas of my expertise and I don't know that we should be discussing the subject at all."

"Listen a minute, please. How would a person set off an explosion with a timed charge rigged to detonate at an exact hour not just a day or two ahead of time but maybe a week or longer?"

"How can I be sure you're not involving me in some felonious project?"

"You don't know the answer?"

"Of course I know the answer. But I'm not certain I should tell you. Can you give me a valid reason for needing such information?"

"You may save a man's life."

"Whose?"

"A person close to me."

He pouched his lips. His eyes fidgeted. I still blocked his way to the door. Had he seen my picture in the papers or on TV? I didn't want to threaten him, but I was in so deep now I couldn't turn and leave.

"I don't like the feel of this," he said.

"I don't either. Give you my word I'm only after information, not a way of blowing up anybody."

"You're asking whether a person could set a charge to explode with a certitude of exactness over a period of extended duration?"

"That's it."

"Easily done," he said, a pronouncement.

"By easily you mean not complicated?"

"Thanks to integrated circuits on microchips, we have timepieces of remarkable accuracy and economy." He held up the wrist and his watch. "You can go to Wal-Mart and buy a digital timepiece cheaply that will lose or gain only a few seconds a month."

"How would it be rigged?"

"Not complex. People set VCRs for TV channels days or weeks ahead. My little watch has an alarm. An extension to a year or even more would be a rudimentary change in circuitry. The longer the time of course, the less accuracy. It would depend on how much precision is necessary."

"You said gain or lose a few seconds a month. That means in a year a variation of less than half a minute."

"Correct," he said as if surprised I could count.

"You could fire a charge like with the timer in your watch or an alarm clock digital radio?" I asked.

"Over a very extended period you'd need a constant, unvarying source of power for the timer." As he talked, his natural pedantry re-asserted itself. "Otherwise you'd surrender variable degrees of ex-actitude."

"Such as?"

"It could be something as simple as regular house current to the timer circuited to deliver a hundred-and-ten-volt jolt to the pri-mary charge."

"Primary charge?"

"A detonator more easily ignited than the base charge."

"Blasting cap?"

"Would be a detonator, yes."

"And the base charge could be dynamite, black powder, or whatever?"

"Indeed," he said and again looked at his watch.

"But house current could be interrupted," I said. "Lightning or trouble at a substation. That might throw off the timer."

At Bellerive there'd been frequent interruptions in the power supply. Lightning knocked out transformers. Limbs blew over lines. A winter ice storm had once cut electricity three days and nights. Schools had closed, and we'd kept all the fireplaces in the house burning. My father'd assigned John, Edward, Gaius, and me the duty of keeping them supplied with split red-oak logs.

"Use house power in conjunction with a battery," he said.

"What kind of battery?"

"Well not a dry cell because dry cells can't be dependably recharged. Over an extended period they deteriorate. A storage battery is fully rechargeable and can provide long, dependable service."

He was talking like a professor giving a lecture.

"Also mercury and lithium batteries or perhaps several types linked in a series with a coil to step up the voltage to the primary charge."

"How long would those batteries last?"

"Kept charged, they could function an indeterminate number of years."

"Years?"

"Beyond doubt. Your everyday industrial and heavy-duty truck batteries have a life of five to ten years."

A tiny bell rang in the laboratory. Dr. Bingham looked at his watch and stood. He tugged at his smock to straighten its snug fit.

"You'll excuse me," he said and with a quick, short stride turned into his laboratory. I lost sight of him among the equipment and counters. A door opened and closed. He was using the bell to flee?

I hurried from his office, out the exit to the Jeep, and wheeled away down the road. I turned off Route 60 onto a Henrico secondary and pushed the Jeep so hard she felt she'd fly apart.

I made it into the countryside and passed a mowed wheat

field where cars and trucks had parked and a tent was being spread. A sign painted on the side of a truck trailer read: JIMMY JOHNS, EVANGELIST.

I swerved in, bumped across the field, and stopped on the far side of the trailer. Now the Jeep couldn't be seen from the highway. I stepped out and walked over to a black man who was naked to the waist. Wearing Bermuda shorts, he pounded spikes. I lifted a sledge lying on the ground.

"Give you a hand," I said, and as he watched lifted the eight-pound sledge and hit the spike so dead on the head it sank a couple of inches into hard clay. One thing I knew was using a maul, another lesson learned at Leavenworth University.

"No money in it," he said as we began to pound the spikes using alternate strokes.

"God's money."

We developed a rhythm. Five swings from each of us, and the spikes were set deep. We moved along the line.

"You pretty good with the hammer," he said. "Work on the railroad?"

"All my live-long days."

"Praise Jesus," he said and grinned. Maybe he, too, was a university graduate. "My name's Luther."

The first state police blue-and-gray Ford LTD sped by, its lights blinking. A few moments later, several county mounties in a souped-up Malibu. They slowed to look over the area and rolled on.

"What you reckon they chasing?" Luther asked.

"They always looking for something."

"Who ain't?"

When the spikes were all sunk, we gathered to raise the tent. Jimmy Johns himself appeared. He wore white boots, a white suit, and a white Stetson.

"Have I hired you, brother?" he asked, his voice Southern country.

"Happy to lend a hand to the Lord's work," I said.

"May He bless you and keep you," Jimmy said.

More police cars passed, and a helicopter swept over, not necessarily after me, but it was possible. When we had the tent up and anchored, I helped carry folding wooden chairs inside and lined them in rows. We assembled and bolted together the pulpit platform. At the rear we stretched a red banner that had a message on it in white block letters: TAKE UP YOUR BED AND WALK.

I ate hamburgers and beans the cook provided on an outdoor grill. Two women stepped from an aluminum trailer. They wore white vests, white skirts with golden tassels, white boots, and held speckled guitars.

At twilight Luther and I lit torches on either side of the billboard proclaiming REVIVAL! Inside the tent the two women tested the PA system. Jimmy Johns himself played "Rock of Ages" with a heavy beat on an electronic organ.

Cars and pickups turned into the field. Luther, now shirted and slapping at mosquitoes, used a flashlight to direct traffic. I slipped away and drove back toward Richmond, hoping the law would believe I'd gone the other direction. At Mechanicsville I stopped at a Burger King that had two pay phones. I got change and first dialed Edward's number in hope of questioning Juno. She answered.

"It's Charles," I told her.

"Mr. Charles, I can't talk," she whispered.

"Juno, you were working for my mother at the time I was born, weren't you?"

"When she come carrying you from the mountains."

"Trying to locate my birth certificate."

"I'm hearing Miss Patricia in the other room."

"You wouldn't know anything about where it'd be?"

"Mr. Charles, don't ask me none these things."

"What things, Juno?"

"I just work in Bellerive's kitchen. What I know?"

"Juno—"

"Who's on this phone?" Patricia interrupted. "I want to know who's called this house!"

I hung up and first tried Walter Frampton's office and then his house. He picked up his phone on the fifth ring.

"You get a police report?" I asked.

"A partial copy of the state's investigation and had to talk fancy," he said. "Benson wanted to give nothing unless he got something in return, that something being your whereabouts."

"The explosive."

"I got it here in bureaucratese," Walter said. "'Examination of powder residue indicates the base charge blasting agent used was dynamite of low conflagration thirty to forty percent nitroglycerine, the remainder ammonium nitrate and wood meal of a type no longer marketed. The detonation was incurred by a primary charge of azide encapsulated in wax.'"

"Azide?" I asked, remembering what Percy and Edgar's father had told me about blasting caps.

"Right, whatever that is."

I felt a jolt of excitement. I'd also learned from the Gunner a 30/70 dynamite mixture would've produced a cool burn for its slow heaving effect, a combination once commonly used in coal mining.

"What else?" I asked. "How about wires, a timer?"

"Mortar, bricks, fragments of bakelite, plastic—"

"Hold it. Is that plastic an explosive or plastic the synthetic compound?"

"Not differentiated in the report."

"Well if the compound, it could be from a battery casing. The same for bakelite, which is also a plastic."

"No final determination on their source in the report," Walter said. "Pending."

"How about lead or lithium?"

"Lead yes, according to the report possibly a component of the detonator."

"But also possible from a storage battery."

"We playing a game of possibilities?"

"Any copper?"

"Fragments of copper and several other metals and alloys as well as rubber."

"Anything else?"

"It's not a final report. The police lab's still working items down in Richmond."

"Nothing about how the detonator was fired?"

"No."

"We got to find that out," I said and straightened as I saw a blue-and-gray Impala speed along the highway. "It's the big answer I need."

32

THROUGH THE NIGHT I drove south to North Carolina, staying off Interstates, and then turned west along winding narrow roads that led into small, drab towns where lonely lights burned in darkness.

At Oxford I spent the last of Blackie's money and part of Zeke's for gasoline, corn dogs, coffee, and a tin of Copenhagen Snuff. I continued on to Asheville, up to Abingdon, then headed north-northwest to Kentucky before turning back east to West Virginia.

I met the dawn past Bluefield and ached from the long ride. Road jolts rattled my teeth. When I passed Beckley and drew close to Shawnee County, I'd been on the road thirteen hours.

I figured if I met a roadblock, it'd be set up for people leaving the county, not anybody entering. I was part bearded, bedraggled, and drove a rattling vehicle that might've belonged up any holler and carried West Virginia plates. I could pass for a native.

I drove the mountain to Cliffside and by the town limit sign, ELEV. 3190 FT. Traffic moved, with no indication of a slowdown. Around a curve the bar-lighted Cougar waited, parked on the far side of the road. Too late for me to double back. The mountie smoked and leaned against a fender. I cocked a foot on the Jeep's door frame and slumped as if easy riding.

He watched. I kept my speed constant and spat out the side. I caught his reflection in the dirty, quivering side mirror. He looked after me but didn't get in his car or reach for a mike. I wiped palm sweat on my thighs.

I made it past the courthouse and through Cliffside, favored by meeting a green on its only stoplight. Then down the mountain, where I slowed at the Pit. The red neon tubing hadn't been switched on, and no cars in front. What day was it?

I continued on to Persimmon Creek, geared to four-wheel, and climbed the switchback path to Aunt Jessie's. The Jeep bucked and tilted. A gray fox ran across the trail toward the witch hazel thicket. It carried a rabbit in its mouth.

Below the cabin I switched off the engine and set the brake. Rattler barked, chickens and guineas raised a fuss. The dog came running and snarling at me. Aunt Jessie's Holstein grazed along the split-rail chestnut fence. I smelled smoke from the stone chimney.

She stood in the cabin's doorway. She'd taken off her bonnet, and her white hair was long, thick, and rich.

"Come sit," she said, peering at me with those blue eyes that belonged to a young face instead of buried among age's creases. "Wasn't sure I'd ever be seeing you again."

She toed open the door and hushed Rattler. The room felt hot from fireplace coals.

"Came just to visit you, Aunt Jessie," I said and sat at the table. The lamp was unlit, but I smelled kerosene. Wild daisies had been arranged in the mason jar.

"You ain't got much to do if you come just to see me," she said and settled across from me, her clawed hands dropped into her lap.

"Present for you," I said and laid the tin of Copenhagen before her on the table.

"Why, you nice to do that," she said, drawing it to her. "I been having gum itch all the long day."

"Aunt Jessie, would you again let me see that notebook of Lupi Fazio's?"

She hesitated, her eyes almost disappearing among the furrows, but stood to move in her rocking gait to her bedroom. When she opened the leather trunk, it creaked like a saddle. She brought the flimsy spiral notebook.

I turned pages first to sketches of Bellerive, the wings and different views of the house, and finally the portico. The word again, *compire*. "Compare"? While at the college I should've tried to find an Italian dictionary.

Then back to the beautifully intricate mechanical drawings, the meshed cogs, hoist wheels, driving gears, the ventilation fans, weigh scales, coke ovens, cleaning screens, water tanks, and the stone powder house.

I found rudimentary sketches of electrical hookups, yet nothing to indicate Lupi might be dealing with unusual power circuits or sources. Curled wires led nowhere. Finally the flat bean with the word *seme* beneath it. Had he been that day dreaming of a sunny Neapolitan garden?

"Aunt Jessie, I have to ask you some questions."

"Figures," she said. She'd untaped and twisted open the Copenhagen to fit a pinch of snuff between gum and cheek. She offered me the tin, and when I shook my head she snapped the lid shut.

I wondered about her hair when she was young—blond as ripe wheat I imagined, and she could've been beautiful.

"The feeling I been getting from you all along is that Lupi Fazio should be given a lot more credit than he received for putting the High Moor mine on a paying basis."

"Practically took Boss John by the hand and led him to the bank. Lupi drew up the layout for hauling coal out the mountain, sending it down to the tipple, and loading it. Built the shaker screen for sizing before washing. Designed the trolley between the tipple and the coke ovens."

"Also did the electrical work?"

"Most of it."

"I just see a few drawings of that here," I said, lifting the notebook.

"He had other drawings. They gone now. I picked up the notebook after he died. Something to remember him by. Squatters broke into the old office and used most his papers to light stove fires."

There were no dates on any drawings, no way to place them in time. I again turned pages, more slowly, unable to make sense of the mathematical notations and the Italian words, many abbreviated.

"And the first thing my father did when he came to High Moor was fix the clock."

"I told you he took it to pieces but needed Lupi to put it together."

"Lupi had to know clocks."

"He knew most things."

"And he'd ride the train down to Virginia to help work on Bellerive?"

"Now and again," she answered and tightened her lips to juice up her snuff.

Many of the mechanical drawings were detached and detailed, though apparently connected with others on the same page. I again examined sketches of Bellerive. Above a front view I made out faded tiny words: *raggio di sole*. *Sol* the Latin for sun. Something of the sun? "Rags"?

And then back to *seme*, which could be from the Latin *semen*, yes: "seed," not "bean." A seed to grow what? It had no place in the notebook. I showed the page to Aunt Jessie.

"It mean anything to you?"

"All chicken scratching to me."

"You ever see a seed like it?"

"Don't look like nothing planted 'round here."

"Aunt Jessie, about Lupi and my father. They were close friends?"

"Never'd put it 'xactly like that."

"But Lupi did everything for him."

"That ain't always friendly. Friends goes both ways."

"I don't understand what you're telling me."

"Lupi believed in Boss John, and at first they was close. If Boss John was happy, so was he. Boss John worried, Lupi's face frowned. He didn't have much. What he got came through others. Made him easy to use."

"My father used him badly?"

"Not at first maybe. Your daddy was too scared of going broke. But after money started pouring in, things changed. Lupi no longer ate so often at your daddy's table. They have a party with the Philadelphia bankers that came down to look over the High Moor operation, Lupi wasn't invited. When he went to Virginia to work, he didn't stay in the big house either but slept and mostly ate with the other hands."

Lupi in the old slave cabins my father had restored, perhaps the one I'd shared with Rajab Ishmael.

"Lupi resented that?"

"Would you? Give yourself to another man, save him at the bank, and then he gets too proud for your company. Your daddy paid him good but wasn't much inviting him in the front door."

"So they stopped being close?"

"Close ain't necessarily friends. I been close to people I'da liked to push in the gorge."

I couldn't fit it together. She seemed to be saying two things at once, and I felt her holding back. Yet she met my eyes with no evasion.

"Lupi died when?" I asked

"I told you it'll be three years come January."

"Did Lupi go to my father's funeral?"

"Nobody 'round here went. High Moor'd emptied out by then except for Lupi. Your daddy carried the money to Virginia with him and never came back to say hello. Washed his hands of us."

"People angry about it?"

"Not so much angry as hurt. All the years your daddy pretending to be everybody's best buddy and then not even sending a Christmas card once the mine closed."

"Yet Lupi'd still travel down to Virginia to work on the house. Not friendship, just the money."

"Lupi never did anything just for money. He was dog-loyal to your mama. He went to her funeral and seen you under guard and cuffed at the grave. Told me you looked hard and thin. Fretted him."

"I don't much remember anybody except my father and brothers on the other side. I wasn't allowed to stand with the family."

"Lupi seen your daddy hit you to the ground the summer you all fought. Told me he heard your daddy cuss you and shout he'd given up on you, was sorry he'd ever fathered you, hoped you'd leave and never come back. Which you kept to except for your mama's funeral."

"Why would he be fretted about how I looked?"

"I told you he thought the world of your mama and built that cradle for you he carried her in Virginia."

"When did he finish work at Bellerive?"

"Early summer after she died. Come back on the train and stayed for good."

"Aunt Jessie, you already told me I was born in Shawnee County."

"I did, and you was," she said and stood to spit in the fireplace, causing coals to sizzle and smoke.

"At a hospital in Cliffside?"

"Wasn't then no hospital in Cliffside."

"Another county?"

"No."

"At the High Moor house?"

She didn't answer but acted as if she hadn't heard. Sunlight through the doorway failed to penetrate the full depth of creases in her face. Her hands, still cupped around the Copenhagen can, could've been made of sea-leached driftwood.

"Aunt Jessie?"

"Not too far from the house," she said.

"The company infirmary?"

"Nope," she said. Just the slightest shift of eyes.

"Where then?"

"Don't make no difference to a baby where it comes into this world."

"Aunt Jessie, you slipping my questions."

"Not my job in this life to tell everything I know," she said and tightened her lip against the snuff. She looked out the doorway. The screen shredded the sunlight in which dust motes spun and drifted.

"I bad need to know."

"You wasn't born under no roof but up on the mountain. Likely near the cliffs."

"What was my mother doing there?"

"She liked to hike about."

"While she was hiking I was born prematurely?"

"I don't know nothing about premature."

"Who helped her?"

"She done it herself," Aunt Jessie said and faced me again. The eyes steadied.

"My mother delivered her own baby?"

"Most like."

"An accident?"

"Yep, an accident," she said and opened and closed one hand.

"How'd she get back to High Moor?"

"She come down in the night with the baby."

"Nobody was caring for her?"

Again Aunt Jessie turned to the doorway. Her fingers gripped the Copenhagen can, and her eyelids lowered as if the sun were too bright.

"Lupi didn't have much for all the work he did 'round High Moor," she said.

"Why you changing the subject on me?"

"My house, I change if I want. Lupi worked hard, read his books, drew his drawings. He believed in your daddy. Had your daddy, your mama, and Esmeralda. The three big things in his life."

"You lost me."

"Lupi lost too."

"I don't see a connection."

She stood and walked to the trunk. She returned and uncovered the cardboard sketch of Esmeralda. She laid it on the table. The wild girl, long tangled hair, huge brown eyes of a faun ready to flee.

"She misses Lupi," Aunt Jessie said. "Still comes down in the late evening to where he'd leave food in the little house on the post. She'd take candy from his hand. Loved them lemon drops. Everybody knew that."

I waited. She turned to me, her eyes no longer hooded but fierce.

"You determined to know everything, ain't you?"

"I got no choice."

"Another man coaxed her close. Just as you would a scared hungry cat. Toss her scraps to draw her in. Only it wasn't a cat, but Esmeralda. And one day if you was the man who'd been drinking big and had her within reach—"

She stopped as I raised my eyes from the sketch to her.

"Lupi got out his bed the first kill frost morning of October and a baby lay on the stoop of his house. It was wrapped in an old sweater he'd given Esmeralda. He heard her keening up on the mountain. He carried the baby to your mama."

"What'd my mother do with the baby?"

"She got driven to Hinton the same night, climbed on a C&O train, and took the baby down to Virginia. Your mama, daddy, and Lupi kept the child secret in High Moor, but Lupi let it slip while him and me was drinking a bottle of his persimmon wine. Before that I figured the baby'd been fathered by a hunter or 'bo along the tracks."

"My mother reared the baby down in Virginia?" I asked.

"She did."

"A boy?"

"Skinny, howling, full head of dark hair."

I looked at the sketch of Esmeralda, her dark hair, thin untamed face, and enormous eyes. She might've allowed my father to coax her close using candy because she knew or sensed Lupi trusted him.

At High Moor a baby kept secret, while in King County people believed my mother returned to Bellerive with her natural child.

I don't know what happened in the High Moor house that night, but my mother must've shamed or threatened my father into letting her keep me, and maybe Lupi, too, had something to do with forcing the decision. It explained much about the way my father had treated us over the years. My mother'd had to pay a high price.

"Lupi changed," Aunt Jessie said. "He'd always smiled and called to people. He became quiet and stayed to hisself more and more. Stopped coming to visit me or anybody."

"Yet still worked for my father?"

"Only once after your mama died."

I thought of my father facing me daily after the Christmas I witnessed what happened beyond the lighted gap of a bedroom doorway. From my birth as well I'd been a reminder of his having ravished an innocent retarded girl, my presence giving the lie to his life as a refined Virginia gentleman.

I thought, too, of Lupi deceived, outraged at my father's betrayal, Lupi a man of hot Italian blood fired by ancient genes of feud and revenge, that blood ablaze, the flames patient, devout, and above all artfully cunning.

Esmeralda my mother, and Lupi, who loved her, would've also cared for me.

33

I CHOSE A different route to return but didn't want to travel during daylight and in Marlinton found a motel. I pulled the blinds and was so tired I slept till near midnight. I gassed up, ate a sandwich, again hit the road. West of Lynchburg a trooper swept past and onward. At dawn I circled Richmond before pulling into a Texaco station to phone Walt's house.

"You again rang me out of the sack," he said.

"I'm coming in openly. Meet me at the jail."

"I'll let Rutledge know."

"Tell them not to shoot," I said.

I thought of again trying to phone Juno. Yet she could tell me little if anything I didn't already know.

I drove into King County and was less than a quarter mile across the line before I heard the siren. Cole in the black Galaxie barreled from pine shadows. He'd been waiting. The rack of blue and yellow lights flashed.

I slowed to a stop on the shoulder. He cut the Galaxie in ahead of me, sprang out crouched, and pointed his .357 S&W magnum over the top of the door.

"Slow and easy and spread 'em!" he ordered.

I obeyed. He approached and yanked my left and then my right arm behind me to clamp on the cuffs. He patted me down, spun me, and pushed me back hard against the Jeep.

"Could clean up your mess right now. Claim you tried to run. Only thing keeping me from it is I'd rather see you sizzle. I'm putting in for a front-row ticket."

"I'll see you receive a complimentary pass."

He punched me in the stomach, causing me to bow to him. The blow hurt, but not as much as if I hadn't anticipated it and tightened my belly muscles. He took my wallet, change, and Old Timer. Also the Jeep's keys.

He bent and kneed me into the Galaxie's rat-wire cage and locked the rear door before crossing around to the driver's side. He reached for the mike.

"Sonofabitch in hand," he said.

"Bring him on," Sheriff Rutledge's voice answered.

Cole heavy-footed the Galaxie to eighty before slowing at the town limit. A glimpse of the pale green Axapomimi, the King County Bank, flags raised and sagging in front of the courthouse.

Word had gotten 'round. People stood along River Street and on the courthouse steps. They walked from shops. Troopers, deputies, the sheriff, and Benson Falkoner waited. No Walter Frampton. A cameraman and reporter climbed from Channel 14's gaily painted van.

Rodger, the pigeon-toed deputy, opened the Galaxie's door. He'd drawn his 9-mm Ruger. Cole jerked me out by hair at the back of my neck. Somebody in the parking lot booed, and the crowd joined in.

"Charley, looks like you lost weight," Benson said.

"Lock him up," Rutledge said.

Cole and Rodger held my arms and moved me fast inside the jail to the cell block. The barred door waited open. They jammed me inside, banged the door closed so forcibly it rang for a time, and locked it.

"Want to see Walter Frampton," I said. I was still wearing cuffs.

"Nobody gives a diddly damn for your wants," Cole said and hitched up his uniform pants. He turned to Rodger. "Watch the prick every second."

"Best duty yet," Rodger said and unfolded a metal chair. He set it in the corridor at the front of the cell. There were no other prisoners.

"Take off the cuffs?" I asked.

"Suffer," Rodger said.

I used an elbow to release the latch that held the cot folded against the wall and sat. The steel door to the block clanged, and Cole came with Walt.

"Sure you want to talk to this piece of shit?" Cole asked.

"Life has its crosses to bear," Walt said.

Cole let him in. Walter carried his attaché case. I stood. Cole and Rodger didn't leave.

"Don't I have a right to talk to you without being overheard by them?" I asked Walt.

"You do," he said and looked at the deputies.

"I'm asking the sheriff first," Cole said and left.

"Well you been around," Walt said to me. He looked at my soiled clothes and unshaved, scabbed face. "Hope you got a good story. Cigarette?"

He fitted the Winston to my mouth and lit it with his Bic. Cole returned, aggrieved.

"We wait at the head of the block," he said. "No fucking funny stuff in there."

He and Rodger started away.

"The cuffs," I called. "Need to use the john."

"Piss down your leg," Cole said.

"Hey now, fellows," Walt said. "I'll get an order if I have to."

"Nothing but piss anyhow," Cole said and entered the cell. He unlocked the cuffs and backed off to relock the cell. He and Rodger moved away along the block.

"You got to get us out to Bellerive," I said, speaking just above a whisper.

"No chance," Walt said. "They not letting you out of this place. You're under twenty-four-hour guard."

"I know who blew the portico. If they'll take me there, I can prove it."

"Start by convincing me."

"The explosives were laid after my mother died, while I was at Leavenworth, three to four years ago when the portico was built."

"One more time," Walt said as we both glanced toward the head of the block where Cole and Rodger waited.

"An Italian immigrant from High Moor. He worked at Bellerive and had reasons to hate my father."

"That long ago he set explosives under the portico to go off at the exact time the LeBlancs gathered?"

"He knew the family well. This was to be the big celebration, two hundred and fifty years since Jean Maupin Leblanc set foot on Virginia soil. If my father hadn't gotten himself killed, he'd likely have been alive to die too."

"You're telling me an explosion could be timed that accurately?"

"Didn't need to be accurate to the minute. The LeBlanc celebrations lasted several hours. All that's necessary was a microchip timer, a heavy-duty battery, and dynamite. Checked it out with a physicist."

"You're coming at me too fast. No battery lasts that long without a charge."

"Use a voltage regulator and tap in into a basement circuit. Plus around Bellerive there were plenty of batteries on trucks and construction equipment that'd go the distance."

"You're expecting me to believe this worker could get in under the portico, set the explosives and timer, and leave them undiscovered over a period of years?"

"I believe he was the builder, drew the plans, knew every inch of space. He planted the dynamite and bricked up the area so nobody could find it."

"And you want to go to Bellerive to do what?"

"Find some evidence of a power source or connection that would've kept the battery or batteries charged."

"Benson and Rutledge won't go for that story. Neither do I."

"I came in voluntarily. I know if I'm wrong, for me it's all she wrote. They got to see that."

"They not looking to see." He tossed his cigarette into the seatless crapper, lifted his attaché case, and stepped to the cell door. "I'll do some talking, but I expect to hear laughter that'll shake this jail."

Cole let him out, cuffed me, this time at the front, and relocked the cell. Rodger had again drawn his Ruger. Cole walked Walter to the steel door.

"Ten lawyers ain't gonna help," Rodger said as he sat to watch me.

I stood above the toilet bowl and tongued out the cigarette, which had burned my lips. It hissed in the water.

"You ever see them serve up the juice down Richmond way?" Rodger asked. "When it hits, men buck so hard they break leather straps. Bones crack, skin pops, and smoke shoots out their ears. Their eyes bubble and fry behind the mask."

"Appreciate that information."

"Some fight and scream."

I unzipped my fly to take a leak.

"Do what you're doing and more," he said. "Stinks worse than butchering hogs."

34

I LISTENED TO the mill whistle, pigeons cooing, the sound of outboards cranking up and sputtering along the river. Chances were I'd never again hook a striper or drop a black duck in the blowing golden marsh. The saw blades stilled at Axapomimi Lumber.

Deputy Mary Beth Bains, gray hair pulled tight, still wearing white-beaked barn swallow earrings with her uniform, served both Rodger and me a cheese sandwich and a Dr Pepper. She avoided my eye and didn't speak.

At mid-afternoon they came—Benson Falkoner, Sheriff Rutledge, Walt, and Cole. Rodger stood from his chair. Cole unlocked the cell for Benson, Rutledge, and Walt to enter. He and Rodger kept hands on their pistols' butts.

"Well, Charley, you tell quite a tale," Benson said, his drooping, ruddy flesh soft and shiny. His seersucker jacket had sweat stains under the arms. "You ever thought of taking up scribbling books? Science fiction I mean."

"Just ride me out to Bellerive a few minutes."

"But that'd hurt our feelings," Rutledge said. He ran a finger along the side of his nose. The Panama he'd tipped back had left a red horizontal stripe across his forehead.

"I gave up voluntarily," I said.

"With my help," Cole said from the corridor. "And Mr. Smith and Wesson's."

"I didn't resist arrest."

"Ain't the way I saw it happen," Cole said.

"Take me to Bellerive and I'll show you what blew that portico. You want it right, don't you?"

"We heard from Walter," Benson said.

"A real good yarn," Rutledge said.

"I contend the law has a duty to check it out," Walt said.

"Don't particularly want any more duties," Benson said. "Trouble Charley's caused."

"About run the county out of money," Rutledge said.

"If you don't comply," Walt said, "I promise the Commonwealth's failure to do so will be vigorously pursued in court."

The first time I'd heard that tone and an element of belief from Walt.

"Your job, not mine," Benson said.

"The State Police Investigator's report mentioned plastic and bakelite fragments in residue of the explosion," I said.

"So?" Benson asked.

"What were they?" I asked.

"Could've been an old cup or thermos," Rutledge said. "Something the workers discarded or forgot."

"Or a battery case," I said.

"Shot in the dark," Benson said.

"What about the traces of rubber, lead, copper, other metals?" I asked.

"Nails, an old shovel, anything left or tossed under the portico when it was closed up," Benson said.

"Why was it closed up? Wouldn't it make sense to leave passage for ventilation?"

"Sense ain't always the order of the day," Rutledge said.

"There's ventilation slits in the brick," Benson said. "Nothing more necessary."

"And the lead?" I asked.

"Lead's common and don't make it a battery," Rutledge said.

"Plus the cap was lead azide," Benson said.

"A cap ought to be demolished," I said. "The insides of a battery would be partly protected by the casing."

"Solder," Rutledge said.

"What'd need soldering under the portico?"

"Water pipe to a faucet," Cole said.

"Is there a faucet?" I asked Benson.

He hesitated, then "No."

"There was something else though," Walt said.

"Not of consequence," Benson said.

"In my situation everything's of consequence," I said.

"Traces of fiberglass," Walt said. "Could be insulation."

"You didn't tell me about any insulation," I said.

"At the moment that didn't seem significant."

"What would the insulation be used for if there's no water pipe under there?" I asked.

"What's it always used for?" Benson asked. "To insulate."

"No need to insulate under the portico," I said. "It's not living space and already bricked off from the basement and rest of the house."

"The insulation could've been packed around dynamite," Benson said.

"Why if the dynamite was set to go off in a day, week, even a month?" I asked. "Dynamite don't have to be kept warm or dry for that span of time. Same with a metal or waxed cap used as the detonator. But if it was meant to explode years later, it'd make sense to pack it against moisture and cold. And insulation around a battery would help maintain its charge during freezing weather."

"Boy's got imagination, I'll hand him that," Rutledge said.

"Plenty of time to make up a bunch of stories where he's been and going," Benson said. "Least till they pull the switch."

"There had to be some kind of electrical connection from house current to the battery," I said. "My guess is we'll find it searching the basement."

"His guess," Rutledge said and looked at Benson.

"The basement's already been inspected by experts," Benson said.

"But they didn't know exactly what to look for," I said. "Lupi was a clever man."

"Lupi?" Benson asked. "The I-talian?"

"Lupi Fazio," I said. "I've seen his drawings. I believe he designed and built the portico as well as had the opportunity and ability needed to set the dynamite."

They stared, not believing. Maybe not even Walt did fully. I raised my hands to them, palms up, a plea.

"If I'm wrong, you won't have any trouble killing me," I said.

Benson gazed at Rutledge. A hot breeze blew in the shrill and chimes of Axapomimi Lumber's sawmill blades. Rutledge spat into the crapper. They nodded to each other.

"Cuffs on," Rutledge said. "Shackles too."

AS COLE AND Rodger walked me along the corridor and from the jail, they gripped my arms. The clanking shackles required short, shuffling steps. They locked me in the Galaxie. Rodger drove, and Cole, his .357 drawn, sat half-turned to watch me. Ahead, Benson and Rutledge rode in the sheriff's silver Oldsmobile 88. Walt followed in his VW.

"You getting lots of the poor taxpayers' money spent on you," Rodger said.

"At least electric don't cost much," Cole said. "Real bargain in this case."

Bellerive's gates were closed and padlocked. Rutledge had the key. We drove the winding drive, branches of the black walnut trees hanging listlessly over the road, the leaves already yellowing. I looked across pasture to the restored slave cabins and thought of Lupi hatching his plan.

The second set of gates was also locked. Grass needed mowing, and flowers of the garden had tipped and dropped petals and blooms. Roses dragged the ground. Periwinkle climbed among the box bushes. Something had overturned the sundial. Torn yellow police tape fluttered, and a flicker rapped the plywood of a boarded-up window. The bird flew to the top of a water oak.

Cole and Rodger jerked me from the cage so fast I'd have fallen, shackled, without their grip.

Rutledge had a tagged key to the side door under the porte-cochere. When he opened it, a cool stream of lifeless, mildewed air flowed from the house. Cole entered first. He knew the location of the circuit box in the pantry and closed breakers to switch on lights. A single chandelier burned in the back hall. White shrouds covered furniture in dusk of undamaged rooms.

"What now?" Rutledge asked as we stood on the landing between the English basement and the first floor.

"Check the wall separating the front of the house from the space under the portico," I said.

"Acts like he's running the show," Cole said.

"Let's get it done and over," Benson said.

Rodger opened the basement door. The steps were narrow. Heart-of-pine beams exposed the rough, ancient strokes of an adze.

A feeble sun shone through smeared windowpanes. Cole cut on lights.

We walked through what we'd called the game room. It contained a stone fireplace, a pool table, and a cleaning bench for the sporting guns that'd been kept in racks—L. C. Smiths, Parkers, Lefevers. The racks were empty. From a ceiling beam hung a pair of bobwhites I'd mounted. I was surprised my father and John had left them all these years.

"Where next?" Rutledge asked.

I shuffled toward the furnace room. Cole looked for a light. I remembered the switch—over the doorway instead of beside it. We crossed past the great boiler that had provided steam heat to Bellerive, first using coal and apparently later converted to oil. I'd learned to roller-skate on the concrete floor around the furnace. During winters when I returned wet from duck hunting along the Axapomimi I'd often come here to undress and thaw out before laying my clothes over hot pipes to dry.

Behind the furnace, another room once used for storage of implements, fertilzers, seeds, sprays my mother had needed in her garden. Cole found the drop string to the ceiling's single low-watt bulb. There remained rows of clay flowerpots, a rake, a watering can. The space still smelled of soil and bone meal.

The front wall of the room divided it from the area beneath the destroyed portico. Bellerive's double courses of brick had not buckled or given to the blast.

"Okay, what we searching for?" Rutledge asked.

"No major damage to the wall," I said.

"Meaning?" Benson asked.

"You'd think we'd find loose bricks, broken mortar, maybe a bulge," I said.

"We'd think?"

"Unless the dynamite was directed upward under the portico by a person who knew explosives and set them in a shaped hole to do the job. And the wall's been changed. There used to be a small, low-doored passageway that gave out under the old veranda. It's been closed up. You can see where by the bricks with a lighter cast."

"To support weight of the portico's columns and slate floor, it's likely the foundation would've been bricked up and reinforced," Benson said.

"This wall carries no weight of the portico and wouldn't need to be reinforced by closing the passageway," I said. "But what if somebody hid something underneath he meant to make sure nobody found?"

"You making things up as you go along?" Benson asked.

"Just tell us what we're searching for," Rutledge said.

"A wire or conduit. It'd feed through the wall somewhere to what was a battery or batteries under the portico. Probably insulated copper."

"Another probably," Cole said. "He's stalling."

"Let's check the wall," I said. "Any slight opening could be it."

"Give the man a chance," Walt said and adjusted his glasses to squint at the wall.

"Yeah, do it," Rutledge said. "Too dark in here. Get the flashlights."

Rodger left for the flashlights and came back. He and Cole shone them on the wall. I raised my cuffed hands and ran fingers horizontally across bricks.

"It don't make sense," Cole said. "The only power source reaching this far would be a line from the ceiling fixture. There's no splice to a feed-off."

"Keep looking," Benson said. "Let's lock this thing up tit tight."

Walt searched beside me, careful of his khaki suit. I stooped and felt along the junction of the wall with the concrete floor. No hole or breach. The others began to slack off.

I asked for a flashlight. Rutledge nodded, and Rodger handed me his. I methodically followed the mortar joints of every course of bricks.

"Got to be here," I said.

"No it don't," Rutledge said.

"The ceiling next," I said. "He might've drilled through the floor joists."

Rodger took the flashlight back, and he and Cole shone them along the heart-of-pine joists and subflooring. We moved about with raised hands. Lupi Fazio, the mechanical genius, would've had a artful way of rigging the wiring to keep it from being discovered and leading back to him.

"Zero," Benson said and lowered his hands from a sill to dust them.

"The floor," I said. "He could've laid a conduit under the concrete."

Flashlights shone at the floor.

"This concrete ain't new," Cole said. "You can look at it and see it's been here a bunch of years. If he'd laid wire under it, patching would show."

I let down on my knees and rubbed fingertips across the coarse grit of the floor. I swept away shards of a broken flowerpot as I moved forward and bowed to within inches of the concrete.

The others watched. Even Walt had quit. He'd pulled out his handkerchief to wipe his hands.

"All right," Benson said, "enough."

"The power source didn't have to feed in from down here," I said. "It could've originated upstairs."

"Just shitting us," Cole said.

"What can a few more minutes hurt?" Walt asked, but he sounded disheartened.

"My feelings," Cole said.

We walked back through the basement, up the steps, and into the hallway. I rattled along in shackles.

"What you want us to do?" Benson asked.

"Go through the front rooms and see if we can find a wire spliced from a wall fixture down through the floor," I said.

"That's crazy," Rutledge said. "John LeBlanc or somebody in the family would've noticed."

"Inside the wall it wouldn't show," I said. "Check all the outlets."

"We going to keep listening to him?" Cole asked.

"Screwdriver," Benson said to Rodger, and Rodger left.

Shoes ground plaster. Some wiring had already been exposed by the blast. Cole twisted his knife blade to remove a white socket plate over a parlor outlet. When Rodger returned, he carried two screwdrivers. He and Rutledge used them. No splices found.

"Upstairs front," I said.

"Just do it," Rutledge told Cole before he could bitch.

Aroused dust of broken plaster hazed the air of the master bedroom. Two outlets on each wall. Rodger and Cole detached the plates and shone the flashlights into the receptacles. Again nothing. The same in my mother's sewing room. I looked at the cradle Lupi had made for her.

"Satisfied?" Benson asked. He brushed bits of plaster from shoulders of his seersucker.

"Outside," I said, but hope drained. "Could be wiring nobody noticed."

"He ain't never going to be satisfied," Cole said.

"Have us looking on the moon," Rodger said.

"Got to leave anyhow," Walt said. "Circle the house while we're doing it."

We left by the porte-cochere door, which Cole relocked. He and Rodger held my arms as we all walked around the house checking the brick exterior. Only ground wires to lightning rods and two electric lines stretching from the transformer on a power pole beyond the serpentine wall to the house connection under the kitchen's eaves. No indication of tampering.

It was finished. Either I was wrong or Lupi had been too smart to be beaten. I slogged along, the shackles chafing my ankles. When I stumbled taking too long a step, Rodger and Cole righted me roughly.

"Party's over," Benson said, his face flushed and sweat-beaded.

35

I SAGGED AS they moved me to the Galaxie. Rodger and Cole dumped me in the cage. Engines fired up, and Rutledge's Olds, antenna whipping, led the way down the lane. Walter brought up the rear.

As we drove away I looked back at Bellerive—my last view. The house stood red in sunlight but already had an aspect of loss and desolation—the overgrown garden, the rear windows stark and sightless, a quick glittering reflection off the piebald weather vane enclosed by ironwork on the roof's crown.

Wait a second. What was there to cause a reflection? The piebald stallion had been added after I left Bellerive and appeared in Lupi's notebook—the front sketch of the house with portico completed. Again a flicker of light from the vane. After all these years there'd be no gloss unless recently repainted.

I remembered tiny handwritten Italian along the sketch's top. *Sol.* The Latin word for sunlight. *Raggio di sol.* Then *seme,* from the Latin *semen* or "seed," alone on a page with the drawing of a pale flat bean. But *semen* was also another kind of seed, the planting of a child and posterity.

Raggio di sol. Something of the sun. Rags of the sun? Tatters? I could think of no Latin derivation. *Seme* and the drawing of a bean.

Beans. Beams. Sunbeams. *Raggio* equals "rays." In the bay I'd fished past channel markers a hundred times, their blinking lights battery-powered and kept charged by canted flat panels of solar cells.

"Stop and go back," I said. "I saw something."

"No dice," Cole answered and raised the .357.

"It's got to be," I said.

"Won't work," Rodger said.

I turned to the rear window and Walter in his VW. I waved, twisted to my knees, pressed my face and hands to the glass. I banged my palms, head, and cuffs hard against it.

"Hey, fuckface, turn around," Cole ordered.

"I'm telling you I know," I said and kept pounding the glass. I began yelling.

"You listen and I ain't bird turding," Cole said and aimed the .357 at me.

"Shoot, goddammit, if you won't stop."

Rodger slowed the Galaxie, and Walt, his horn honking, pulled alongside. I was still waving. Benson and Rutledge halted at the left side of the lane.

"I'll do it," Cole warned again and rapped the revolver's barrel against the rat wire.

Rodger braked the Galaxie. Walt legged out of the VW and bent to my window.

"What?" he called.

"Gone ape on us," Cole hollered to Rutledge, who jogged toward the car and held to his Panama. "I'll put my twitch on him."

"I KNOW," I shouted at Walt.

"You gonna be sorry," Rodger said. He'd drawn a baton from the floor.

"What's the problem?" Benson asked, puffing along behind Rutledge.

"Ape!" Cole said.

"Take me back and I'll show you how Lupi did it," I hollered.

"Want me to subdue him?" Rodger asked. He pushed out of the Galaxie and whacked the baton against the roof.

"I'll handle it!" Cole said and had the twitch off his belt ready to clamp on my wrist.

"I'm telling you I see how he did it," I pleaded with Benson and Rutledge.

"He's bulling again," Cole said. "Let me turn him off."

"I'll bring him to heel," Rodger said and again banged the baton against the Galaxie's roof.

"Hit him and I'll make a complaint to the court on his behalf," Walt said.

"Everybody quiet down," Rutledge ordered. He pointed at me. "You too."

I did. I brought my knees forward and sat obediently.

"All right," Rutledge said, "what you got?"

"It's in the attic," I said.

"Shitting us," Cole said.

"Shut up," Rutledge told him.

"Drive him back," Walt said. "You owe him that."

"Don't nobody owe him nothing!" Cole said. He held the twitch in one hand, the .357 in the other.

"I told you to shut it up!" Rutledge said.

"If you won't take him back now, I'll come with an independent investigator," Walt said. "And if we find evidence ignored, it'll appear the Commonwealth was negligent in its duty."

"You watch how you talk, son," Benson said.

"Big-ass college boy scaring us to death," Cole said and spat.

"I got to hit you in the mouth to make you shut up?" Rutledge asked Cole. He knuckled back his Panama and looked to Benson. "Already wasted a hunk of day. Another ten minutes can't end the world."

"All right, if it'll finish this mess once and for all eternity," Benson said.

They got in the cars, and we turned around at the tractor road to the hay barn. Cole unlocked the gate. We again drew up under the porte-cochere.

Cole and Rodger held hard to me as we entered. I felt their anger through their fingers. We climbed the damaged and plaster-strewn grand staircase to the second floor and the confined steps to the third—servants' quarters used in my time by Juno and Gaius.

"How you get to the attic?" Rodger asked, looking at the ceiling.

"Juno's room," I said and showed them. I'd played in the attic as a boy and remembered her closet held a ladder that led to a ceiling trapdoor. The room was empty except for a pile of aged *Life* magazines and a bare iron cot.

Rodger opened the closet. Two empty coat hangers hung on the rack in front of the ladder.

"Take a look-see," Rutledge ordered Rodger.

Rodger climbed the ladder and pushed open the trapdoor. It fell over with a crash, and dust spiraled and drifted downward.

"Too dark," Rodger called.

They hadn't brought flashlights. While Cole held me, Rodger ran down for them. Benson began to sneeze. Fear chunked around my belly. Cole felt my trembling and smirked.

Rodger came back carrying the flashlights. He gave one to Cole and again mounted the ladder. Half his body disappeared into the attic. He, too, began sneezing as he played the light around. He climbed higher and vanished beyond the rectangular darkness.

"See anything?" Rutledge called.

"Dirt daubers," Rodger answered.

"Let me show him," I said.

"Watch it," Cole ordered and held me back.

"I'm sending Charley boy up," Rutledge hollered to Rodger. Then to Cole, "You follow. Don't let him kick you."

"Let him try," Cole said.

The ladder's steps were too far apart for me to climb wearing shackles.

"Take them off," Rutledge ordered.

Cole glared as he knelt to unlock the shackles. He tossed them back into the room where they clanked to the floor and spumed more dust.

"Any lights up there?" Benson called to Rodger.

"Not I been able to find," Rodger answered, his voice distant. He walked, and floorboards creaked.

"Any power?" Rutledge asked.

"Don't see no wiring," Rodger answered.

Benson and Rutledge gazed at me.

"There's power," I said.

"Nothing but dirt dauber nests," Rodger hollered.

"Okay, here he comes," Rutledge called. Then to me, "Git."

I climbed the ladder, my wrists still cuffed. Cole followed. As I crawled over into darkness, I felt the sun's heat on the slate roof. Rodger shone his flashlight at me. The disturbed dirt daubers pinged the ceiling. Their broken pods lay on broad, undressed planks and crunched under our feet. Cole stood behind me, his flashlight in my back.

"Anything?" Benson called from below.

"Bat shit," Rodger answered.

"Let me use the light," I said, coughing from aroused dust, and held out my hands to Rodger.

"No chance," Rodger said, still sneezing.

"Then shine it where I tell you," I said.

"Look who's giving orders."

I shuffled toward the center of the attic. I had to bend under oak trusses that'd been numbered using Roman numerals when Bellerive was built. Stale air drew hot into my lungs.

"Point your lights up," I said.

"Why, what we looking for?" Rodger asked.

"A hole he can crawl through," Cole said. He, too, was sneezing and coughing.

"The base of the weather vane," I said.

I searched the roof where the vane should be bolted through.

"Shine along here," I told them.

"Funny how he can tell us what to do," Cole said.

"Like we work for him," Rodger said.

They missed it with the first sweeps of their flashlights.

"Slower this time," I said and glimpsed a metallic sheen. I stood under it. "Both lights there."

"Say please," Cole said.

I said "please." They focused their lights on the six iron bolts capped by hexagonal nuts. But where was the wire? God, let there be wire. I couldn't find it in the dazzle against the boards.

"Ease off a little," I said—and remembered: "Please."

They drew the lights away but there was still no wire.

"Hold me up—please," I said to Rodger.

"Hell no," he answered. He was coughing.

"It's no trick, I got cuffs on, and I need to see closer," I said.

"I don't like touching you," Rodger said and turned to Cole. "What you think?"

"I think I'll shoot him through the ass if he tries anything," Cole said.

Rodger handed his flashlight to me. Cole again held his .357. Rodger moved behind, gripped me around my thighs, and lifted. I was coughing, and my eyes watered. I shone the light on the bolts. Jesus, no wire.

"A little higher," I told Rodger. "Please."

"Shit on you," he said but heaved me upward so hard my head bumped a truss.

Nothing. Or did a slightly different hue parallel the wood's grain? My fingertips traced a barely discernible ridge. I blinked to clear my runny eyes and held the light right at it. A thin brown insulated wire was grooved into the ceiling and burrowed toward the attic's west wall.

"Got it," I said.

"What's happening?" Rutledge called. His head appeared above the trapdoor.

"Got what?" Rodger asked and let me drop hard.

"Power source."

I stood pointing, my hands and body shaking. We were coughing, our eyes running, the dirt daubers zooming around.

"What you showing us?" Cole asked. He fingered shut one nostril to blow snot from the other.

"The stallion," I said.

"You claiming—?" Rutledge asked. He'd climbed the rest of the way up and clomped toward us. Walt, too, rose on the ladder.

"Just follow the light," I said and tracked the nearly veiled wire along the ceiling beneath trusses to the side of the attic where it angled down between bricks and lathing.

"You see it, don't you?" I asked them.

"How's a weather vane produce power?" Rutledge asked.

"Solar cells," I said. "The stallion's been imbedded with them."

"No lead-pipe cinch," Rutledge said. "The wire could be a ground."

"Too small," I said. "Would burn out grounded, and the vane's protected by lightning rods surrounding it. This wire's hidden. No reason to bring a ground into an attic and hide it. The stallion ought to be still producing current. Easy to prove with a voltmeter."

"Prove what?" Benson asked. He'd come up and was holding a handkerchief over his nose. He sneezed into it.

"The solar cells kept the battery charged up over the years," I said. "The battery in turn provided current to the timer and the voltage needed to set off a detonator to fire the dynamite."

They gathered under the vane and followed my flashlight beams tracing the wire to the side of the attic.

"Well goddamn, there is something," Rutledge said.

"Hold it," Benson said. "Even if the vane's the power source, that doesn't absolve you. You still could've done it."

"The only time I came back to Bellerive was under guard for my mother's funeral," I said. "They were doing work at the front of the house, maybe the portico, but it wasn't finished, and the roof had no weather vane."

"You could've snuck back after prison," Benson said. "While living at the inlet."

"Sure, with John, his family, and servants in the house I climbed up ladders to bolt down and wire the vane and somehow dug under the portico to rig battery, timer, and dynamite."

"Coulda been times since you got out of prison when nobody was in the house—or vacationing—or maybe you had inside help," Rutledge said.

"Shit," Cole said and blew snot from the second nostril.

"What?" Rutledge asked, coughing.

"He wont here. Me and my daddy was mixing and hauling mud for the little I-talian bossing the job. Particular about anybody touching things. Let us go and laid the last courses of portico brick hisself. We figured he was trying to save LeBlanc dollars."

Cole hated saying it. He didn't want it to be true.

"He install the weather vane on the roof?" I asked.

"Yeah, a little wop," Cole said.

36

THEY HELD ME in jail that night but treated me more like a guest than a prisoner. I got a shower, a soft clean towel, white soap, and Mary Beth Bains served me mashed potatoes, black-eyed peas, and meat loaf buried under fried onions and beef gravy. For dessert I received chess pie along with all the coffee I could drink.

In the morning Rodger banged in, yet didn't fasten on the cuffs. We walked side by side to Rutledge's office, not to the windowless room used for interrogations. Benson and Walt snuffed out cigarettes as I entered.

Rutledge sat at his desk. He'd taken off his Panama and hung it on a hat rack. His wiry red hair was wet-combed, the furrows deep and rigid. His smile lifted the left corner of his lips.

"Hope you got some sleep, Charley," he said and offered me a seat.

"Can't tell you how glad the Commonwealth and I personally are that the complexion of events has changed," Benson said.

"You letting me go?" I asked. The chair I sat in had a foam rubber pad on it—a place of honor. Maybe they feared I'd sue.

"Like to go over a couple of things once more," Benson said. "If it's all right with you, we'll record it."

I looked at Walt, who held his attaché case on his lap.

"I'll speak up if I deem there's anything you shouldn't answer," Walt said.

"Good," Benson said and switched on the machine. The reels spun.

The office window was half raised and flies clotted the screen. A fan whirred, feebly pushing the sluggish, humid air. Three men stood outside by a blue Plymouth in the parking lot.

"Newshounds," Rutledge explained. "Wanting to get at you."

"There'll be more," Walt said.

"We'll sneak you out another door if you want," Benson said.

"We got the weather vane down," Rutledge said. "Fire department helped us out. All the spots on that piebald are photovoltaic cells sunk into the metal and wired. Beautiful work, like a jeweler's. State Lab checked the vane. Expect they'd like to hold it. They maintain a police museum down in Richmond for unusual items used in the commission of crimes."

"Probably ask you for it," Benson said.

"That's brother Edward's call," I said. "Doubt he'll agree."

"Well, can't blame him for wanting to protect the family name," Rutledge said. "Also found the wire leading in under the portico. The I-talian chiseled a pencil-size channel along the west inner edge of the basement to the charge. Concreted it over, then rubbed and ground grit and pieces of a broken clay flowerpot on top the channel to tint it to the surrounding surface."

"Impossible to find without breaking up the floor," Benson said. "The point is the Commonwealth's satisfied you couldn't have been 'round to blow the portico. No way you can be connected. Thing we'd like to know is why the little Italian went to all that trouble."

"Before he answers, the Commonwealth should declare it intends to release Charles MacKay LeBlanc and absolve him of all pending charges," Walt said. "Furthermore it should be stipulated that any statement he makes from this point forward will not be used by the Commonwealth to pursue an indictment against him in regard to the August sixteen explosion at Bellerive and the deaths of John Maupin LeBlanc III and his family."

"Damn, you sound like a big-time Richmond lawyer," Rutledge said.

"He's right to ask it," Benson said. "The Commonwealth hereby releases Charles MacKay LeBlanc from accountability in the afore-mentioned matter of the Bellerive-LeBlanc homicides and waives all rights to prosecute because of any statement given during this transcription."

"Good enough," Walt said and again nodded to me.

"All right," Benson said. "This little Italian, Lupi Fazio, why'd he do it?"

"My father betrayed him," I said.

"How?"

"Something that happened out at High Moor years ago."

"Be more detailed?"

"In the beginning they were close and Lupi believed in my father."

"What happened to change it?"

"Don't know," I lied. "Could've involved money. Most things do."

"If he hated your daddy so bad, how come he didn't just shoot or knife him?" Benson asked. "Why go to all the trouble of wiring the weather vane, battery, and dynamite to go off so long a time afterwards?"

"And take out your brother John and his family, who according to Edward had little or nothing to do with him?" Rutledge asked.

"He intended to get Edward too," I said. "The broken timing belt on Edward's car delayed him. If he hadn't been late, they'd all been wasted."

"Whyn't Lupi include you?" Rutledge asked.

"I was at Leavenworth when he set the charge."

"But why would Fazio want to assassinate your brothers and their families and not your father?" Benson asked.

"He meant to kill my father, who had the tractor accident that ended his life after the portico was built and sealed up. Fazio was complicated, a brilliant self-taught engineer from southern Italy where vengeance runs hot and is tied to honor. He must've brooded on whatever injury he believed my father did him, nursed his hate, and planned like the artist he was."

"Still don't understand why he just didn't go on and murder your father direct," Rutledge said.

"Nothing simple and direct would've satisfied Lupi. First he needed to protect himself. A long time span covered that. Second, there had to be ingenuity, for that's how Lupi was built. Third, because of his big hate the vengeance would have to be the worst thing he could think up to do to a man who'd become haughty about the LeBlancs, their name, the family lineage, on the two-hundred-and-fiftieth-year celebration of themselves."

"Which was?" Benson asked.

"What greater injury could be inflicted on a believer in dynasty than to end his line?"

"But you're still living."

"I'm the black sheep, the only LeBlanc meant to be left, a felon and disgrace to the name. Lupi's last twist of the screw."

I didn't believe that. During the night I'd run it through my mind. The court-martial board had sentenced me to fifteen years at Leavenworth. Lupi hadn't figured on a release two years early for good time. He'd thought I'd still be locked up and thus provided with an alibi. He'd allowed me to live not to shame the LeBlanc escutcheon—*Validus et Fides*—but because I was Esmeralda's son and had awarded me life out of his reverence for her.

"You talk like you knew this Lupi," Benson said.

"Heard lots about him. An old woman out in West Virginia told me about him and showed me his drawings."

"Where in West Virginia?" Benson asked. "In case the Commonwealth needs a deposition."

"Near Cliffside, Shawnee County. Name of Aunt Jessie Arbuckle. Everybody knows her. Treat her right, she's a fine lady."

"You ever know me not to treat a lady right?" Benson asked.

"You don't got any idea what your daddy actually did to this Lupi that could make him so mad he'd kill wholesale?" Rutledge asked.

I shook my head. Walt eyed me. No mention made of a nonexistent birth certificate. I'd not serve that one up for them, and hoped it'd never need to surface.

"Maybe we'll run it down in time," Benson said.

I doubted that. They wouldn't learn from Aunt Jessie.

"Lupi musta blown a brain gasket too," Rutledge said.

Yeah, I thought, he'd cared about a young retarded girl he'd taught to take lemon drops from his hand.

"You releasing Charles now?" Walt asked Benson.

"Look, we'd like him to stay around town a few more days," Benson said. "I've already stated the Commonwealth's dropping any action against him. Just to help us out if more questions arise."

"But he's not required to stay?" Walt asked. "We want that understood."

"We don't mean to make it no harder for him than what he's already been through," Rutledge said.

"He's a free man as far as the Commonwealth's concerned," Benson said and switched off the recorder. "Anything we can do to make it easier for you, Charley, let us know."

He held out his hand, and I shook it. Rutledge's likewise. Why not? All I wanted was to be gone.

As I left, Cole stood by the Coke machine in the squad room

and threw darts at the badly punctured Ayatollah Khomeini. Cole wouldn't meet my eye.

The reporters waited—two from newspapers, one from Richmond's Channel 14 TV. They tried to question me while a photographer scampered about aiming a shoulder camera.

"He has no statement," Walt kept telling them as we walked to his VW. When we drove out of the parking lot, he turned his head to me. "If you sticking around a while, I got an extra bed and beer in the fridge."

He drove me to the apartment he rented—half the first floor of a white, gabled Victorian house that had a veranda around three sides.

I remembered the house, owned by Miss Mabel Tascott, who'd been my teacher in third grade and spanked me hard across the back of my legs with a stiff wooden ruler for looking up the dress of a little girl named Rosemary Bondurant.

Walt showed me a room and a mahogany double bed, the posts and headboard carved with vines and grape clusters. A peahen fan covered the fireplace. The Seth Thomas clock on the mantel had stopped running. A bay window gave out onto a rose garden.

"Use the kitchen anytime you want," Walt said. "Besides beer, there's sandwich meat and frozen pot pies."

He led me to his living room where he had a desk, a horsehair settee, a typewriter, and a rabbit-ear TV. Papers and legal quarterlies lay about on the desk and radiator covers. Etched globes of a chandelier had been converted from gas to electricity.

"Plenty of newspapers, books, magazines," Walt said. "Anything you want, call me at the office and I'll bring it or have it sent over."

"You treating me high style."

"I guarantee you'll be collecting on the insurance," he said. "I'd also like you to think I've developed some regard for you and am not doing this altogether for the recovery."

"I'll think it," I said.

He started to leave me and turned back.

"You won't run out on me, will you, Charles?" he asked.

"Not without a croaker sack full of dollars," I said.

37

I SLEPT, HAD a bath, shaved. My face was still bruised, but the scabs had flaked off. I walked naked to the kitchen where I opened a can of sardines, dumped them into a bowl, and sliced a fresh tomato and onion over them. I shook on pepper, garlic salt, and Italian dressing. I drank two of Walt's Coors.

The Richmond newspaper lay on the living-room desk. I glanced through it and found nothing about myself. I tried TV and heard my name as well as an announcement of a news conference at the King County courthouse. I switched off the set.

I drew on a pair of Walt's khaki shorts and a white T-shirt before walking barefooted to the veranda where I sat in a fan-back wicker chair and looked out under pin oaks and a pecan tree to the street. A still, hot day, the heat sticky, the air wavy. Locusts sounded energy-drained. Two boys walking slowly toward the river tried to keep to strips of oak shade. They carried fishing poles. How long had it been since I'd sat on a porch and felt free? I didn't really feel it now.

Miss Mabel Tascott emerged from her side of the house willed to her by her father, a school principal. She was gray-haired, erect, brittle, surely yet a spinster. Despite the heat she wore hose and a blue dress closed high at the neck by a cameo brooch. She held a long-spouted green can to water plants in pots and jars arranged along the porch railing. There were also hanging baskets drooping multicolored blooms. She didn't realize I sat there till she had trouble reaching a basket.

"Do it for you, Miss Mabel?" I asked.

I'd startled her, and she stepped back alarmed, her small mouth rounded as if for a kiss. She studied my face carefully.

"Charles LeBlanc," she said, holding the can close to her breasts as if fearful I might seize it from her. She looked at my bare feet. "I taught you, or tried to."

"I remember. I'm staying with Walter."

"You never behaved in class."

"I'm sorry. Trying to do better now."

"I loved your mother."

"Most everybody did."

"She had magic fingers with roses. And she could make peonies grow on concrete."

"Let me reach the basket for you."

She allowed me to water her begonias. I gave back the empty can.

"How long will you be staying?" she asked.

"Be gone soon."

"You were a bad boy, but I never believed you did that awful thing at Bellerive." She smiled. "I'm glad you're here. I want you to feel at home."

"Miss Mabel, think you could find me an Italian dictionary?"

"You're studying Italian?"

"Just a few words I need to look up."

"I'll try the school library. It's not open, but I'll borrow the key from Amos Boatwright. He's superintendent now."

During the afternoon I drank another beer and slept. When the phone rang in the living room the first time, I didn't answer it. The second series of rings, I did.

"Reporters bothering you?" Walt asked.

"Not so far."

"They've been here and are roaming about searching."

"Keep them off if you can."

"There's somebody else. Your brother Edward. Called and wants to drive over from Richmond to see you."

I started to say no, but then thought, Why not let it all play out? I told Walt to send him on but make sure no reporters followed.

Miss Mabel returned a while later with a small, musty dictionary that had been published in 1934. Not much use for Italian around Jessup's Wharf. First I looked up *raggio*. "Ray" or "beam." *Raggio di sol* equaled "sunbeams." Next *seme*. "Seed," yes, but also "origin" and "race." Finally *compire*: "to finish," "to perfect." I thought about that one. To finish what, the line of the LeBlancs? To perfect a plan that would accomplish that end?

I'd never know for sure, except that Lupi had finished things all right. I returned the dictionary to Miss Mabel, and as I drank a tall glass of her iced tea on the veranda, the black Audi 5000S drew up in pin-oak shade. Edward stepped out carefully, glanced toward the house, and ran a hand over his thin blond hair. He wore a light gray summer suit, white shirt, wine-colored tie. He'd been enclosed by air-conditioning and appeared crisp. He hesitated before coming along the brick walk, his stoop causing his jacket to bunch slightly around his shoulders.

I let him climb the steps to the veranda before I stood. He wore his scholarly glasses. His skin had always been fair and unblemished, causing him to sunburn easily.

"I heard on the news," he said. "Phoned and talked to the Commonwealth Attorney."

"Want to sit?"

"Yes, thanks," he said but looked at the wicker chairs as if he believed they might soil his trousers. He let himself down cautiously.

"Can offer you a beer," I said.

"No thanks and I'm very sorry for the way I've treated you, Charles. In fact I'm mortified."

"Haven't heard anybody use the word *mortified* in many a day."

"Particularly for how I acted the last time I saw you at the house."

He wore the gold signet ring with the LeBlanc crest. It'd been passed down to the eldest living son for generations. The undertaker must've drawn it from John's finger.

"I want to redress the way you've been treated," Edward said. "I suppose you've heard Bellerive's mine through the terms of John's will."

"Yeah."

"I plan to sell it. Already received inquiries."

"Valuable land."

"You don't want it, do you?"

"Me?" I asked and almost laughed. "Rather be shackled again."

"I didn't think so. I don't either. I've become a city person. Always have been, though country-reared. The place has no meaning to Patricia and my daughter and now holds particularly unpleasant associations for me. I'll put Bellerive on the market, and when sold I'll see you receive a share of the proceeds."

"Very generous."

"We are brothers," he said.

I thought of revealing to him we were brothers only by half. It would mean nothing now. Let him believe in our father's goodness. The whistle sounded at Axapomimi Lumber and raised the locusts to a screeching frenzy.

"What did Dad do to that Italian to cause so much hate?" Edward asked.

"No idea. Probably never find the answer."

Edward looked out at his Audi, which glimmered even in

shade. Miss Mabel's blue tomcat walked across the yard and jumped on the car's trunk. Edward frowned before turning back to me.

"Hell of a thing," he said. "Would you like some money now, a sort of advance?"

"Yep."

"How much?"

"Ten thousand."

He didn't blink but reached to the inner pocket of his tailored jacket and drew out a leather-enclosed checkbook and silver pen. Using his narrow thigh as a rest, he wrote out the check, tore it painstakingly, and handed it to me.

"Anything else I can do?" he asked.

"Yeah, tell me who stuffs your shirts."

He sighed and stood. He replaced the pen and checkbook.

"I thought we might make things up a bit," he said.

"Guess we have a bit."

"Will you be around? Patricia asked me to invite you to come lodge with us till you get your feet under you."

"They're under me. Tell her I'll be moving on soon."

"Well then," he said and held out his hand.

I shook it, a polite city hand, and for a second I felt tempted to put the squeeze on it and bring him to his knees.

"Good," he said. "Hope you'll let me hear from you now and again."

I watched him leave down the walk. He leveled his shoulders and shooed the cat off the car's trunk. He drew his clean white handkerchief to wipe away the dusty paw prints. His circular strokes were gentle to the Audi.

38

WALT BROUGHT COLESLAW and warm, crusty fried chicken from the Dew Drop Inn. Over cracked ice we drank his bourbon. He kept a bottle of Old Crow hidden behind the fireplace's desiccated peahen screen to keep Miss Mabel from discovering his nightly thirst.

Two reporters knocked on the oval glass of the front door, and he locked it. They stood on their toes to peek in windows. Walt drew blinds and phoned Rutledge. The sheriff sent Rodger out to forbid the jackals to approach Miss Mabel's house any closer than the public sidewalk.

"You can leave anytime you want," Walt said. He loaned me a pink button-down oxford-cloth shirt, tan cotton slacks, socks, and a pair of shiny black loafers fashionably decorated with kilties. The loafers were too long and narrow.

That night I woke and lay listening to insects whose throbbing swelled in moist, abrasive heat. Miss Mabel's house had no air-conditioning, and Walter switched on electric fans. The whooshes of their revolving blades became part of the night's chorus. I thought of that outsized weather vane Lupi had installed on Bellerive's roof. Not just a piebald horse but a stallion. Irony?

I wouldn't return to Jessup's Wharf. If I couldn't find something in Montana, there'd be another place. In America there was always another place.

During the morning Walt and I drank coffee, and he drove me to the King County Bank when the doors unlocked at nine. I opened an account to deposit Edward's check. The tellers, cashier, and customers gawked as if I'd become a star.

Reporters walked in the bank. The president, a round, glossy man named Granville Grimes, showed Walt and me into his private office to sign the signature card. He told me he'd been a friend of the family. I didn't remember him. He waived the waiting period for Edward's check to clear, and I withdrew two thousand cash.

"I'll deposit the insurance money in the account," Walt said.

"Take your cut."

"The meter's running."

"There'll be more from Edward. Look after it till I send you a postcard."

"You leaving this minute?"

"Soon as I buy shoes that fit," I said, which I did at Jessup's Mercantile—lightweight Gore-Tex hikers. I also paid for white athletic socks, two sets of underwear, two short-sleeve shirts, two pairs of Levi's, and a small canvas duffel bag to hold the purchases I wasn't wearing. I changed, tied on the shoes, and returned Walt's clothes.

He walked me to the courthouse. Along River Street citizens stared and whispered. Reporters and the cameraman followed. They called questions. I didn't answer.

At the jail Sheriff Rutledge handed me the key to the Jeep and a temporary driver's license. He, Benson, Rodger, Mrs. Bains, Walt, and the reporters watched, and the cameraman angled for shots as I started the engine and rolled away. They shrunk to nothing in the Jeep's shaky rearview mirror.

I thought of driving to Bellerive for a last look. There were graves I could stand by, a few good memories to revive, last pictures to load into the mind. But I'd carried too many ugly images over the years. Let the Montana sky erase them.

I stopped down the road and unfastened the Jeep's canvas top. I wanted wind over me, though the hot air scoured my skin. I breathed deep, attempting to draw freedom into my lungs, and glanced behind to see whether I'd really gotten away. The law could be fickle.

I drove 360 to Richmond where I ate a cheeseburger, bought a pack of Camels, but no six-pack. I'd take no chances with the law till I felt beyond its reach. I again thought of calling Juno. What would I say? Thanks for carrying a secret so many years? Better let it all pass.

West of Richmond I picked up 460 and down the road caught sight of the hazy Blue Ridge mountains. Then west of Blacksburg the somber Appalachians rose like a dusky wall. Air became thinner and cooler. My breath drew easier.

I crossed into West Virginia and followed the turnpike to Beckley, where I drove to Zeke's house. He came out holding a paper napkin. Alice Faye stood at the door looking irritable at the interruption of dinner till she realized who I was. She smiled at me and held Suzy Q. close.

"Ready to pay off the loan and buy the Jeep," I said.

"The Jeep ain't much. Eight hundred okay? Nah, that's too much. Five hundred."

"Eight hundred's fine, and I'm writing you a check."

Alice Faye and Suzy Q. kept peeping around the carport door.

"I'm selling the Jeep," Zeke called.

"Hallelujah," Alice Faye answered, and Suzy Q. cheered.

"Make it out to my bride," he said. "But hold it a second. I got a title somewhere. Come on in and visit. There's a chop left on the platter."

"Not this time," I said, and as he also knew, there'd be no other.

Alice Faye helped him find the title. He brought it out and signed it over to me on the Jeep's hood. Using his pen, I wrote the check. We shook hands. Of late, lots of handshaking.

"Keep in touch," he said, the old evasion of good-bye.

"For sure."

I reached Cliffside after dark. I felt exposed, as if I should be slinking through town. Sidewalks lay empty. The half-dozen street-lights shone ineffectually against the mountain's pressing blackness.

I stopped at the Shawnee Food Market for beans, a flashlight, a carton of Copenhagen snuff, and five one-pound bags of lemon drops.

"Party time?" the thin young clerk asked. He parted his hair in the middle, and I saw two fingers of his right hand had been sheared off. He used a thumb to press the cash register keys.

"Ever'day," I said and drove from Cliffside into the absolute night of the twisted, descending road. I passed the Pit, windows dark, no cars or pickups in front. I crossed the bridge over Persimmon Creek and snaked down toward the gorge till my headlights picked up the glitter of water flowing across the road. I parked well off the shoulder, took the Jeep's key, my provisions and duffel bag, and used the flashlight to find the trail leading to High Moor.

As I hiked, streams splashed among rocks and boulders. A large bird flapped from a looming tree. A cool wind disturbed leaves, and the canopy of branches rustled and swayed. I had the same sense of being watched. My imagination or Esmeralda? The flashlight picked out the rusty machinery among weeds at the side of the trail.

I passed the first portal, the grilled iron bars seeming more to keep persons imprisoned than to prevent entry. I shone the light into that devouring blackness and listened to the slow, relentless drip of water.

I thought of men who entered mountains, who daily trod its perpetual night and emerged tarnished into an alien sun.

When I walked from under tree cover, I passed the burned stone remains of the company office where Lupi had put together the clock, drawn his artistic mechanical sketches, saved High Moor for my father, and devised his eternal punishment.

I hiked down the slate steps to the forsaken camp. The moon slid free of clouds and made eerie the collapsed structures along the cindered street.

Shining my flashlight into empty doorways, I located the Jenny Lind where Lupi had lived. The miniature house nailed to a post stood tilted beside the rotted picket fence. I straightened the post and tamped my heel against the bottom before unhooking the roof and emptying a bag of lemon drops inside.

I ate beans cold off my Old Timer blade and drank night-blacked water from the turbulent river. I smoked and lay on the small, shredding porch listening to wind, the pounding rapids, the clatter of coal drags snaking through the gorge, a distant dog bark. The mountainside pulsed with insects, a subdued and sadder rhythm foretelling summer's end and the chilled hand of fall, which arrived early in high country.

I half dozed till I believed I heard Esmeralda slip down into the camp. When I looked along the moon-shrouded street, it lay empty except for shadowy pokeweed and nettles bending to wind.

In the morning I checked the miniature house. The lemon drops hadn't been taken. I splashed my face by palming up rain-water that had collected in the dip of a boulder. I looked toward the massive stones topping the gorge's rim as the wan sun slowly defined their shape.

Then I glimpsed her. Or at least I believed I did. I squinted at foliage growing above the camp till my eyes blurred. What I'd seen might've been an illusion caused by a swipe of sunlight touching moist, wind-agitated laurel, a trick of the mind that ignited a vision of enormous eyes in a wary, fugitive face.

I waited till the sun fully burned away mist. I whistled, hollered, and raised bags of lemon drops. No reply except from crows, which flew cawing toward the cliffs.

I climbed to the cemetery above the burned church. A low, half-collapsed wall supported it against the mountain's weight. Italians were reputed to be great builders using unmortared stones. Maybe Lupi had constructed this one and been buried here along with Angus MacKay, whom I'd believed to be my grandfather.

I found neither. Kudzu grew among and embraced the time-honed and pitted markers, many listing and cracked. I tripped over a tablet lying flat. I made out part of a word that had been chiseled into broken, begrimed marble. I stooped to draw fingers across it as if reading Braille: EL VED. *Beloved.*

Hiking out along the trail, I again heard a dog bark. I paused and called Esmeralda's name. No answer, not even an echo.

I moved on, then turned, hearing what—tree boughs grating, the forlorn plaint of a dove, a distant voice?

No, after a time nothing.

39

I DROVE THE Jeep back to the bridge over Persimmon Creek, where I four-wheeled it up to Aunt Jessie's. She crossed around the cabin, her arms curved under firewood. Her feet left swiping prints in moist grass.

"Well you back," she said as Rattler growled and I opened the door for her. She dumped the split lengths in a wooden box beside her hearth. The warm cabin smelled of bread and earth.

"I'll be moving on," I said.

"Figures," she said. "Blackie come for a visit and told she heard about you on her radio. So you free of the law?"

"Me and Lupi," I said. Our eyes locked, hers a blue that belonged in the face of a lean mountain girl with free-swinging wheat-colored hair. Aunt Jessie might not understand details of how Lupi had blown Bellerive's portico to hell but all the time had known the why.

I set the carton of Copenhagen on the table beside a mason jar filled with a teaberry spray that still had droplets of dew on the petals.

"You again scratching my itch," she said. "And I thank you kindly."

I laid two one-hundred-dollar bills and the remaining four packages of lemon drops beside the snuff.

"Think you can find someone to keep candy in that little house on the post?" I asked.

"She won't take lemon drops no more. She won't let me see her either, though she eats food I leave for her and has kept a blanket."

"Anything I can do?"

"Not hardly."

"Use the money. I'll send more later."

"I'll do that, though nobody 'round here ever going to let her starve. I'll give the lemon drops to chaps down at the church."

"I'd appreciate that. You been good to me, Aunt Jessie."

"You one of ours," she said. "No matter how far you travel and where you end up, remember you got these mountains in you."

"No way I'll forget."

She opened the door of the oven built into the chimney above the fireplace and used her broad wooden paddle to slide out a hot loaf of bread. She wrapped it in a brown paper sack, used a miller's knot to tie the twine, and as she gave the loaf to me, our hands touched and lingered.

"Trust in the Lord," she said.

"It's a thought," I answered.

I walked to the Jeep. I had a last glimpse of her standing before her cabin looking after me, her arms hanging straight, her bonnet a nunlike hood.

The Jeep bumped down to the paved road. I drove to the Pit. The front door hung open. Music and the whine of a guitar-stricken, deep-drawling nasal baritone:

Don't cry me no cries,
Don't tear me no tears,
Just reach me a coffin nail
And another two beers.

Inside, the place was partly stripped—barstools, beer spigots, booths, the pool table gone. The isolated jukebox played. Blackie, her legs crossed, sat smoking atop the counter.

"Well they didn't bury you under that jail after all," she said.

She was barefooted, her toenails still red, white, and blue. She wore cutoff jeans and a denim halter. Her hair needed combing. She had on no earrings or makeup. The red eye patch caught a velvety luster from sunlight angled through the doorway.

"See you been changing things around."

"Closing," she said, the long scar a raw stripe down her face. "Give it all back to the Indians—if they was any Indians. Not worth torching without insurance, and mine got canceled."

Glimmer of tears in the one dark eye. Something more beyond hurt and defeat—an intimation of long-suffering valor not even coal country's savaging could destroy. I felt not pity but admiration.

"Like to come with me?"

"Why'd I want to go anywhere with a thing like you?" she answered and snubbed her cigarette in the sink behind her. She drew a breath to collect herself as she squared her shoulders. Toughness regained.

"Free ride," I said.

"To where?"

"Big sky. More space than the eye can eat."

"In that bucket of bolts out there?" she asked, sneering at the Jeep.

"That buggy has lucky wheels."

"You got money? I don't want nothing to do with a man short on money."

"Buy you a red Cadillac car and a diamond bracelet."

"One day you gonna slip on that slick tongue of yours and break your damn neck," she said as the jukebox clicked to silence. She glanced at it. "They hauling it off today."

"Just leave the door here open," I said. "Come back if Montana don't fit."

"What the hell I'd come back for?" She touched at her eye. "You mean it about taking me?"

"Swear to God."

"Poor God's got a pile of due bills," she said, pushing from the counter to the floor. "What the hell. Pack a few items."

I wondered whether she'd bring her high school diploma and the picture of herself and the sergeant. I smoked as I waited. She came lugging a suitcase, her radio, the Winchester. I offered to help, but she brushed past and set things in the rear of the Jeep beside my duffel bag.

She'd painted her lips and fastened on the looped golden earrings. She wore a pair of black-and-white Western boots, hip-hugging black slacks, the thick leather belt with the Mexican silver buckle, a red long-sleeved shirt, a black spangled vest, a pearl-colored Stetson, and the zebra eye patch.

As I started the engine, she climbed in the Jeep and hooked a boot heel over the door frame.

"Reckon anything good can come of this?" she asked.

"Don't look back," I said.